FIVE DOLLARS and a POCKET FULL of WISHES

Gino Luti

ISBN: (Paperback) 978-1-954341-45-6

(E-book) 975-1-954941-46-3

Writers' Branding
1800-608-6550
www.writersbranding.com
orders@writersbranding.com

"Show Us How It's Done"

"Stick around a minute, Gene; I need to talk to you." My Dad spoke matter-of-factly, with authority. He was not big, but quite solid. In our house if he spoke you listened. He is the monarch of our family. He kept his hair drill sergeant short and his patience shorter. Though I have never seen him do it, there was no doubt in my mind he can knock someone out, no problem, so he scares the shit out of me. I turn, walk back to the dinner table and sit down respectfully. I knew what was coming. Dinner had been quiet with not much chit chat. My Mom obviously told him I came home at four in the morning the night before, visibly inebriated and reeking of pot. He was a pilot and had been away on a trip and just got back this afternoon. Mom is a peanut of a woman. She had no chance of controlling a six-foot one arrogant teenage boy, chock full of himself. Upon being confronted by her, instead of showing any remorse or concern, I tell her to take two aspirin and call me in the morning. After dinner he is having his obligatory cup of coffee and cigarette, when he called me back to the table. He is wearing a face that says; what the hell am I going to do with you? He is lightly tapping and flipping a Zippo lighter between his fingers on the table. I respect him and though he strikes fear in me, his attempts to discipline me are futile.

I am seventeen years old, in the first month of my senior year in high school and probably should have 'kiss my ass' tattooed on my forehead. For instance, no sooner am I told I am restricted to my house when I sneak out the window to hang out with my friends. When my mom finds a roach clip in my jeans, I swear to her its not mine and that, "I am holding it for a friend".

My dad began, "You're a pretty sharp fellow, far as I can tell." He's never opened one of his lectures like this before, and there is something different in his tone, sarcastically upbeat, and this concerns me.

"There's not much you don't know about, as far as I can tell." I desperately search for a retort but come up empty. My mouth is as dry as the Mojave, his delivery is throwing me off my game. I am usually quite good with some sort of apology or something; but for some reason I am blank. He is speaking as if he has something on me this time, a hole card that is going to clean me out. My forehead was heating up. What could he have, what does he know?

"What happened to you joining the Army?" Again, I have nothing, just sat there, staring at the bowl of plastic fruit in the center of the table, completely void of what to say. I am confused and trying not to show it. Over the summer, with my folks' blessing, I went to the Army recruiting office to pre-enlist but was tripping my ass off on magic mushrooms and chickened out at the last minute and hauled ass out of the place. The way he is speaking makes me feel like he is a store detective and I am a shoplifter with various items bulging out of my shirt.

"Well, the way I see it, we're just holding you back. A guy like you needs to get out in the world… so you can show us how it's done." What the hell did he mean by that? Is he actually throwing me out of the house? I feel the blood drain from my face; my mind is a wash of uncertainty and fear. To my chagrin, I now feel like the wizard being discovered behind the curtain by Dorothy and her friends. I lean forward, take a deep breath, and slide my chair back from the table. Resting my elbows on my thighs in defeat, with my head down, staring at my intertwined fingers, tapping the tips of my thumbs together. Glancing up I notice my dad sliding a five-dollar bill across the table in my direction. Puzzled by that, I look at the five dollars, then at my dad. I have not said a word from the moment he asked me to stick around; but now he is quiet and Abe Lincoln is staring a hole in my forehead and I was staring right back him. What the hell could this five-dollar bill mean? My insides are a bubbling caldron of bewilderment and panic. My dad just sat back in his chair looking at me until I could not take it any longer. Cautiously, almost inaudibly I ask,

"What's…that for?"

"That's for a cab ride down the road…you obviously have someplace else you'd rather be, considering how little respect you have for the home, your mother and I provide for you. Oh, and your motorcycle stays here." I am floored. Is he bluffing? I look at my mother in the kitchen doing the dishes a few feet away; she seemed to be ignoring the whole conversation. I want to stand up, walk over to her and ask if she agrees with my dad, but I am paralyzed. In my head I am asking, "Mom, do you feel the same way as Dad?" Though I sat and said nothing. I want to walk in the kitchen, give her a hug and say goodby… that ought to make her feel like shit; But I could not do it. I didn't have it in me. My dad continued,

"You're welcome to visit whenever you like; but you need to find your own place to live." My mind is racing to catch up with his words. Maybe he is testing me. Is he hoping I will grovel and apologize? I'll show him. My eyes begin to well up, but I am not about to let them see me cry. Snatching up the five bucks, I stood up from the table, and walk to my room, defiant. I bet he figured I would not do it. Confused, angry- no furious, I pull my sleeping bag from my closet and stuff all my Levis, my two flannel shirts, socks, and underwear in it. I am wearing my favorite tan work boots, jeans, and a tee shirt. I grab my dress shoes in case I might need them. I roll everything in my sleeping bag as well and use my good school belt to wrap it up. I put on my heavy wool pea coat. Though it is not cold, I knew I might need it where I am going. Though I did not have a clue where that will be; it might be cold there. I head for the front door with my mind swirling, trying to think of a parting shot… to inflict pain. I want to lash out at them but could not come up with a smart-ass line. I throw my pack up on my shoulder and am out the door. Cab ride, hell… I Don't take cabs.

The world has just been handed to me. Be careful what you wish for, began to take on an unwelcome pertinence. My stomach muscles clenched, I can hear every thump of my aorta, and my nostrils were sucking air like a jet engine. I did not know if I should jump for joy or walk back into the house and beg forgiveness. My teenage cockiness rose to the occasion. Exhilarated, feeling like… okay this is it… I tell myself, put one foot in front of the other.

Walking away from my house, the air is different. The smell of Jasmine is thick as ever in the air, the sound of croaking frogs, seemed a little louder, a little clearer. The sunset is a day glow orange ball. I head up the street, with no destination in mind, just going. On one hand I am mad as hell for being invited to leave, and on the other, well… they have just seen the last of Gene Martin. After a quarter mile of walking I begin to collect my thoughts, and decide to go to Food Spot, a convenience store where my friends and I hang out. Life is for the living and I plan on doing plenty of it. Yep, look out life, because here I come. It is October of 1971 and I am about to embark on a journey for the ages. Miami, Florida is about to become where I am from. And the entire world is where I am going.

My dreams were of freedom and the open road. Living at home is simply cramping my style. I am bored as a cat with a dead mouse. I agree with the mantra, "Don't trust anyone over the age of thirty." I read J. Krishnamurti's,

Think on These Things. Jack Kerouacs's On the Road and they inspire me. Bob Dylan, Jimi Hendrix, and Jim Morrison are my heroes. I want to be like Kerouac and Dylan, traveling the roads, hitchhiking from one adventure to another. Maybe getting kicked out of my folk's house is just what I need.

It is about 6:30 in the evening. I try hitchhiking but end up walking most of the way to Food Spot. As usual, a few of my friends are hanging out, sitting on the curb smoking cigarettes, waiting for someone old enough to buy them beer. Paul Collins, Matt Myan, and Matt's girlfriend Deanna are there. I greet them,

"Hey you guys, I just got kicked out of my house." As if it was something cool or an everyday occurrence. I sit down on the curb and bum a cigarette. Paul looks at me with a silly grin and asked, "Looks like your folks didn't let you take your motorcycle. What are you gonna do now?"

Full of chutzpah I proclaim, "I'm gonna hitchhike around the country… see the world."

That's when Matt, asks with a grin, "That's great, but what are you gonna do tonight, smart guy?" Ignoring his condescending tone, I say,

"I'll find a place to crash and take off in the morning."

Matt asks, "What about high school? Aren't you in your last year?"

"Screw that, I hardly go to class anyway."

After hanging out with my friends a while, Don Stein shows up. Don is another friend, one of the "Food Spot flies." That is whom we are, night after night buzzing around the front of a convenience store. Don has a car, already graduated from high school, and is working, though he still lives at home with his folks. When he hears I was kicked out, he offered to let me spend the night in the back seat of his Impala.

Later that evening another friend, Phil Sanchez, shows up at Food Spot. I begin working on Phil to take off with me. In spite of my bravado, I am still scared to hitchhike alone. I said to Phil,

"I'm planning to take off for California tomorrow. Didn't you say you wanted to see the west coast? Why Don't you come with me? We'll see the world, hitchhike across the country. Come on man, it will be a fuckin' gas." Phil, ever the cynic responded, "Oh yeah and how are we supposed to eat?"

"We can get jobs along the way; you know how easy it is to get a job. We can get work doing anything, anywhere." Phil looks at me skeptically, took a drag off his Marlboro, and spat. He is thinking about it. Phil is a great guy with a good sense of humor, and we get along. Like me, he didn't get along with his dad. Phil stayed out too late, is getting lousy grades in school, drinking beer, smoking dope, and his dad didn't like it. I figure Phil is ripe for taking off with me. Phil's dad gave him a Volkswagen bug to use to go to school and work. Phil fixed it up with mag wheels and pin striping, so it looked cool. Like my folks with my motorcycle, Phil's dad used the car for leverage, taking it away the minute Phil pissed him off.

Phil has shoulder-length black hair and always seems to have a smirk for no particular reason. Girls like him, so I thought he would make a good traveling companion, though he made it clear he would rather take a car than hitchhike. His idea is to take the V'dub, regardless of the fact that the car was in his dad's name. He suggests we go to Detroit where his cousin Candy lived and after that, head for California. I thought, if he would rather take a car than hitchhike, I'm game... anywhere, but here. As for stealing his dad's car, I am fine with that. It is his dad so it isn't really stealing.

Paul and Matt are asking various adults to buy them beer, and finally one did. We go behind Food Spot to the "big tree" to drink. This is another hangout where my friends and I gather. It is on the edge of a golf course, secluded from the General public. Phil, Don, Paul, Matt, and I, along with a few other flies, spent the evening drinking and smoking until around midnight. I left with Don, who lived a few blocks away, and at his suggestion I climbed in the back seat and scrunched down before he pulls up to his house, not wanting his folks to see me. He parks on the street in front of his house and I thank him again.

Lying there in Don's car, my mind is full of questions. Did I really want to be out on my own? Would this work out for me? Have I got myself into something more then I'm ready for? I am in turmoil and looking for ways to justify being out of my house, and on my own. To comfort myself I thought, my folks Don't need me and I damn sure Don't need them. It's time for me to get out in the world and embrace the unknown. I Don't feel bad enough to cry, and I Don't feel like smiling because I am not really happy. I feel anxious as I lay there, in the back seat of my friend's car.

I thought about my mom who had been through a lot in her life. I wondered what she was thinking and if she was going to miss me? She had seen the Great Depression, World War II; right up to World War me. I thought about how she would spend evenings out on our patio reading. How I would go out there and engage her in conversations that I would inevitably turn into a debate. Telling her things like how I will be glad when I will not have to go to high school anymore. Telling her there was so much I want to do and see and that school was just holding me back. My mom would respond with encouragement. She would tell me if I would just go to school and apply myself, I was smart enough to be a lawyer or anything I wanted to be.

"Who wants to be a lawyer?" I shot back.

"They're nothing but a bunch of stuffed suits taking advantage of people who Don't know any better. I want to travel the world." I know my mom is smart and only wants the best for me. Still, her advice pisses me off. I love her, but I cannot stand her. I am determined to go against her; the arguing empowers me, makes me feel dominant. I do the same thing with my teachers in school. I goad them into a debate at every opportunity. I want to be thought of as an intellectual, a philosopher and someone unique.

It's funny when I think about it; but I have been talking about taking off and traveling for quite some time. I made it known I wanted to hit the road and how I was going to travel all over the country, working my way from one town to another. Now that the time is here I felt overwhelmed, why? This is what I want, so why did it feel like I had bitten off, not only more than I could chew, but also more than I could swallow. I am gagging on my own dream. Here I am in the back of a friend's car with absolutely nothing more than a sleeping bag, some clothes, a couple bucks and a pea coat. I am having trouble organizing my thoughts. I am cold and hot at the same time. I should be thrilled to finally be enjoying my first taste of freedom. Instead I am scared. I go over in my mind the conversation with my dad. Thinking about how shitty I treat my mom. It almost makes me feel sick. At the same time, I am cringing at the thought of going back home. Being told when to come home at night was so damned annoying. I never want to be told when to come home again.

Eventually I calm down with the thought of my friend Phil and I taking off together. We'll look out for each other… it will be great. Next thing I know it is morning and I am waking up in the back of my friend's car.

I awake with an ashtray in my mouth and there is no bathroom sink to brush my teeth. My body feels a little stiff and itchy, but there is no shower. Well, welcome to the street. After peeking out the windows to see if anyone is looking out the window of Don's house, trying to keep my head down, I open the door on the street side and slip out of the car. Phil and I agreed to meet at Food Spot. It is a short walk from Don's car. Phil showed up a short time later. It is about seven a.m. Phil snagged his coin collection and any other money he could get his hands on. I still had $3.00 left after buying cigarettes and a coke, and, with that, we take off.

I thought to myself, we can do this. I had a dozen jobs under my belt; yardman, dishwasher, gas station attendant. To get a job I would practice being interviewed in my mind, then walk in to the Burger Castle on Dixie highway and apply. Being tall and thin with my hair pushed back behind my ears and a confident smile, I expect people to like me. I reveled in introducing myself and asking for a job. Using lines like, "I've always wanted to work here." Or, "This would be the perfect job for me, it's close to where I live and I can work nights and weekends." I know how to deliver my lines with sincerity; I can bullshit anyone. So, traveling and working along the way is going to be a piece of cake. Besides my teachers and parents concerns for me were a constant pain in my ass. Like static on a cheap radio, no matter how I try tuning them out, there they are. I am filled with mutiny and want a ship of my own, even if that ship is a Volkswagen and belonged to my friend's dad.

First stop a gas station. We need to fill up and get a map. I wash up in the men's room sink, splashing soap and water on my upper body. It is not a shower, but it was something. I remembered to pack my toothbrush, though I forgot toothpaste, and thought about brushing my teeth with soap… but water would have to do. After checking the map, we pick Highway 27 and head north, talking about all the great things we are going to see and do.

I said with the excitement of a little boy, "L.A., San Francisco, the beaches, the girls… man, this is going to be great." The day is clear, the sun is shining, the temperature is in the seventies, and I feel good. The scenery coming out of Miami is uninteresting for the most part. I had seen it before, a few businesses and undeveloped open fields of high grass on either side of the highway, though it looks great to me. It looks like liberty. After three or four hours of driving, we catch I-75 North. Near Ocala we stop for lunch at a What-A-Burger, where Phil paid for our burgers and cokes.

Reaching the north border of Florida, we begin to encounter rolling hills. Georgia has some great scenery; the woods look lush and seem to be cheering us on with their branches waving in the breeze. The farms are real Americana; I am expecting to see the Real McCoy's trotting through the woods along the highway. By now night is approaching. I offer to drive, but Phil said he was fine. We have been on the road about thirteen hours when Phil finally is tired of driving. It is nine p.m. and we are in North Georgia, just south of the Tennessee border, according to our map. We pull over at a rest stop that has picnic tables, a rest room and some grassy areas. It is our oasis in the night.

We are more than halfway to Detroit and the temperature is in the fifties. We roll out our sleeping bags to sleep on the cool damp ground. Lying there, gazing up at a sliver of a moon in a clear star-filled sky, my mind wandered. I am not worried... I am full of anticipation. Thinking about the fact that we are in Phil's car and he had most of the money, made me feel a little uncomfortable. My contribution is $3.00 at best. I said to Phil, "We're in this together man. What's mine is yours and what's yours is mine." He didn't respond; though I did not really expect one. I dozed off.

In the morning we awake, both of us cold and shivering. We are on the road and driving before sun-up. The scenery became more beautiful, mountains, rivers, streams, and vast stretches of forest. I thought about how cool it would be to just get out of the car and walk off in to the woods forever. The farther north we venture, the more interesting the landscape and the more we like it. Living in South Florida where the terrain is flat, we are intrigued by the change in topography. We cruise through Tennessee and then Kentucky. There are mountains all around us. Up and down, left and right, winding our way through tall trees with gold and red leaves or bare branches that spoke of fall and it all feels so good. We get into Ohio; looking out the car windows at rolling farmland with silos standing tall and saluting our arrival. Eventually in some places it becomes almost as flat as Florida, though not nearly as boring~ probably because it is new to us. My friends and I always talk about how boring South Florida is when it came to scenery. Stopping only for gas and fast food, we make good time.

We arrive in Wyandotte, a suburb of Detroit, late in the afternoon. We give Phil's cousin a call, and she gives us directions to her house. Wyandotte is a working-class community with nothing special about it. When we arrive at Candy's she came outside to greet us. Candy is a beautiful black-haired sixteen-year-old. I immediately begin trying to impress her. She is about five-four, with a killer body and an angel face. She has natural looking tan, silky jet-black hair falling halfway down her back. As she speaks she smiles coyly; she has a habit of reaching up and twirling a few strands of her feather like hair around her index finger next to the side of her face. God, she is sexy. I immediately had designs on her. Her mom and dad, Phil's aunt and uncle are not home.

"We're off to see the world," I tell Candy, doing my best I'm somebody special act. Phil looks at me like I am a fool; she already has a boyfriend and is not impressed by my posturing. No sooner do we arrive, when Candy suggested the three of us go over and meet her boyfriend... so the three of us hop in Phil's car and go to her boyfriend's garage apartment. He is what my friend's and I refer to as a plastic freak, a guy with a long yet obviously professionally cut head of hair, wearing mod clothes— the kind the department stores sell. He is a wannabe; he was not an authentic hippie, so Phil and I are not impressed. His only redeeming quality is turning us on to a great rock and roll piano player/singer by the name of Lee Michaels.

Been fourteen days since I Don't know when
I just saw her with my best friend
Do ya know what I mean?
Lord, do ya know what I mean?

After a couple beers, a joint, and some small talk we are bored, tired, and ready to head back to Candy's house.

Phil's aunt and uncle are at the house when we get back and glad to see us. Phil's aunt had a pot of chili on the stove and fixed us each a bowl and it tasted as good as it smelled. After eating we talk; tell them we are on our way to California for a vacation. Phil's uncle is visibly concerned for his nephew. Both of us being seventeen are hardly old enough to be traveling on our own cross-country. He knew something was up, but he didn't say anything. Eventually they show us the basement, a kind of rec. room. It is nice enough, with a ping-pong table and a few couches, along with a small black and white TV. Phil's uncle said we could sleep down there for the night. I am not sure what we were thinking; here we are at Phil's uncle's house, the house owned by his father's brother. It wasn't long before Phil's uncle came back down stairs with some news.

"I called your dad and told him you were here." Phil said nothing just looked at his feet while sitting on a couch.

"He's worried about you, Phil. Said he is flying up tomorrow. He wants his car back and he would like to talk to you when he gets here." Continuing he said,

"He wants you to give me the keys to the car." Phil obliged without so much as a word, it was obvious he was embarrassed.

After Phil's uncle left the room, I said to Phil fearlessly,

"We Don't need a car, we can hitchhike." With nothing more said than that, he agreed. I am a little surprised. I guess the thought of facing his dad was motivation enough. It was about 9:30 at night. We pack our stuff into our sleeping bags and creep out of the house undetected, without so much as a goodbye. We talk about asking Candy to go with us but come to our senses.

We trekked toward the Interstate or at least the direction we thought it will be. Walking away it soon dawned on us we don't know where the Interstate is. About a mile down the road we decide to hunker down behind a white concrete building to get our bearings. It doesn't provide much shelter, though it does break the wind, which is blowing cold. Sitting on the hard, crunchy ground with our backs against the cement wall, we each lit a cigarette. Phil begins complaining about the cold. I look up to notice a time and temperature sign flashing in front of a bank across the street. I nudged Phil, pointing up at the sign, and his response was.

"Huh?" Then he shook his head in disgust, looked down at the ground and spat. The sign read 10:02, forty-one degrees. A minute later, 10:03, forty degrees, and by 10:04, it is thirty-nine. I can tell Phil is quickly losing his wanderlust. He is not taking the elements well, and to make matters worse, I say to Phil,

"Check it out man, every minute the time changes the temperature drops, watch." By 10:08 it was 36 degrees and not looking good for a couple of self-proclaimed adventurers. I said,

"Let's go, man. We gotta find the Interstate and get a ride in a warm car."

Defeated Phil said,

"Nobody gonna pick up two dudes this late at night, screw this; I'm going back to my aunt and uncle's. He stood up. I am not staying out here freezing my ass off; let's leave in the morning when it's not so damn cold." I try talking him out of going back, but he is having no part of it. He, in turn, tries to convince me to go back with him,

"Come on man… come back with me. You're gonna freeze your nuts off out here." I would not hear of it… I did not want to go back with him because that would be admitting I could not make it without a car. Remembering my dad challenging me to, "Show him how it's done." I knew going back with Phil meant I did not show my dad shit. I also would feel pretty embarrassed to have to face Phil's aunt and uncle. Did they know we left; was the door we slipped out of now locked? Would we have to knock on the door when we got back and say,

"Oh hi, we were taking off for California, but it got cold so we're back until it warms up?" I was too proud for that; I told Phil I was going to California on my own. He gave me ten bucks, stuck out his hand and said,

"Good luck Gene, you crazy fucker." I took the ten, shook his hand, gave him a nod and we walked off in opposite directions.

Walking away I wondered when I would see Phil again and how awkward it will be for him when his dad confronts him. Well, I cannot think about that now, I need to find the highway and find it fast. The cold wind is showing no mercy and a car will be my only refuge. I cannot sink my head far enough down between my shoulders to hide my ears in the collar of my coat. If my fists were any deeper in my pockets I would rip a hole in them. Still, I walk along feeling good; I was doing what I wanted. That's when I notice two shadowy figures in a nearby doorway.

COLD FEET

The lines of a song hit me:

Nobody's ever taught you
how to live on the street
And now, you're gonna, have to get,
used to it
Bob Dylan, *Like a Rolling Stone*

It seems I am in a rough part of town. The two figures I notice, are a couple of men who appear hobo-like, standing in the doorway of an old run-down building. They are wearing tattered old winter coats, talking, rocking from foot to foot, with their arms folded tightly against their chests and steam coming from their lips. Noticing a small lighted cross, above the doorway, I decide it will be a safe place to ask directions. I walk up, "How ya doin' what is this place?"

One of the guys responds,

"It's a mission."

"A mission, what's a mission?" The less scruffy one answers, "Well, we'll give you something to eat and a warm place to sleep if you sit down and listen to a sermon."

Skeptical, but cold and hungry, I ask, "When does the sermon start?"

"In about five minutes. Go in and take a seat."

I decide I'll get directions later. Once inside, I notice about a dozen disheveled looking men, sitting on metal folding chairs in a fifteen by twenty room. Doesn't look like anyone here is as young as me, but I don't feel out of place. One guy turns out to be a woman. Her face is a reddish brown with deep distinct wrinkles, like state highways on a road map. Her eyes are small, bloodshot and cloudy. Her hair is short, and an unkempt mixture of browns and grays with wisps of white. The plaid wool coat she is wearing is worn, tattered, and soiled. I wonder how long she has been on the street, what she might look like if she had a place to live, clean clothes, and a reason to care. She is probably someone's mother or grandmother for God's sake. At the moment, she is barely distinguishable as a woman, from the shabby men in the room. I feel bad for her.

I thought about my grandmother, Grandma May. She is a nice old gal, who enjoys sitting at her dining room table in her fourth-floor flat in Brooklyn, drinking Miller Highlife. Her face will twitch and her hand will quiver as she picks up her glass of beer. She is always interested in what I am up to. Upon my telling her what I have been doing, she will always nod approval with her trembling smile. I do love her, though I have not seen Grandma May in quite some time. I sat staring at the old lady in the room and wondered how my grandmother was doing. A few minutes passed, and the fellow at the door who invited me in, stepped to the front of the room.

"Welcome everyone." He smiled. He doesn't look much better off than the people in the room. He took off his coat and introduced himself as the minister of the Word of Hope Mission. He began talking about Jesus. "Jesus is Lord," he says. It is a relatively Glennric sermon, I remember something about being thankful and counting your blessings. Looking around the room I wonder, how many blessings do these poor hoboes have? After a ten or fifteen-minute sermon, he invites us all to sing, held out his hands, and gestured for us to begin,

"Aaamaaazing grace, how sweeeet thou arrrt, to saaave a wretch like meeee…" I know the song, and mumble along. After a painful rendition by "Drunks in midnight choir" to quote Leonard Cohen; we are invited to the adjoining room for refreshments. There is a folding table set up against the wall with sandwiches and pitchers of Kool-Aid. We are told the sandwiches are peanut butter and honey on white bread. The Kool-Aid turns out to be mostly water. I help myself. It is not much in the way of dinner; but it is free. Folding cots are set up around the perimeter of the room. The other wayward souls and I are told we are welcome to spend the night, but no alcohol would be allowed. I went over, sat on a cot, and am thankful to have a warm place to sleep.

I lay on my cot thinking about Phil going back to his uncle's and having to see his dad the next day and am glad not to be with him. I thought about myself, going to California. It is going to be quite an adventure. Thousands of miles across country, hitchhiking alone; I will have stories to tell for days.

The next day came and I am up early. I spirit out into the day, working up the courage to hit the highway. I thought to myself, I can't go to California from here. It is far too cold to cross the northern part of the country this time of year. I'll go down south and cross along the southern states. I decide to take I-75 South for now. I am standing at the entrance ramp with my thumb out pondering. Wouldn't it be funny if Phil's dad drove by and he and Phil picked me up on their way back to Florida in the VW? Would he pick me up? No, that would not be funny; not funny at all.

It is not long before an eighteen-wheeler pulls over. Reading the name on the side of the trailer: *Mary Carter Paint Company.* Climbing in the truck is like climbing up in a tree fort. Getting in an eighteen-wheeler for the first time is somewhat intimidating. It is so high, you have to climb using your hands and feet, being careful to look where to grab and step, the motor is noisy and distracting. The driver said, in a strong voice, over the drone of the motor,

"I'll take you as far as Chattanooga, Tennessee."

"Sounds good." I had no idea how far that is, but I don't care. As we begin to roll, we jerked and rumbled. The cab seemed to be lunging and struggling to pull the trailer with each change of gear. I could picture a single dog dragging a huge sleigh and trying furiously to get the load moving, pulling and contorting his body up, down, and side to side, up down side to side. I am watching the driver, his right foot working quickly between the gas and clutch, his right hand shifting the walking cane long stick shifter and his left hand steadying the huge hula-hoop of a steering wheel. It seems every three seconds he is changing gears, *mmmmm, crunch clunk, mmmmm, crunch clunk, mmmmm, crunch clunk*, until fifteen shifts later we finally reach cruising speed and things smoothed out. The driver tells me his name is Bart. His leathery tan face, slicked back grey hair, and dark stubble made him appear to be in his mid-forties. He is wearing a western style tan and brown shirt with shiny snaps instead of buttons. His jeans looked brand new and seemed to fit tight on his skinny, boney legs that protruded out from under his pronounced gut. He has on some kind of reptile skin cowboy boots and is sporting a huge belt buckle. There is the ripe aroma of body odor mixed with diesel exhaust in the cab, though it quickly fades. We trade small talk and the next thing I know I am listening intently. He had a clear speaking voice and plenty to say. He told me about the farm he grew up on, the rubber plant he worked at in Akron, his theory that Castro and the Mafia killed Kennedy.

"JFK's Brother Bobby was digging into Mafia business and doing his damnedest to bring the mob down. Castro was still pissed off about his brother JFK making him get the Russian missiles out of Cuba, so the Mafia and Castro got together and hired Oswald. After Oswald shot Kennedy, they had Oswald knocked off by Jack Ruby. So, there was no tracing Oswald back to anyone. Yeah, those bastards really pulled one off." He is a great story teller and I can be a good listener.

After two hours into the ride, I begin to nod off, still tired after spending a restless night in a room full of strangers. No sooner am I dozing when Bart says, in almost boss-like fashion, "Hey, I picked you up to keep me awake. Don't go passing out on me now." Snapping to, I sat up in my seat, a little embarrassed for not doing my job. A moment later he is holding out a clenched fist to me, saying,

"This should keep you awake." Opening my palm, he dropped two black capsules in it… some sort of speed, I assumed.

"I need something to wash them down,"

"Use your spit," he chuckles. He shares his philosophies on life. "If a man says he's going to do something, by God he ought to do it come hell or high water. I've got no use for a man that can't keep his word." And, "If you make a plan you need to see it through to the end. Don't quit 'cause it turned out to be harder than you thought."

I thought about my own situation and how I was sticking to my word, becoming a hitchhiking adventurer. It made me feel good to be able to fit into one of his philosophies. I want to interrupt him and tell him, but he is on a roll, so I let him continue. One story is about an eighteen-wheeler loaded with paint, crashing and permanently marking the highway in multi-colored semi gloss, as he put it.

"Yeah," he said proudly, "We'll know where Jesse lost that load for quite some time to come." As if splattering hundreds of gallons of paint across the interstate was something to be admired. Hmmm, I think I agree…

Bart is a good guy and I like him. We stop to eat and he offers to pay for my food and though I had money I did not offer to pay for my own. Felt a little guilty but kept my mouth shut. We stop again and this time I pay for my own. At a truck stop outside Chattanooga, Bart tells me this was as far as he was going. I have been with him about nine or ten hours and am sorry we have to part. I have grown attached to Bart. He is my first real cross-country ride and road mentor. He was kind and made me feel safe in an unsafe environment. I thank him, bid him fare well and walk off. Wondering what my next ride might be like, another eighteen-wheeler, or a family car, another nice guy or a psychopath? It is a gamble to stand on the side of the highway and it felt different from hitchhiking around town back in Miami. In my home town, I would have the advantage of knowing my way around and only going short distances. Out here I am really out here. Taking some real chances; gambling for sure. It reminds me of playing blackjack with my dad and brother. After pushing pennies, nickels, and dimes back and forth across the table, we would eventually get to the point where we would go for broke on a last hand. I would sit there, anxiously looking at my dad's face as he held the deck of cards. Mischievously he would look at me and say, "You want another card, while making a small circle with his middle finger on the back of the deck of cards… you sure?" Then, "POW!" He would flip the card off the deck and slap it on the table. Only on the road, the flip of the card was not for a pile of change, it's for keeps. I am inviting anyone to pull over, pick me up, and take me away— either down the highway to my destination or brought to the middle of nowhere, beaten, tortured, bludgeoned to death and buried in a shallow grave; the choice is theirs. These are my thoughts, my fears, as I head for the next entrance ramp.

I stick out my thumb and am picked up by a guy who said he is an assistant D.A. going back to Atlanta. A coat and tie guy, probably will not be giving me any speed, but I am still wide awake from what Bart had given me. We begin to talk and he asks me if I have heard about people suing fast food restaurants I try to appear interested, to be polite, so he went on.

"Just walk in any fast food restaurant and look for a wet spot on the floor. Slip and fall and just lie there. When people come over to try and help you up tell them you can't move your legs. If they try to help you up, yell in pain. They'll call the paramedics and when they get there tell them you can't move your legs. When they put you on the stretcher, moan. When you get to the hospital tell them you can't move your legs, they'll have a doctor examine you. A few days will go by and an insurance man representing the fast food restaurant will show up telling you that they will take care of all your expenses. He'll offer you a check for your pain and suffering if you'll just sign a release form; sign and take the check. After a week or so, slowly get feeling back in your legs. Take a few days, maybe a week, then be on your way."

This guy is unbelievable; here's an officer of the court telling me how to beat the system. I wish my mom, the lawyer lover, could hear this guy. It is amazing how candid he is. There is something truly unique about being a hitchhiker. The people who pick me up were complete strangers and they knew they would not be with me for long, and most likely, never see me again. It is a perfect opportunity for them to say anything without consequences.

In turn, I could tell them about myself and how I felt or thought. This was a very cool aspect of traveling I never expected.

A few hours down the highway he turned off and I am back on the side of the Interstate. I know Atlanta was not much further down the road, but from the looks of things I am still very much in the country. It's eight or nine at night; I am cold, tired, and a little scared. I thought how hitching at night is relatively fruitless because people are just too nervous about picking up someone they can not clearly see. Standing on the side of the road, I notice a building with a steeple above the entrance. Remembering Bart, the trucker, telling me about churches and the "wayfarer's door." He told me, in some rural parts of the south, churches will leave a door unlocked, a wayfarer's door for cold and weary travelers in the night. I decide it is worth a try, so I hoofed it for the church. As I approach, its dark and foreboding and I had to remind myself it is a church, nothing to fear here. I try the front door, but it is locked, I walk around to the side and make my way to the back, where there is a single light bulb above the back door. Walk up cement steps and am startled by a cat that rambles out from under the church. Watching it head off into the high grass, I realize it is not a cat. It seems to waddle, and I had never seen a cat waddle. Maybe it was a giant rat or an opossum. Try the door knob and… Eureka!

It's open… Bart was right! I am happy to get out of the cold night air and have no hesitation about going in; they had left this door open for me.

I step inside, careful not to move too quickly, find a light switch. The distinct smell of cedar fills my nostrils. Don't think the heat was on, but it is warmer inside this church than outside in the cold Georgia night. Looking around I seem to be in a back room. I notice a few pieces of old furniture and what looks like a hot plate on an old tan Formica counter. After checking out the rest of the church, I unrolled and stretched out my sleeping bag on one of the pews. To give myself comfort I tell myself, I'm in God's house and God was good with me. Lying there thinking this is so bad; I could be outside on the ground right now. Though I am tired and in unfamiliar surroundings, I feel safe. I slipped into dreamland.

In the morning, I am awakened by a lady about my mom's age. I nervously got to my feet and began to explain why I am there. She said she was there to clean and didn't seem at all concerned with my presence. A soft-spoken southern lady with her hair pinned up tightly, wearing a faded blue smock. She had a friendly smile and a face like Aunt Bea. She offered me coffee. We talked a little; I drank my coffee, thanked her, and went on my way.

It is a nice morning, felt like it is in the fifties and looked a little cloudy. It felt good to walk out in the crisp cool air. I am proud of the fact that I had found shelter for the night. I could not wait to tell my friends about the wayfarer's door.

Back on the highway I catch a ride with a couple of prepp*y*-looking guys, with freshly pressed button-down shirts, and short hair cuts, parted on the side. We had a little, where ya from, where ya going conversation, and one of my least favorite songs came on the car radio. The guy in the passenger seat gets excited. "Wait, wait, turn this up, I love this song." I thought, he must be kidding, but then he started singing along,

"*Winnie the Pooh doesn't know what to do,*
got a honey jar stuck on his nose."

Holy crap, this guy really does like this song. I wondered what it would feel like to leap from a car doing seventy miles an hour.

We eventually get to their exit and I happily bid them farewell. Still had money from the ten Phil had given me. There is a gas station at the exit, so I went in and bought one of those little apple pies wrapped in wax paper and a coke. My next ride is a young couple in an old tan colored, beat up Plymouth Fury, probably a '65 or '66. Before getting in I ask through the open window, "How far are you going?"

The girl in the front passenger's seat said, "Near Lake City,"

I said, "Great!" I thought, that's where I was going to catch I-10 to go west, according to my map. I open the door and the girl in the passenger's seat slid over and invited me to sit in the front. She is good-looking, so I gladly accepted the offer. She is wearing tight jeans; her shirt is skin-tight, and she is *built...* with bleached blonde hair and a nice smile. There is trash— fast food wrappers and cups— on the floorboard and on the dashboard, but I didn't mind.

She said, "I'm Jill, and this is Tommy." She has a bit of a southern accent. Tommy is a little heavy-set, with pork chop sideburns, and needed a shave. Had a mole next to his right eye, flannel shirt cut off at the shoulders, and dirty jeans, along with old cowboy boots.

"Hi, I'm Gene," I said.

"You like to drink?" Tommy asked me.

"Beer and wine," I said. "But it's a little early for me."

"What about something homemade?" He spoke like he hadn't heard what I just said or didn't care. I look over and he has a bottle of Mountain Dew between his legs.

"Homemade?" I ask curiously,

"Oh yeah, here, take a belt off o' this." He handed me his Mountain Dew bottle, so I decide I'd be sociable, considering they have just picked me up. I unscrew the top, gave it a sniff, and it smelled like liquor, though it is clear as water. I put the bottle up to my lips, took a sip, and it is smooth as any whiskey I'd ever tasted, not that I'd tasted very much. A warm rush came over me, like warm water being pumped through my veins. It's a fantastic feeling.

Surprised and impressed, I said, "Damn, that's some of the best tasting stuff I've ever had. What is it?"

Tommy laughs and says proudly, "That's 'shine boy, white lightning'—some of the best there is. Take you another belt, go ahead." I did and could already feel a buzz; this stuff is strong— real strong. I went to hand the bottle back to Tommy, when Jill took it from me, took a swig, and put it between her legs.

A few minutes later, Tommy said, "Let me get one more."

Jill said, "You've had enough. You know how you get."

Tommy, of course, isn't going for it, and said, almost whining, "Come on baby, lemmie get one more?"

"All right, but then I'm putting it away 'til we get home." She handed him the bottle. He unscrewed the cap, held the bottle up to his lips, and started to chug,… *gluck, gluck ,gluck, gluck, gluck*. Sounded like a German Shepard at his water dish.

"That's enough, Tommy." Jill reached for the bottle, he came up for air and let Jill have the bottle back, then he let out, "*YEAAAAHOOOO MOUNTAIN DEW, DAMN THAT'S GOOD!!!*"

Jill looked over at me and held up the bottle. I said, "No thanks, I gotta be able to walk when I get dropped off."

"Walk? Hell…" Tommy said, "I'm driving and I can't even see." He laughs, drunkenly.

We have been on the highway for a while, talking about nothing, when Jill reached in the glove box and rummaged around for a moment, then pulls out a bag of weed. I was slightly taken aback because I didn't think these rednecks looked like the type that smoked weed. She opened the bag in her lap,and being careful not to spill any, she reached in and shook the pack of orange zig zag rolling papers, removing some weed that was sticking to them. She rolled a joint the size of my pinky, and I thought, "Damn, she sure ain't tryin' to make that bag last."

"You do smoke hootch?" she said with a half smile, head cocked sideways, eyebrows up.

"Sure," I said. As we cruised on down the Interstate smoking the joint, Tommy said, "Hey man, you wanna come to our place and party?"

Now I didn't have a good feeling about this, but I also thought, "What the hell, if I'm going to be an adventurer, I need to go on an adventure— take a chance now and then." There was also the fact that Jill was damn cute; so, against my better judgment, I accepted. As we left the highway I was hoping this wasn't going to turn out bad for me.

Being stoned helped to fuel my paranoia. Not far from the Interstate we pull off the paved road onto a dirt one. There are no houses or buildings of any kind. We were out in the sticks and I am beginning to regret my decision. We pull up to a trailer out in the woods. A couple of mangy looking mongrel dogs were chained up in front, barking at us as we walked toward the trailer. A pretty nice looking blue Camaro was parked on the side— a '68 or '69 with wide white racing stripes and Crager SS mag wheels— very cool looking car. The trailer is your typical singlewide, pretty rough, rust stains around the trim, aluminum foil on the windows, and cement blocks propping up the corners.

Walking up to the trailer, Tommy said, "Come on in dude, we got a new color TV, a twenty-seven incher."

At that moment Jill spoke up and said, "Shit Tommy, we're out of beer and I ain't drinking that 'shine all night." We stepped inside the trailer and Tommy turned on the T V and I thought, "What the hell am I doing with these yo yos?"

Jill said to Tommy in a bossy tone, "Tommy, go get me some beer… now. In a little while you'll be too drunk to go anywhere." At that moment, Tommy stood up, walked over to Jill, and drew his hand back as if to hit her. She flinched, and he laughed.

"I'm takin' your Camara'," he said.

"Go ahead, just don't wreck it or you'll buy me a new one." He walked out.

Jill walkd over and plopped down on the couch, right next to me. "Oh shit," I thought, and then she said with a devious grin, "You like girls, doncha?"

I thought, "Now this is not cool at all. I'm with a big redneck's girlfriend and she is now hitting on me." I liked her and thought she was good-looking, but when the reality of getting with her right there and then hit, I suddenly wanted no part of her. Just listening to the rumble of the Camaro's motor pulling away made me uneasy.

"Yeah," I said, "but what about Tommy?"

"What about Tommy?" she said with a tinge of disdain. "He doesn't give a shit what I do and I don't care what he thinks."

"Really?" I said, nervous and surprised, not believing he wouldn't mind if Jill and I got cozy. This was a tough decision for me. Here was a good-looking girl, who had the classic nightmare of a boyfriend. I was torn between my libido and my well being.

"Hell no, as a matter of fact, if you're so worried about him I'll fix that." She got up walked over to the phone and started to dial. I thought, "Who the hell could she be calling?"

"Hello… is this the sheriff's office?" My eyes got big, and I thought, "what the…?

"This is Jill Banks and I'd like to report my car stolen… I guess I left my keys in it… I was sitting in my trailer and heard it pull away just now… Hell if I know, a car thief I guess… It's a 1970 Camaro, blue with white racing stripes… what? Hold on." She set the phone on the counter and began looking through a kitchen drawer.

I got up and walked over and said in a hushed voice,"What the hell are you doing? Are you telling the cops your boyfriend stole your car?" I was freaking out, to say the least.

"Don't worry about it," she said, "He deserves it… Here it is." She picked up the phone again. "Are you there… It's FYN 098… I live in a trailer at 147 Tompkins Rd. just, that's right, west of the Interstate… No I don't think so… it can't be too far from here, it hasn't been five minutes… Okay, I'll be here." She hung up turned to me and said, "Now, where were we?"

I am not feeling any better than before she called, and in fact I feel worse, this crazy chick was going to have her boyfriend arrested… so she could get with me? It made me think, if she could so easily screw her boyfriend over, she could just as easily pull some sort of crazy shit with me.

"Are you nuts? You just called the cops on your boyfriend when you know damn well you sent him to the store. This is not cool atall. Suppose they don't find him. He'll be back."

"Oh, you worry too much." She took my hand and pulled me over to the couch. She started to tug at my coat.

"Take your coat off and stay awhile."

"Wait a minute, aren't the cops gonna come by and ask questions or get a report or something?" I was not feeling relaxed… at all.

"Oh hell, this is the country. They won't be here for who knows how long." Looking for a way to stall, I asked, "Well, you got anything cold to drink?"

She huffs, gets up and goes to the fridge, and looks in. As she bends over I could see her butt clearly. She had a nice figure… that was one sexy girl! Damn, I thought, she probably would be fun to…

"Oh hell no. Are you crazy?" I thought to myself. Even if the cops didn't show up, Tommy could easily get the beer and come back at any moment.

"You want some juice?" she asks.

"Yeah, that's fine." She came back over to me, and as I sat there on the couch she stepped over me, straddling my legs, sat right in my lap, handing me a glass of juice, leaned into me with her body, and began to kiss my face. I was beginning to break down. I had to think fast, so quickly I said, "I need to use the bathroom."

She smiled slightly, and then climbed off me. I got up, went into the bathroom, stood at the commode thinking about if I could fit out the window. Damn, my pack was in the living room. This was so uncool, having no options. I went back in the room. The phone rang, and she answered and had begun chatting with someone, when I heard a car pulling up to the trailer. Jill leans over the counter and pulls the curtain back to peer out the window.

"I gotta go; I'll talk to ya later." She hung up the phone and walks toward the door. There is a loud, *RAP RAP RAP.*

"Sheriff's deputy!" Nonchalantly she opens the door, then stands there leaning against the door frame with her arms folded. There are two sheriff's cars and three or four deputies. It had not been fifteen minutes, and they had their man. The one who knocked on the door said,"You the one that called in the Camara'?"

"Yeah, that was me," Jill said.

"Well this fellow says you know him." There was Tommy on his knees, with his hands cuffed behind his back, missing his shirt, a deputy on either side of him holding him by the arms.

Tommy looked up with a bloodied face and said, "Jill, you fuggin' bitch, tell these pigs who I am."

One of the deputies said,"Watch ya' mouth boy!" The one holding him on his right; gave him a jab in the gut with point of his billy club. Tommy moaned and buckled over. Jill said, in a very matter of fact way,

"I've never seen him before in my life… where's my car?"

"You fuggin' bitch," Tommy said.

"Hey, wud I tell ya, boy. *Whack*! Tommy took another to the ribs, and the deputy at the door said,"Well really don't make no difference 'cause he's DWI and going to jail anyway. You have to come to the sheriff's office and fill out some paperwork. Your car's goin' to the impound."

They drag Tommy away with him whining,"Come on baby quit fuggin' around and tell him who I am."

They threw him in the back of one of the cars and were gone. Jill shut the door and turned around and said, "He won't be botherin' us. Now we can relax."

I jumped to my feet. "I can't believe you just did that."

"Oh fuck him," she said. "He ain't worth spit." I reached down and grabbed my pack.

"Where you going?"

"As far and as fast as I can." I hit the door and I am hoofin' it.

She calls from the trailer, "You ain't gotta leave. Come on, ain't nobody gonna bother us now." I didn't look back. The walk to the highway is not as far as I had thought. Soon as I hit the highway, I catch a ride to the Interstate entrance ramp. Damn that was nuts..... absolutely nuts.

Standing at the entrance ramp I began to think about my friends back home and wondering if maybe I should hold off on going to California right now. Miami was only about five or six hours south from here. Yeah, maybe I should go back and see if anyone might want to go out west with me. Though I am on the road and loving it, I was missing my friends and the familiar surroundings I had left behind. It is not long before a car pulls over and I am out of there. The very next exit was I-10 and I said nothing as we blew right on by, so it is back to Miami for me. I didn't feel like I chickened out, just felt like I changed my mind… or at least that's how I justified my decision, which as a free man I had every right to do. In reality, I got cold feet.

A guy in an old Porsche 912 picked me up. It is in bad shape, which surprised me, considering it is a Porsche. I figured anyone owning a car like a Porsche would take care of it. There were cracks on the dash, a scratched windshield, and the exterior is not any better. This guy is not much of a talker, though I did not care, I am just glad to be getting on down the road. I began to think about what I am going to do back in Miami. Maybe I can talk my friend Paul, or maybe, into to taking off with me, or I can get a job and rent a little place, save up money, and then take off. Well, whatever I did, it will be my choice… nobody is telling me what to do. I am on my own. Porsche Dude is in his early thirties, white collar type, dark short hair, sunglasses and a business look. We had some light conversation, then after about thirty minutes into the ride he asked me, "Do you ever lose sleep because of worry?"

I took the bait. "Yeah, I have… why?"

"Well, in my case it's because my kids live in Utah with my ex-wife and I live in Ocala with my new wife. I'm worried that they're going to grow up not knowing me,"

"How often do you get to see your kids?" I asked.

"Not enough," he says, sadly. "Not nearly enough."

"That's tough all right, so what keeps you and your new wife from moving to Utah?"

"Her parents live here in Florida and she doesn't want to leave."

"Man, you're in a spot, unless you can convince your wife that your kids need you more than her parents need her. Does your ex-wife have a new husband?"

"Yeah, she does," he says, "and they're already calling him "Daddy George."

"Well, if they're young enough, they'll eventually think of the new husband as their dad, simply because he's around… and you're not."

"I'm afraid that's already happening."

"Yeah, well don't hold it against them, kids have a need to attach themselves… makes them feel secure."

"Sounds like you've been there?"

"I have, I sure have."

"This is where I turn off," he says.

I thank him and wish him luck.

"Take care of yourself," he said as he drives off. It felt funny…. me, a kid, on the highway giving a grown man my opinion, like I had something to say worth considering. Well, I was pretty worldly for my age. I thought, I'm a lot more aware than most kids my age.

It was interesting to me, that all the people I met, except for maybe Jill and Tommy, seemed genuinely concerned for me. I was young, on my own, there was no denying it. Most of the people I came in contact with, advised me to be careful and take care of myself. Only I can tell they mean it. Half the time they offer to buy me something to eat or give me money with out my even asking. The world was not such a bad place and people, for the most part, are good.

Right outside Ocala; I pick up Highway 27. The same highway Phil and I took on the way up. Twenty-seven was not an Interstate; it was a two-lane highway that wove in and out of small towns. This is rural Central Florida. There were fresh fruit stands, an occasional old house or rickety wooden structure, some barely standing. The highway wound south past horse farms, orange groves, and a lot of open space. I was getting rides, mostly from locals traveling short distances, but I didn't mind. They were completely cool to me. It is starting to drizzle, but I am so close to Miami I didn't care.

I stick my thumb out and in less than five minutes catch a ride with some construction workers, said they are

on their way to Homestead. Which is south of where I want to go, so I am set. There are three guys, longhaired red neck Florida crackers, crowded in the cab of the pick-up. They tell me to hop in the back. I climb in, finding a spot between scrap wood and toolboxes. No sooner do we get moving, when the clouds clear and the sun comes back out. Once again things are going my way. Along with toolboxes, saw horses, and extension cords is a spear gun. Apparently one of them is a skin-diver and that brought to mind a haunting memory.

It was about two years ago, and I was fifteen years' old living in Miami with my folks, in a subdivision called Green Hills. My dad had an eighteen-foot tan-colored, fiberglass tri-hull boat with a very big Mercury out-board motor. When we were not boating he kept it on a trailer parked in the back yard. My dad was proud of that boat, the whole family was for that matter. I was in a skin-diving club that would take boat trips to the Florida Keys with kids, my own age and a few adult chaperons. We would camp, skin-dive, and spearfish. For a teenage boy, it was an absolute blast. Recently my folks gave me a spear gun as a gift. I borrowed one on my first skin-diving trip, so for my fifteenth birthday, my parents, in all their thoughtfulness, gave me one of my own.

I was up in the back of my dad's boat with my spear gun,shooting at a target made on a cardboard box, set up twenty or so feet from me out in the back yard. It was a relatively powerful spear gun. It had double bands and was capable of killing a good sized grouper or whatever. I was quite happy and enjoying a newly acquired lethal weapon. Even if it was just cardboard boxes being put to death.

My little sister Judy, whom was nine years old and a neighborhood kid by the name of Elizabeth whom was about seven, wondered in the back yard and asked me what I was up to. I invited them both to climb in the boat with me. Elizabeth said her parents were in our house visiting parents. She was a very cute little girl with chestnut hair and a shy smile. I knew her from the neighborhood because she would occasionally hang out with Judy. Judy always seemed to be in a good mood and always curious about whatever her big brother was doing. Today was no exception. With Judy and Elizabeth looking on, I loaded the spear gun and pulled back both bands, turned toward them with the spear gun ready to shoot. I said,

"You see this spear... it could go right through you." While giving them an, *I'm about to kill you*, sort of look, pointing the spear gun in their general direction. Now I was not an evil kid, just not very smart when it came to certain things, such as a loaded spear gun. Casually waving it back and forth between them, while smirking. Their eyes got wide and they were nervous. Then for some unknown reason, other than to get a reaction, I pointed the loaded spear gun directly at Elizabeth's chest. I have absolutely no idea why, except that I was an utterly stupid kid, showing off. Elizabeth looked terrified, trembling, wincing, and holding her hands up in front of her, trying to protect herself backing up, as if her tiny hands would be any defense against a steel spear traveling at forty feet per second at point blank range. There was no place to hide, the tip of the spear was inches from her tiny chest. My arm was extended with the spear pointed directly at her heart. I said,

"Watch," and I pulled the trigger. I am not exaggerating. I put my index finger on the trigger and squeezed. She was looking at me scared as hell and I was enjoying the fear, I was evoking from her. I squeezed the trigger again.

"See my finger, I'm pulling the trigger," I said, casually, while actually flexing my index finger against it. I did this with complete confidence because the safety was on. There was absolutely nothing that could happen...

Then turning the spear gun away and pointing it at my cardboard target while keeping my eyes on Judy and Elizabeth, in a menacing tone I asked,

"You know why you didn't get shot, why you didn't die just now?" Judy and Elizabeth looked at me nervously, unable to speak, eyes as wide as their face muscles could make them, fearfully shaking their heads no.

"Because I had the safety on. Now I'll turn the safety off.", my words dripping with superiority, as if divulging a magician's deep dark secret. While extending my right arm toward the target, I reached over with my left hand clicked the safety off, never taking my eyes off Judy or Elizabeth. I squeezed the trigger. Knowing the quiet yet distinct dull snap sound of the bands releasing was about to be heard as the spear shot toward the cardboard box. Then to my surprise, nothing...nothing happened. No sound, no "thump", turning to look at my gun and squeezed again, still nothing. I was perplexed. Why is it not shooting? Turning the spear gun to get a better look at the safety, I could see it was in the on position. The hair on the back of my neck stood up. I had actually just turned the safety on *after* pointing it away from Elizabeth. Which meant when I had the gun pointed at her chest and was pulling the trigger, the safety was actually off. The trigger had simply jammed. By sheer luck or divine intervention, the trigger simply stuck.

I began to shake and shudder as the blood drained from my head at the realization of what just happened. Dread washed over me like a tsunami. I just came within a centimeter of killing an innocent little girl, because I felt the need to show off. I was weak and I began to quiver. I felt unsteady. It was as if my bones turned to straw and could barely hold my body in an upright position. It was easily the most mind numbing, gut wrenching feeling I had ever experienced. I wanted to hide in the deepest, darkest hole I could find.

I carefully pulled on the bands to disarm the spear gun and had barely enough strength to do so. Making a point not to look at Elizabeth and Judy. I silently climbed down out of the boat, with my spear gun and walked to the garage. I stood there for a moment thinking, then pulled out a ladder and climbed it, placing the spear gun high in the rafters. I Came back down and slipped in the house and went to my room to lie down.

I lied on my back with my hands behind my head, staring up at the ceiling. I could hear Elizabeth's parents chatting with my mom and dad in our family room. I almost put a twenty-eight-inch steel spear right through their little girl's heart. I thought to myself, am I stupid, am I insane, what the hell was I thinking? I almost had to walk in that room and tell Elizabeth's parents, I'm sorry, but I just killed your little girl, she's in the back yard with a steel spear stuck in her chest and I put it there... I remember feeling sick to my stomach, the image of Elizabeth sitting there with a vacant look on her face and a spear sticking out of her, was imprinted in my mind's eye. I felt my eyes watering. At that moment my mom glanced in my room . . .noticing me, she asked,

"Are you feeling okay? You don't look well."

"I'm just tired," I rolled over to hide my face. I moped around for the next two or three days. At night it was hard to fall asleep. I thought how my family member's heart's would have broken, and how I would have destroyed Elizabeth's family. I imagined her smiling, happy mother, crying for the rest of her life, all because of a completely senseless act, by me. There was a constant ringing in my head I could not escape. I considered sitting down with my mom and explaining to her what happened, in the hope she would have some magical thing to say that would make everything all right. Though I never did. I never told anyone what happened. I finally told myself it was not Elizabeth's time to die, that God said, no, not now. When he wants her he'll take her, now be thankful and get on with your life.

As I sat in the back of the pick-up going down the Highway, I pondered how different my life might have been had my spear gun gone off, had that trigger not jammed. I might have been put in a juvenile facility for a very long time, or maybe I would have had a complete nervous breakdown and been put in a mental institution. At times the memory could overwhelm me if I let it. So I learned not to allow it. Like at this moment, sitting in the back of this pick-up truck, speeding toward Miami.

The Fisheries

The construction workers drop me off in Perrine, South Miami, down the street from Food Spot. My first cross-country experience has been a good one. I met some interesting people and some I hope I never meet again. Saw some beautiful country and really enjoyed myself. I know it won't be long before heading back out on the road again. I am hooked. There is a fire within me and traveling seems to fan the flames. I hitchhiked fourteen hundred miles by myself, and if I can do that, California will be no problem. This is what life is about and I am intoxicated by the mere thought. I am the adventurer I always wanted to be. In my mind this truly is my proudest moment.

With my pack slung over my shoulder and feeling emboldened, I walk up to Food Spot. A couple of my friends, Paul, Bub Markowitz, Bub's girlfriend, and a couple other assorted Food Spot flies greet me. They are curious about what happened to Phil and me. It's funny… I had hung out with Paul at Food Spot the night before Phil and I left; now, four days and 2,800 miles later, I am right back here with Paul again. Paul is this tall thin kid with a bit of a southern accent. He is seventeen and had quit school in the tenth grade. He has a nose like a beak, and for that his nickname is "Bird." Pauly Bird lives in Homestead, fifteen miles south of Perrine, and we became good friends over the past months, I am glad to see him again.

"How was it and why the hell are you back so soon?" Paul asked smiling.

"It was very cool. We got all the way to Detroit… that's when Phil's uncle called Phil's dad and told him where we were."

"Oh shit," Paul said chuckling.

"Yeah, Phil and I decided to hitchhike to California, but we were freezing our asses off before we even got going, so he went back to his uncle's and I took off and hitchhiked back here."

"Now what are you gonna do?" Paul asked.

"Oh, I'll find a place to crash until I get a job, and then I'll rent a place. Seen Glenn lately? Is he still living in the apartments behind Food Spot?" I asked. Glenn Jarred was my oldest friend.

"Yeah, I saw him earlier today… over at the Fisheries."

"The Fisheries? What's that?"

"It's this place over on Old Cutter Road where some of us have been hanging out lately. A guy by the name of Jeffery Joe has a one room apartment there."

"So its apartments, called the Fisheries?" I was puzzled.

"Well, it used to be a tropical fish hatchery, but the owners gave up on the business and turned the main house into one-room apartments."

"Really? Huh."

I heard about the Fisheries before Phil and I took off but had no idea what it even was. Paul said, "Come on, hop in my car, I'll take you there. Maybe Jeff will let you crash at his place."

We jump in his faded green '64 Oldsmobile and head for the Fisheries. We hit Dixie Highway and head south, take a left at Franjo Road, then Old Cutter Road, ten minutes later there is the Fisheries. Pulling up in the driveway, I am intrigued by how secluded it is—the place is dark and ominous.

"Damn, Paul, this is a trip. People live here?"

"Yeah, pretty cool huh? Follow me, I wanna show you something." He is like a little kid with a secret to share. I watch my step; it is difficult to see. There is a crumbling cement walkway and Paul leads the way along the side of what I assume is the house where the rooms for rent are. Crickets chirping, frogs croaking and the grass had not been mowed in years, though I can see there once was landscaping by the way the bushes and shrubs bordered the walkway. Now weeds, vines, and trees engulf everything. Stepping in the back yard there are rows of rectangular tanks made of concrete. They are about two feet wide, five feet long, and three feet deep, with barely enough room to walk between. There are fifty or sixty cement tanks lined up, ten or twelve across, one behind the other, stretching thirty to forty feet from the back of the house. With only the moon for light, it looks like rows of water filled cement coffins with no lids. The eerie glow of the moonlight reflecting off the black water in the tanks is creepy as hell . . . but I liked it. I said to Paul,

"So this is where they must have kept the fish, huh, the Fisheries… makes sense."

"Franjo Fisheries," Paul said.

We wander among the tanks, and I thought what a great place it would be for a horror flick.

"Man this is creepy." I could envision zombies rising up out of the black water, skin falling off, with slimy algae running down their faces, roaming the neighborhood in search of human flesh. I walked zombie-like toward Paul, my arms extended in front of me and my head cocked to one side. I bumped my knee on one of the tanks and wince. Paul just shook his head, forced half a laugh and said,

"Let's go see if Jeff's home."

Following him back around to the front of the house, I am curious about the inside. The whole scene felt surreal, with the moonlight shinning through the vine-laden palm trees. Paul pointed toward the front yard.

"There's a huge pond right there. You can't really see from here, but it's like a giant bowl of black bean soup." I look in the direction he was pointing but could not see a thing. Stepping up to the house, Paul opens a screen door minus the screen that led to a patio in front of the house. We step through the door to a terrazzo floor, following Paul across the front of the house. It is a little darker on the patio, though there is a single dim, naked light bulb at the far end. To our right are remnants of torn screens along the front of the house, the remains of what once had been a big screened-in front patio. To the left is a curved front wall of the house, with thousands of tiny mosaic tiles, creating scenes that were indistinguishable in the faint light and though many of the tiles are missing, you can tell it had been quite impressive in its day.

Every ten or twelve feet there is a door with a number. Paul stopped at the second to last door, which displayed a number seven and a dimly lit bulb. We hear Jim Morrison's voice accompanied by the distinct sound of the electric organ of the Doors, relieving the otherwise creepy silence.

The time to hesitate is through
No time to wallow in the mire
Try now we can only lose
And our love become a funeral pyre.

Paul knocks, and in two seconds the door swings open. There stands a guy, shoeless in cut-off shorts and a white tee shirt. He has a big thick mustache and a high forehead, with thinning blonde hair combed back, a big smile, dragging on a cigarette. He is easily twenty-five or twenty-six years old. I wonder what my friends were doing hanging out with this strange brew of a guy. Paul spoke first.

"Hey Jeff, what's going on?"

"Nothing really... Come on in." Jeff stepped back holding the door with his left hand, picked up his right foot and placed it on the inside of his left knee, now standing on one leg in a stork-like pose. In a comical way, he bowed his head slightly, and swept his extended right hand across the open doorway, gesturing for us to come in. At first, he looks like somebody's dad, but then, his mannerisms and the way he spoke is tentative... almost childlike.

Jeff's apartment looks like a cheap motel room. The smell of cigarettes and stale beer permeates the air. The room is about twelve by eighteen feet with a card table and a couple folding chairs to our immediate left. There is a shoebox-size Am/Fm radio on the table, along with some Icee cups, packs of Pall Malls, and a full ashtray. Against the wall, to the right of the card table, is an old burgundy couch with a coffee table, with a couple of overflowing ashtrays and some cans of Old Milwaukee. There is an end table next to the couch with yet another ashtray, more cans of beer, and a half-empty bag of Wise potato chips. In the back corner of the room is an unmade bed that took up most of the wall, flanked by a rickety nightstand holding a small lamp with a crooked shade, yet another overflowing ashtray, and an old paperback lying face down open to the page where I assume the reader had left off. At the foot of the bed is a jalousie door, a rear exit I assume. We sit down on the worn shabby spring less couch.

Across the room from the couch on the opposite wall is an open door, next to the rear exit, and I could see a small sink, so I assume it's his bathroom. Directly across the couch from us is a TV perched on a dresser, showing the Beverly Hillbillies with the sound off. Damn that Ellie May had a body! To the right of that is an open door—a closet, I presume. Jeff went to the card table, put out his cigarette, which he smoked down to a very short butt, pulls out a chair, and sat, leaning forward, resting his elbows on his knees, smiling at us with a puppy dog demeanor, nervously waiting for us to say something, or throw him a bone.

Paul spoke first.

"This is a friend of mine, Gene; he just hitchhiked down from Detroit." Jeff's eyes got big, he stuck his hand out for me to shake, and I did. He is enthusiastic and uncertain at the same time.

"So you hitchhiked all the way from Detroit, Michigan? Wow, that's pretty gutsy."

"Yeah, took a day and a half." I said it as if I did it all the time.

"Damn, is that where you're from?" He picks up a pack of cigarettes off the card table and offered Paul and me one. Paul declined, but I took one. I notice his middle and index fingers are seriously stained a yellowish brown. He is undoubtedly a heavy smoker.

"No, my parents live here in Miami, but I went to Detroit with a friend." Paul interjected,

"Hey Jeff, Gene needs a place to crash. Can he stay here with you?"

I was a little taken back by Paul's forwardness, but before I had a chance to say anything, Jeff said,

"Sure no problem, he can have a piece of floor." He smiled, and I thought, Damn, this guy is laid back as hell or really hard up for friends.

"Thanks, man." Now I am still a little curious about a twenty-five-year-old hanging with a group of sixteen and seventeen-year olds, but I am not going to be too curious and talk myself out of a place to stay.

After a short while, someone knocks at the door, and Jeff hops to his feet and swings open the door with the same exuberance as when Paul and I showed up. There stands Glenn and Don—Don who let me sleep in his car my first night on the street after my dad gave me my walking papers, and Glenn, my friend since the seventh grade at Glades Junior High. Glenn is a well-built dude, with thick, long, unkempt blond hair, long side burns, and an easy smile. His blue eyes turn blood red after two hits off a joint, and girls like him. Don has slits for eyes, always dressed in a tucked in button-down shirt, and chain smoked—but it is obvious he doesn't inhale. Just thinks it makes him look cool. He is a big guy, but not well built, and the girls don't think much of him. Don is always trying to fit in, and the fact is either you do or you don't. A person who has to try to fit in comes across as a phony, though I'd always thought of him as an all right guy. At the same time, something about him bothers me.

Happy to see them, I say,

"Hey you guys, what's up?" And we shake hands. I do like my friends... a lot. I find the kind of comfort and caring from my friends I don't feel at home. I tell myself... Paul, Glenn, and Phil... they are my family. It is as if I want to choose my family, not just accept the one life had thrown my way.

We sit around drinking the beer Glenn and Don brought over while I tell tales of hitchhiking… feeling rather worldly, being the center of attention and loving it. Don seems jealous… questioning me, like he has his doubts about my stories. He is that kind of guy… afraid someone might be more interesting than him. Don was known to accuse Glenn of lying about having a stepfather and used to say Glenn's real father had never died. Not to Glenn's face, but he liked talking behind his friend's back. Seemed to have a need to put down anyone, friend or not. Don is my first real encounter with a passive-aggressive personality, and it is annoying.

Don asked me, his voice dripping with skepticism,

"So, you stood on the side of the road and stuck your thumb out and got rides all the way here from Detroit, Michigan?" He is giving me this, yeah right, kind of look.

"Right up to Food Spot, to be exact," I say with pride.

Glenn, on the other hand, is impressed I had the guts to do it. Glenn and I have been friends for a long time, so we had a history. He knows when I am bullshitting and when I am not. Glenn has a great sense of humor. That is one of the qualities that make him so likeable. We have a standing joke between us about him moving out of his house. Yeah, Glenn would say, Gene helped me to move out of my parent's house one night. He would look at me, smile and nod because he knew; I knew exactly what he is talking about.

It was about three months earlier. I went by Glenn's house late in the evening, quietly creeping up to his bedroom window and knocking. He was still awake and he let me crawl in. We sat there smoking weed, carefully blowing the smoke out the window. Glenn got the bright idea to sneak his dad's car, a '66 Ford Fairlane, out for a drive. I said,

"Glenn you're nuts! Your old man will kill you if he catches you."

"*If* he catches me; come on, I do it all the time. We'll just push the car away from the house so he won't hear when we start it." It was about eleven o'clock at night and his parents are already in bed. He got the keys and we pushed the car about a block from the house, hopped in, and started it up. First thing we did was head for Food Spot, where we get some older dude to buy us beer. We drive around town drinking, smoking weed, and knocking on the bedroom windows of various girls we knew, hoping they would sneak out with us. We went by Colette Munsky's, but she must have snuck out already, because she wasn't in her room and it was almost midnight.

We finally found Robin Thorton home and convinced her to come out. She rode around with us for a while, and I tried putting the moves on her, though she thought of me only as a friend, so we weren't connecting. Glenn got so drunk he could hardly drive, so I tell him we need to drop Robin off back at her house. Before we take off, I thought it would be best if I drove, so I convince Glenn of the wisdom of allowing me to take over. Robin helped me coax him out of the driver's seat. He is drunk and he knew it, so we bade Robin farewell and headed back to his house, myself at the wheel.

Driving away from Robins I am not sure which way to go to get out of her neighborhood. After a few minutes of driving and a few turns that led nowhere all of a sudden, the road ran out. Now in Miami at the time this was not uncommon, because there were so many new subdivisions adjacent to wooded areas that had yet to be developed. We are on grass before I have a chance to react, and we hit something hard, real hard—it's a huge log, at least two feet in diameter. *CABOOOOOOM!!!!!* I never have a chance to touch the brakes. We smack the log and the log didn't budge. The front bumper and frame of the car imbedded in the log, and the rear of the car went straight up in the air. A little more momentum and we would have flipped over on the roof; but when the car became perpendicular to the ground, instead of flipping over, it came back down and crashed to the ground on its wheels. Yet another, *CABOOOOOOM!!!!!* By shear luck, we were not going fast enough to flip all the way over, which would probably have killed one, if not both of us.

We sit there, stunned, and look at one another in shock. Glenn lifts a big hunk of the dashboard off his lap and set it on the seat between us. Unable to open the doors, we climb out the windows. Miraculously, we had nothing more than minor cuts and bruises. The impact on the log had smashed the front wheels back up into the car, and the bottom of the front of the car was flat on the ground. As I am looking at the car from the side, all I can see was the bottom half of the front wheels. The car looks totaled; there is smoke and steam coming from every crack and crevice. It is hissing like a locomotive that had just pulled into the station from a coast-to-coast, non-stop run, and I am scared shitless about what has just happened. I went up to Glenn and say,

"Glenn, you gotta say you were driving. If my parents find out about this, I'll never drive again." Some friend I am. I have just wrecked his dad's car and I am asking him to take the blame— more concerned about my own driving privileges then the fact that I just put my best friend in one hell of a predicament.

Glenn didn't respond to my plea. Instead, he went around to the rear of the car and began trying to push it, and in a garbled drunken slur said,

"Cccome on… help me… get this thing… out of here." God bless him, he looks desperate. Now I'm sure Glenn has pushed his dad's Fairlane many times, but this was not going to be one of *those* times. Standing there, I notice we are not twenty feet from a canal, which meant if we had not hit that log we would have gone straight in the water.

At that moment, a middle-aged man in a bathrobe and slippers came trotting up, obviously concerned, and asked,

"Is everybody okay?" I answered,

"Yeah, we're alright." I was standing there with my arms folded, head down and leaning with my back against the car. The bath robed man said,

"I've called the police and they're on their way."

At that moment, Glenn looked up at me from behind the car with his eyes wide and scared, he mumbled,

"Pppolice?" Completely disgusted, I muttered,

"Yeah, that's what he said." Glenn slowly turned and started to stagger away from the scene. I walked up behind him and said,

"Wait man, you can't leave," not wanting him to get in any more trouble then we were already in..

The bath-robed guy called out,

"Hey, you can't leave, the police are coming." By now, Glenn was stumbling away and I was walking along side him holding him up, trying to convince him not to take off.

"Glenn, you gotta stay. They're gonna know it's your car." He said, unsteadily walking away,

"Fuck that…I'm not…gggoin' to jail."

We heard a siren off in the distance, I began thinking damn this was bad—really bad. Glenn started to trot and I was trotting right along with him thinking, if he leaves the scene, he'll end up regretting it.

He started slowing down and the sirens were getting closer. That's when I said,

"Run Glenn, run, you can make it." I had a change of heart; we trotted along the canal and came to a school where we hid as the cop cars flew by with their sirens blaring and lights flashing. At that point I realized Glenn wasn't gonna make it any further on foot, so I told him, "You wait here I'll go home and get my mom's car and come back and get you."

I walked and jogged all the way to my folks' house, about two miles. When I get there I quietly snuck in the house, got the keys to my mom's Plymouth Valiant, and drove back to the school where Glenn was lying passed out next to a puddle of puke. I pick him up, help him to my mom's car, and take him back to my house.

The next morning we get up before my folks awoke and told my brother Johnny about what happened. He was two years older and a lot more responsible. My folks trusted him; he listened to the story and responded with,

"You idiots are lucky you didn't get killed." I then said,

"Hey, Johnny, let's go drive by where we wrecked. I'd like to see it." He agreed to take us, and though Glenn didn't want to go, he reluctantly got in the car. I gave Johnny directions to the area where I thought the wreck happened. As we went around a corner, Johnny abruptly stopped and said,

"Oh shit, look." Both Glenn and I did, and were freakin'. Across the canal, a good thirty or forty yards from where we stopped, was a tow truck hooking up to the Fairlane, with Glenn's dad and a cop looking on.

From the back-seat Glenn said, ducking down,

"Get me the hell out of here, now!" I glanced at him huddled in the back seat. He looked like a small child who had just seen the boogieman and knew if the boogieman saw him, it was over. Johnny put the car in reverse and slowly backed up. As we drove away, Glenn said in an accepting tone,

"Well I won't be going home any time soon…"

He never did go home after that. He started living with some guys in their apartment in a complex behind Food Spot, and has lived there since. So, in his opinion, I helped him move out. I guess I would have to agree.

Sitting there in Jeffrey Joe's apartment, I am glad to be back among friends. Then who should come to the door but Phil Sanchez and Matt Myan. Phil just laughed and shook his head when he saw me, not surprised. Myan on the other hand was interested to hear how I got back. Matt asked,

"So when did you get back, you crazy fucker?"

"I was just dropped off near Food Spot not more than an hour ago." Myan then asked,

"You hitchhiked all that way; were ya scared?" He is smiling.

"Not really, I was more intrigued by the adventure."

"Intrigued huh?"

"Yeah, I met all kinds— a trucker, a lawyer, and a couple of Georgia rednecks who took me home with them."

"Took you home with them, what the hell was that about?"

"It was a guy and a girl and a trailer… Well let's just say I was lucky to get away from them in one piece." They laughed and shook their heads. That was yet another of my routines. I would tell my friends a small part of a story and then leave the rest to their imagination. It was my way of creating a mystique.

Myan reminded me of an outdoorsman, or at least that's what he aspired to be. He is a big healthy guy—not fat, just big. He always seemed to be in a good mood. He likes to hunt, camp, and fish, and is really a good guy. I asked Phil,

"So what happened when your dad showed up in Detroit?" He didn't really answer me. He said,

"My dad and I just got back a few hours ago. What happened to California?"

I responded, trying not to sound like I'd chickened out.

"I decided it was too cold to hitch out west, so I came down here… maybe wait until the spring." Yeah, I was back and it feels good, though the road still beckoned. It is only a matter of time before I will be leaving again, but at the moment I couldn't feel better. I am with my friends. And I love my friends.

My Yellow Brick Road

Before long Paul, Glenn, and I are all staying at Jeffrey Joe's apartment. I am having a good time hanging out. If I want to stay, I can, and when I am ready to go, there is no one to tell me I can't. This new-found freedom really appeals to me, and I am not missing my folks at all. "It's my life and I'll do what I want." sang Eric Burdon of The Animals and I agreed. I am living life on my terms, making my own rules, of which I had very few; a joint to smoke or beer to drink and a good time.

After a few days, I decide to get a job. If I am going to stay here at Jeff's, I will need to pay my share. I am not a mooch, and do not like being thought of as one. I hitchhike up to U.S. 1, just a few miles away, to look for a job. U.S. 1 has quite a few restaurants in close proximity to one another, and I know with my skills at acquiring a job, I can just walk along applying until I find one. After a few attempts, a Lum's restaurant hires me. In a week, I get my first check and immediately give Jeff money for rent, bought beer, Pall Mall's, potato chips, and Spaghetti-O's, paid my friends back the money I owed them, and still have a few bucks left.

It is a little crowded at Jeff's apartment, but he doesn't care; he likes having my friends and me around, and at one point he even asks, "Would you teach me to be cool?" How does someone teach someone else to be cool? If I thought of myself as uncool, could I actually ask someone to teach me to be cool? Hell, that would be uncool! What a funny guy. I conclude Jeff is just a bit slow when it came to social skills. He is more like a fifteen-year-old, than a twenty-five. No wonder he likes hanging out with us. Jeff has a pudgy sixteen-year-old girlfriend by the name of Trudy— she would not be my choice for a girlfriend, but it seems to work for Jeff. She came around with snack food and cigarettes she snatches from her house. She has a girlfriend, Susie, she brings with her, who is fifteen years old and damn cute. Susie has jet black hair, a sweet face and a nice body— a sexy little Italian/American girl, who enchants the hell out of all of us. Though being fifteen had us all a little gun shy.

In Jeff's efficiency, there is a good-size walk-in closet, and I decide to put a bunk bed in there. I find some pieces of scrap wood in the back of the Fisheries and build a platform. I find an old mattress in one of the nearby vacant apartments and create my own sleeping quarters. Though it is only a closet, it is like having my own room. Next thing we knew, Paul is all over Susie and she in turn took to him. They would borrow my closet and play "hide-the-sausage." Never mind the fact that Paul has a girlfriend by the name of Katie, and if she finds out Paul will catch all kinds of hell; but at the moment, teenage libidos were in charge, or out of control, depending on your perspective.

It's not long before Glenn, Phil, Matt, Paul, and I are all using the closet for extracurricular activity with any willing girl. Jeff would take Trudy in the closet as well. Now considering Jeff is at least nine years older than Trudy, who is a minor; that worried me. I envisioned Trudy's dad coming over with a shotgun looking for Jeff and making Swiss cheese out of all of us. Unsettling as it is, it is not enough to make me look elsewhere for a place to live.

One evening Phil came by the Fisheries looking for a bag of weed. I too want to get stoned, so I suggest he check with the hippies from Ohio who live in a rental house next to the Fisheries and of course offer to introduce him. When I first met the Ohio hippies, they said they had torn up their draft cards in their hometown up north and took off, ending up here in Miami. I became friendly with them because they smoked weed. The fact that they were draft dodgers meant nothing to me. They were all a few years older than my friends and me and were kind of biker types—rough characters— though they were cool, I cautiously trusted them. We go over, knock on the door and a good-looking girl opened it. We ask her if anyone has a lid for sale. She simply turned away leaving the door open and sat down on the floor, so we step in the house. There are five or six guys and girls lying around, getting stoned right there in the living room. There is a motorcycle in pieces, with the parts spread out in very organized rows on the floor. I thought about my mom getting upset with my brother and me for tracking grease in the house from working on the family car. She would have had a cow at the sight of this. Phil addressed the group and asked if anyone had a bag for sale, though no one responded. They just sat there stoned and looked at us. We could hear music coming from a room off the living room. It is Steppenwolf playing 'Magic Carpet Ride'. The cute girl, who answered the door, is on the floor just a few feet from where Phil and I are now standing. She slowly cocked her head back, demurely, looked up at Phil, and said, "Hi." Phil nodded to her, and then becoming slightly irritated by the lack of anyone responding. He again inquired,

"You guys got a lid, or what?" The cute girl reached up without saying a word and cupped Phil's groin in her hand while coyly smiling. Phil put his hands on his hips, turned his head to one side and coughed (twice). Everyone in the room busted up laughing; it was funny alright. Phil was quick like that. They sell us a lid and we split.

Rarely is Jeff's apartment ever unoccupied. There is always at least one of us here, and on this particular night, I am that one. Startled by a loud, rapid, almost cop-like knock on the door, I open it cautiously and there stood a short, fat, bald, Italian-looking man in his forties, wearing a white tank top and a face that says: I am one pissed off mother fucker. My first thought is, oh shit, some girl's dad is here... and he's not happy. He didn't have a shotgun, but he did have a hammer in his right hand at his side and is gripping it tightly. At the sight of the hammer I could immediately feel sweat beading up on my forehead. With what sounded like an Italian accent he says,

"Wairz Paul?"

"Paul?" I responded, scratching the back of my head, acting perplexed. "He's not here." It dawned on me that this might be Susie's dad. Placing the back of his hand on my chest he gently but firmly moved me to one side so he could look in the room.

"Not here huh?" Stretching his neck looking in, "Wairzee ?!?"

"I don't know," I said quietly and respectfully. I was about to shit my pants. I knew he was one irate daddy.

At that moment, a car pulls in the driveway at the other end of the Fisheries, the head lights caught the mad Italians attention, and he turns and walks in that direction. I follow at a safe distance. As luck would have it, it's Paul, and he is walking right toward his judge, jury, and executioner. As Mr. pissed-off, stepped toward Paul, I call to warn him, "Paul... Look out!" Paul froze in his tracks. The man is ten steps from him and moving swiftly in his direction.

In a loud voice the Italian says,

"You sonovabitch!" Paul, being light on his feet, jumped back and ran behind his car, positioning himself with his hands on the trunk, his legs spread, rocking from foot to foot on the balls of his feet as he peered over his car to see.

Paul said, sounding scared,

"What…what'd I do?"

'Mister pissed off' holding up his hammer and shaking it at Paul yelling,

"I found da rubbers in Susie's purse, you skinny bastid!" This confirmed to me it is Susie's dad. The chase is on… around the car they went, and as slow as Susie's dad is, I worried he might get close enough to hit Paul. Paul, hoping to quell the situation, says,

"I promise you, they're not my rubbers."

I watch the action, from a safe distance, careful to stay out of harms way. Around the car they went, Susie's dad chasing and cursing Paul.

"She tol' me you were her boyfriend, you piece o' shit…Comear, I got something for ya!!" He is shaking his hammer in Paul's direction, then drawing it back, Paul staying one step ahead. It becomes comical; although I'm sure Paul would not agree. I thought, Paul must have gone by Susie's house at least one time and that's how her dad knew who he was. Either that or I gave him away by yelling his name. Then again, Susie must have told her dad about the Fisheries… otherwise, how else would he have known where to look for Paul? Stupid girl…

Paul takes off for the back of the Fisheries, Susie's dad right on his tail. Paul is dancing through the old cement fish tanks like a young Fred Astaire in faded blue jeans. Susie's dad is becoming winded, but not giving up. Down through a row of tanks they went, then up the next row. I watched from the corner of the building and I am thinking, look at the fat cat chasing the skinny mouse through the maze. Paul eventually gets through the tanks, all the way around the house. I go back around front and saw Paul heading to his car, while Susie's dad tries desperately to catch him. I went for the passenger's side. Paul jumped and slid across the hood to get to the driver's side, gets the door open, and in an instant, is behind the wheel. We are doing thirty miles an hour in reverse before Susie's dad knew what happened.

"You skinny bastid… don't you ever come near Susie." His voice fades behind us. "I kill you!"

He probably threw his hammer at us, because I could hear something clanking on the street as we drive off, escaping into the night. Paul's Oldsmobile screams down Old Cutter Road.

After a few miles, and once Paul is sure we weren't being followed, we went over to Food Spot to collect ourselves. We run into Glenn and his girlfriend, Denise. Glenn has some blue mescaline and asked me if I want half a hit.

"Sure," I said. Now I have eaten some magic mushrooms before and figured I could handle it. I also decided if it was good enough for Glenn… We go behind Food Spot to the tree on the edge of the golf course to drink beer. I tell the "Paul and Susie's dad" story, adding a few embellishments, which have all of them, including Paul, laughing their asses off. After a little while the mescaline starts to kick in and I start seeing tracers of lights and begin laughing for no apparent reason. Paul knew enough about it to know I am in the early stages of a mind-altering experience, and begins messing with me, flicking his hand in my face, attempting to freak me out.

Paul and I leave Glenn and Denise and get back in his car. By now the mescaline is going good in my head, and Paul could see it in my eyes, so he decides to take me on one of his Paul Collins trademark joy rides through the near by subdivision. Not sure why, but I got in the back seat of his car. He takes off and rounds the first corner, with me hanging on for dear life, through front yards, sideways, wheels spinning, sliding, and ripping out shrubs, like a yardman gone wild. Paul is looking at me in his rearview mirror smiling, not saying anything, his face looks distorted as he watches my reaction to his driving. I'm sure I look terrified, pleading with him to slow down and laughing at the same time.

"Come on Pauly… take it easy, you're gonna mess your car up if you keep this up." But he doesn't care; he is having too much fun. On we went, tires spinning across the lawns, then screeching as they hit the pavement. Eventually he became bored with landscaping the neighborhood and we head back to the Fisheries.

Upon arriving, he is careful to drive by before pulling in. There is no sign of Susie's dad, so we decide it is safe. We walk up to Jeffrey Joe's and listen at the door, just in case, we knock and stand back, still a little jittery. To our relief, Jeff is there and in one piece. We tell him the Susie's dad story and he is not happy about it—but what could he do? Jeff informed us that Don Stein had told him he was sick of listening to his parents bitching at him and is going to rent the apartment next door. Speaking of parents, I'd been back more than a week and hadn't even wanted to call to let my parents know I am okay. I have a real chip on my shoulder. I'm not mad at them… just didn't want to talk to them.

Don Stein moved in next to Jeff, and Glenn moved in with Don. The partying got even more regular, and between Don's and Jeff's apartments there is anywhere from five to ten to twenty-five teenagers hanging out on any given night. Susie quit coming around… I guess her dad put the fear of God in her; but with all the other girls hanging out now, we really didn't miss her, and we damn sure didn't miss her dad.

One night, after working maybe three or four weeks at Lum's restaurant, I arrive for my shift, only to be hustled back outside by one of my co-workers. He says, "Wait a minute, man. I'm not so sure you wanna go in there. Come out back with me." The serious look on his face had my attention and I followed. He began, "The other night after you got off work, you forgot your shirt."

"Yeah— so what?" Not understanding why leaving my shirt meant anything important.

"Well, Mr. Gomez, who you know doesn't like us leaving our clothes on shelves in the kitchen, saw your shirt and picked it up and asked who left their shirt. Not thinking anything of it, Jill, the cashier said, 'It's Gene's' and right then, a bag of weed fell out on the floor."

"Oh shit! What'd he do… am I fired?" Now I was freaking out.

"Well, he picked up the bag, looked at it, and started cursing in Spanish."

"Oh, Christ, what'd he do? Ooohhh shit…" I just knew I was screwed.

"Believe it or not, he walked out front and emptied it right on the flat-top griddle, muttering under his breath."

"You gotta be shittin' me. It was only enough for a couple joints. Didn't it start to burn?"

"Oh yeah, it burned all right. That was his intention; except it started to smoke up the restaurant with the smell of weed. There were some long haired freaks in the dining room eating lunch, and they started laughing and saying things like, 'Hey, fix me one of those hotdogs, they smell deeelicious.' Gomez started to get nervous and embarrassed, he poured some grease on it and swished it in the trash. So, I'm not sure you wanna go in there." By now I am completely bummed out and feel stupid for having left that weed. I had visions of cop cars, jail, and a restaurant full of people getting high on my weed.

"Well, thanks for warning me, man. Guess I'll just head home and wait for the cops to come get me or whatever." I walked off in a daze not really sure what was going to happen.

On my way home to the Fisheries, walking down U.S. 1, I pass by a restaurant called the New England Oyster House. I see some young guys emptying trash and asked them if the manager is there. They said he is, so I walked in. After I filled out an application, this serious looking, short Cuban man walked up to me and said, "I need a dishwasher, when can you start?" I told him, "Soon as you want."

"Be here tomorrow, four o'clock… and don't be late. You're on the night shift."

I thank him and leave. I walk along thinking I am one damn lucky guy; one minute I'm worried about my boss finding weed in my shirt, the next minute I get a new job, and I'm feeling like a cat with a bird in his mouth heading home.

When I get back to Jeff's, a few people already are hanging out. The Fisheries had become almost as popular as Food Spot, maybe more. In fact, ever since we found the Fisheries we pretty much looked down our collective noses at the kids who still hung out at Food Spot. I tell Jeff, Paul, Stein, and the others what happened at Lum's and everybody had a good laugh. When I said I got another job on my way home, Don Stein accused me of lying. He said,

"You are such a bullshit artist, can't you ever just say something, without adding some of your homemade bullshit." That pissed me off, so I came back at him. "Don, why would I lie? What do I have to benefit by lying about getting a job and what business is it of yours anyway, asshole?"

"Not paying rent maybe?" he said, in an accusatory tone.

I turn to Jeff,

"Jeff, do I owe you any money, have I not chipped in for rent and food?" He nodded and said,

"Yeah, you have, you don't owe me anything." I turned to Don and got in his face, the hair on the back of my neck was up,

"So what are you talking about, Mr. Busybody; as if paying my rent has anything to do with your ass?" He gave me one of those, condescending smirks he was famous for, left, and went next door to his apartment.

Later in the evening Don has some acid— yellow sunshine— and gives me half a hit. I think he s feeling guilty about what happened between us. That is his way of saying he is sorry. Paul showed up, and Don convinced him to take half a hit. Now Myan is there and he is not happy about it at all. He said to Paul, "Bird, don't do that stupid shit, you don't need that." Matt liked to drink beer but nothing else, no drugs for Myan. He thought we were all dumb-asses getting stoned and taking acid and is not afraid to let us know how he feels. I guess seeing Paul going down that road rubbed Myan the wrong way. Now for Paul to take acid kind of surprised me, because Paul really didn't even get stoned, so for him to take acid is a real leap; I think I'd better keep an eye on him. It is the usual evening— music blaring, freaks coming over, getting drunk and stoned, running around the Fisheries like it was a loony bin.

Now at the moment I find myself sitting in front of Stein's little bedside radio, and no one else is in the room. Every song sounded so damn good, I can't believe it. This tiny radio is creating some of the most incredible sound I ever heard; then this song came on, and I recognized it as a song I normally did not like; hated for that matter…

Sunshine goes away today
Don't think, much about playing,
This old man he's trying to run my life,
These ain't dues I'll be paaaying.

I thought, damn, this song is fantastic, and he's one of the best singers I've ever heard in my entire life. You see, that's the way it is when you're on acid… it fools you into thinking, no believing something is way better or worse than it actually is. If something happens to send you in a good direction, it seems to feel that much better, and if something occurs that triggers you to go in a bad direction, you go there with a vengeance. Once I remember finding one of my friends in the bathroom mirror picking at something on his cheek. As I took a closer look I noticed there was blood all over his fingers and he had basically picked a small hole in his skin trying to pop a zit. It was all I could do to get him to leave it alone and put a Band-Aid on it. He probably still has a scar there. During a trip when something goes awry, it can become a "bad trip." Some bad trips were worse than others. Rumor had it; some people became so lost in the trip that they never came down, and would have to be institutionalized, or spend the rest of their days wandering the streets on a never-ending trip, hallucinating 2-4-7. You would think the possibility of that would have kept us from fooling with the shit... But of course it did not. We were indestructible, we were teenagers.

Paul came in the room, I begin telling him how cool this song is, and he responded with a blank stare. I tell him to have a seat and that I want to show him something. Once he looks comfortable sitting on Don's couch I tell him, "Look at the wall the blank wall; do you see the devil's head?" He looked up and said, "No."

"You're not looking hard enough; see the horns the eyes the big smoking nostrils." At that moment, his eyes got real big and with an almost child-like voice he said,

"No… No I don't wanna look." And he ran out of the room. I thought, Nice Gene. And you were gonna look out for the guy…"

By now I have been at the Fisheries a couple months. I still have not spoken to my folks, though I know, they know I am in town. A few weeks back, my mom had gotten word to me through Glenn's mom to ask me to come home for Thanksgiving. I never responded, and the holiday came and went; now it is right before Christmas and she gets word to me again that she would like to take me to lunch. So I call the house and told her I would go. The next Saturday, my mom and my little sister Judy show up to pick me up from the Fisheries. I wait out front; I don't want her to see how I am living. We go to a nice restaurant and had lunch. She talks to me as if everything were normal, even though we both knew it wasn't. On the way back to the Fisheries I tell her I will probably be joining the Navy sometime in the near future, but that I had a few things I still want to do. She thought that is a great idea and hoped I would follow through on it. I had been thinking about the Navy and I knew that would make her happy. Guess I was throwing her a bone.

About five months ago when I was going to pre-enlist, all I had to do was show up for the physical. The recruiter said I could get my high school diploma in the Army. On the night before the physical, I was hanging with my friends, when somebody brought some magic mushrooms, and of course, I had to eat some. We had a good old time running around Coral Reef Drive and Food Spot, freaking out on everything and everyone; hallucinating was a real thrill for me. Some of my friends were afraid of tripping, and I think the thought of that emboldened me to want to do it even more… Like you really have to have your shit together if you were going to trip, and I have been telling myself I have my shit together for quite some time.

The day after I ate the mushrooms I am still tripping as I left home with my mom, who dropped me off at the enlistment office. I walked into a room of distorted-faced creatures who sounded like they had marbles in their mouths when they spoke. I was nervous, barely able to respond to their questions, I wondered if they were going to find out I was tripping on mushrooms. When they took my blood pressure, it was high. The doctor asked a few questions and moved me to the next checkpoint. A few minutes later, all the recruits gathered in a room. Next thing I know, the Army officer at the front of the room said, "Raise your right hand and repeat after me." At that moment, I slipped out of the room and then out of the building. When I made it back home, I lied to my Mom and said my blood pressure was too high and they told me to come back in two weeks.

That night at the Fisheries, after the lunch with my mom and sister, I am feeling a little melancholy. Should I go back home and try to live like a normal guy… go back to high school? No, that just wouldn't work for me. After a few beers, a joint, and hanging with my friends for a while I am right back to being my old self. It is the usual carrying on— beer, weed, other assorted drugs, flirting with the girls, and music. Don Stein had just got a Black Sabbath album and is playing it— loud of course,

He was turned to steel in the great Atlantic field,
Running as fast as they can, Iron Man lives agaaaaaaaaaaain…

Some girls show up, Paul's on-and-off girlfriend Katie, her friend Janet, and a cousin of Katie's named Kim. I take an interest in Kim right away. She is cute and from Minnesota. I began telling her tales of the road, as if I'd been hitchhiking all my life. I guess Don was right when he'd accuse me of being a bull-shitter. Kim and I hit it off that night and she came over a few more nights after that. Before long, we are in the infamous closet trying to consummate our relationship. The only problem is with all the commotion—noise, and people knocking on the door— we never do the deed. Man, I am disappointed. The next few days Kim and I never really had another opportunity to be alone. She said she is leaving to go back home, and I of course, was bummed. I said,

"Maybe I can come up to Minnesota to visit." She's excited.

"Would you, could you?"

"Sure, why not? I'll hitchhike."

"But what will you do when you get there; my parents won't let you stay with us."

"I'll get a job at a restaurant and rent a place somewhere. I can get a job anywhere." I am so full of myself… I Told her I'd see her in the spring, and we hugged, kissed, and said goodbye.

Christmas came and went uneventfully, I tell myself Christmas is for kids, though in my heart I did miss it— the family, the tree, the good feelings. Oh well…

After working at the Oyster House about a month, I start to get restless. I spoke to Kim on the phone a few times and was really missing her. I began to consider going to Minnesota sooner, not waiting until the spring. Tommy, the boss at the Oyster House was a real hard ass, always riding me. One evening after a long night of dishes, pots, and pans, the other dishwasher and I decided to quit. We tell each other we can get better jobs anywhere.

One of our duties at closing time is to climb up on the lighted sign and spell out the next day's special with big plastic letters. The sign is about ten feet up in the air and has a built on ladder, so it is really no big deal. Tommy would give us the special, written on a piece of paper, and we would climb up and adjust the letters accordingly. After locking up with Tommy and watching him drive out of the parking lot, we were about to blow off the sign altogether and just split, when I turn to my co-worker and said, "Wait, I've got an idea." I climb up on the sign and take out the letters I want, I spell out,

FUCK YOU TOMMY

I QUIT

I leaned back to look at it and laughed so hard I almost fall off the sign.

I get back to the Fisheries and tell everyone about the special on the sign at the Oyster House. I convince Paul, Glenn, Don, and Jeffery Joe to ride down U.S. 1 to see my handiwork. We pile in Paul's car and drove back. There is the sign, lit up for the world to see. We are laughing… howling and Don Stein couldn't believe it, he wanted to go back to the Fisheries and get his camera.

On the way back to the Fisheries, the car stalled and wouldn't start. We pushed it off U.S.1 and were standing there looking under the hood, trying to figure out the problem, when the cops pull up. A few minutes earlier Paul had just given me his bag of weed to roll a joint, so I stealthily knelt down and slid under the car. The two cops nonchalantly walked toward us and started asking questions.

"What's going on fella's?"

Don responded, "Our car broke down and we're trying to fix it." I slip the weed out of my pocket and up into the frame of the car. One of the cops squatted down and shined his flashlight on me.

"What do you think you'll find under there?" he asked me. I thought quickly.

"I'm looking for the fuel filter, it must be clogged"

"Come out from under there." I slid out and stood up, brushing myself off.

"Okay you guys, turn around and put your hands on the car, all of ya. Come on." One cop stood back with his hand on his gun while the other one frisked us. After checking our I D's, looking in the car and asking us twenty questions, they left. As they pulled away, Paul knew I had his weed. They all knew. Paul asked me with his teeth clenched,

"What did ya do with the weed?" At that, I jump down and slid back under the car, reached up in the frame, and grab it. Stood up, wearing a stupid grin, hand the bag to Paul, like I was sooo slick. Glenn says,

"Shit, I just knew we were busted." We get the car running and made it back home.

That night I tell everyone I will be leaving in a few days. They are asking things like, where will you go, how will you get money? They are probably concerned for me, because I am about to do something they would not even consider doing by themselves. I love it… love appearing fearless, I reply in a cavalier tone with lines like, wherever the road leads me and I'll make it on my wits. Knowing perfectly well I would be heading straight for Kim's house in Minnesota.

Glenn responded,

"You can't eat wits." Though I am so full of piss and vinegar, nobody can tell me anything. I thought, I am invincible… I am a teenage adventurer.

Over the next few days, feeling somewhat intrepid about my decision, I ask a couple of friends if they will to take off with me. Phil declines. He and his dad have patched things up at home and his dad gave him the down payment on a cherry red, Chevelle SS 396, as long as he promised to finish high school, so he isn't going anywhere. Glenn just smiles at me and slowly shakes his head back and forth, not interested. Paul said he wants to save up some money before he took off. Well, I knew that could take years, so I decide I will be on my own. I guess after talking about being an adventurer for so long, I convinced myself that I am one, and that I really didn't need anyone or anything. I will just make do along the way. My wits and will were all I need to get me through anything.

It is early January and the fact that it was cold as hell in Detroit just a few months earlier and that is basically what drove me south, never crossed my mind. I am going. I call Kim one more time and I tell her I am on my way.

The night before I leave, I ask Glenn to give me a ride to my folks' house, not to say good- bye, but to get another warm jacket. He takes me over on his bike and I get him to let me off half a block away so I can creep up to the house quietly. I knock on my sister Judy's bedroom window; she wakes up and sees it's me. I ask her to go to the hall closet and see if our sister Patty's St. Bonaventure hooded sweatshirt was still in there. She did, and it is. She slipped it through the window to me and I thanked her and told her I'd see her soon. She was a little upset, obviously concerned for me. She asked, "Where are you going?"

"Don't worry Judy, I'll be back... You'll see me again, I promise." And I left, back to where Glenn is waiting. We head for the Fisheries. My idea was to wear the sweatshirt while I hitched, looking like an all-American college kid. The sweatshirt was dark blue with big white letters across the front that said St. Bonaventure and much thicker and warmer than a normal sweatshirt. I'd just wear two or three flannel shirts underneath, depending on how cold it got.

Going to sleep that night I thought, "Well Glenn, this is it. You are about to embark on the journey of a lifetime. The trip you told yourself you would be taking some day." Well that day was here and I am about to take that first step into the great unknown. Wow, this is going to be so cool; I will see the whole country before I am through. I will end up being as worldly and knowledgeable as anyone anywhere. Yep, this is it; I groomed myself for this for months... no... years. Everyone, including my parents will have to respect me once they hear what I am doing. The true adventurer within me is about to be unleashed and I couldn't have been more excited. Like a nomad, an explorer, this eagle was about to spread his wings. As I doze off, I can feel a huge smile spread across my face.

The next morning, I roll up my few belongings in my sleeping bag, tie it with my belt, put on my St. Bonaventure sweatshirt, and counted my money, twenty-four dollars and change. I am ready. I leave my pea coat in the closet at Jeff's. I decide it is simply too bulky to take with me. I have the essentials: jeans, shirts, underwear, socks, my toothbrush, and a tiny tube of toothpaste. I am a little more hygiene-conscious then your average hippie. Energized and exhilarated, I could not wait to get started. The night before I asked Paul to give me a ride to Krome Avenue, and he is ready to go. Krome runs straight into Highway 27, the highway Phil and I had taken when we left for Detroit. I took 27 South when I came back from Detroit, so I felt comfortable on it. Highway 27 was like an old friend, so it will be a great place to start my journey. It later became known as "Bloody 27," due to the frequent fatal car accidents that occurred there, but right now, it is my 'yellow brick road.'

MY WIFES FUNERAL

It is not long before a thirty-something-year-old guy in a fairly new sedan picks me up. Says he is going to Orlando. He is a little on the heavy side, with a bald forehead and thin, curly, long hair on the sides. Like Larry of the Three Stooges. He is dressed in a button-down shirt and jeans, and wearing loafers with no socks. His look is normal enough, but he has an aura that had me on guard. We make small talk and then it gets quiet. That's fine with me; I would rather say nothing and gaze out the window, than engage in meaningless small talk. Not far from Orlando he asked me, "Got any weed?"

"No," I said.

"That's okay, I do." He pulls out a joint and lights it. I feel proud that I look like someone who obviously smokes weed. It's like a badge of honor. Yeah, I thought, I'm a real hippie and it's obvious.

As we roll down the highway, I am pretty stoned when the guy speaks up again. "Do you masturbate?" I thought now, what kind of a question is that to ask a perfect stranger? Guess I was right about feeling the need to be on my guard, but also feeling the need not to be intimidated I answered.

"I have," I said, dryly, looking out the window...

"Every day?"

"Well, not every day." Now he is starting to make me nervous.

"You will," he said. I said nothing, this really isn't a subject I felt comfortable discussing with a dude who just picked me up hitchhiking. He continued, sounding like that of a school teacher at the front of the class, "Grown men masturbate everyday. If they say they don't, they're lying." I thought, jeez, I wish this guy would cool it, and pick another subject. I am becoming annoyed and uneasy at the same time. Why does this guy feel the need to make this point? Is he leading to something? Luckily, the next thing he says is, this is where I turnoff. I thank him for the ride and gladly get out. Christ, I thought, you meet all kinds.

That ride reminded me of one of my fears. The thought of being picked up by a pervert who would take me out in the woods and have his way with me; torturing and then killing me. Even a non-confrontational guy who seemed to be gay would make me edgy, because I equate being gay with being perverted. I remember while working at the Bodega restaurant in Miami, one of the waiters accused one of the cooks of being homophobic. Upon learning what homophobic meant, I remember thinking, well, what do you expect a straight guy to be; aren't all straight guys homophobic?

My next few rides are with regular people—no probing questions. No offers to get high either, just pleasant non-confrontational human beings. I make it all the way to a small town south of Atlanta when it starts getting dark. I am making good time and it really isn't that cold— maybe fifty something. I am on I-75 near a truck stop, so I feel that my chances of getting another ride are good. It is well lit at the entrance ramp, and even though night was bringing a chill along with it, I feel prepared with my thick wool, St. Bonaventure sweatshirt. Sure enough, I catch a ride in a semi.

Before climbing in the cab, I notice there is no name on the trailer, which is not uncommon for these big rigs. I hop in. It feels good, like I'd done it before. My confidence is building; I am becoming a seasoned traveler. This guy is cool, said his name is Rod… Wore one of those western style shirts, jeans, and cowboy boots… sporting a brown leather vest. He tells stories, gives me advice, and all kinds of good stuff. I have to laugh, because I have only been in two big rigs so far and both the drivers were similar in many ways— their clothes, the way they both had stories and opinions and liked to voice them. It is yet something else for me to think about… and I just loved thinking about things… pondering… philosophizing.

One of my heroes, the philosopher J. Krishnamurti, wrote a book called, 'Think on These Things', and I loved that book. I want to be thought of as a philosopher myself, so I would think about things in depth… Think about all the possibilities of whatever the subject was… all the pros and cons and gray areas. That way when the subject came up I would have a well-thought-out opinion… a philosophy. At times, my friends and family would find this annoying, but strangers seemed to find it interesting and charming… and how I love to charm.

Rod told me when as we get to Chattanooga I will need to switch over to Interstate 24 North… he said it will bring me closer to where I am going, since I am heading for Minnesota. Listening to a trucker felt like the right thing to do. I consider these guys to be the kings of the road. He let's me out in Chattanooga, and it is cold… in the mid-forties. I thought about Bart dropping me off in Chattanooga on my trip down from Detroit. I make my way to a gas station and get myself a coffee and snack and start chatting it up with the attendant, so as not to have to go outside in the cold. He is a nice guy and didn't seem to mind my presence. I tell him my situation, hitching to Minnesota, and that I needed a place to stay for the night. He suggests I go to the bus station and hang out there. He said, "You can probably get some sleep, like you're waiting for your bus. The sweatshirt you're wearing makes it look like you're a college kid."

"That's why I wear it," I said, pleased he gets it. "So how far is the bus station from here?"

"I get off in about a half hour; I'll give you a ride there."

"Really?"

"No problem, just hang out and wait; my relief will be here soon enough."

It is not long before his replacement shows up and we leave. He takes me right to the bus station. I thank him and he is gone. I thought once again, that people can be good for no apparent reason, other then it makes them feel good to help a young traveler along his way.

The bus station is dimly lit and dingy, but warm. I find a chair off in the corner, sit down and try to get comfortable. It smells like a cross between cigarettes and Mr. Clean. I sit there thinking about my friends back at the Fisheries and wondered who was hanging out tonight. I lit a cigarette and pictured the Fisheries with Glenn, Paul, Don and various other friends partying. I wonder if they are thinking of me. Looking around, I notice two motley looking people huddled next to their belongings stuffed in shopping bags. I thought about my mom and the fact that she has no idea where I am right now, and what an inconsiderate prick I am. I really should give her a call— collect. Eventually I nod off. I get some sleep, sitting in a chair slipping in and out of consciousness. About six in the morning a bus station employee asked me to show him my ticket, and since I didn't have one he told me I would need to leave. The sun is just coming up so I didn't mind.

I head for the Interstate with renewed energy on a cold, clear morning. Find an entrance ramp, and don't have to stick my thumb out long before three long-haired country boys, in an old primer-gray '66 Chevelle pick me up. I thought about my friend Phil, back in Miami and the Chevelle he is now driving. The long hairs took me to Nashville. There is something about these three that didn't seem right, I have the feeling I am with guys who had either been up to no good or were about to do something bad. I am relieved when they let me out. It made me wonder how many of the people I catch rides with might have just committed a crime, or on their way to commit one. There is no way of knowing. Oh well, I know who I am and what I should and should not do. I can't worry about everyone in the world; I need to worry about myself.

Soon as I get to Nashville it starts to rain... a lot... pretty much ruins my whole day. I sit under an overpass.... quivering, cold, and disgusted... smoking cigarettes, wishing the rain would quit. An entire day and never even get out of Tennessee, I am pissed. By night fall the rain let up, so I try hitching; But no luck. It is just too dark and too late. I walk off to the closest gas station and hang out, but the attendant isn't as friendly as the one the night before. Eventually he runs me off. I thought where is a church when you need one? There is not one as far as I can tell and here comes the rain again, hard as ever. There is nothing but a lot of closed doors and dark buildings. I get the impression that this is a bad part of town and that is not good. Lucky for me the rain seems to be keeping all the nefarious types inside.

I find an abandoned car, behind a vacant building. It has four flat tires and looked like a junker, so no harm in getting out of the rain, I thought. I try the passenger door and it is open. The car still has all its windows, so I decided what the hell, it was shelter. I climb in and knock whatever was on the seat to the floorboard. Roll out my sleeping bag, get in and try to get warm. Feeling beleaguered as I lay there with the smell of mold and mildew, shivering like a wet puppy. It is dark and difficult to see, but I notice what I assume is the make of the car spelled out in raised letters on the glove box. I reach up to touch the letters, running my fingers across them, *PONTIAC*. I remember my folks once owned a Pontiac—a Safari station wagon— I loved that car. Not sure why. Maybe it is because my brother and my dad and I worked on it together or maybe because we took many a family vacation in it. Whatever the reason, just knowing I am in a Pontiac felt good to me... felt familiar... felt safe. So, while the rain drops steadily pelt the rusty old shell, like pebbles on a tin roof, I doze off.

By morning, the rain has stopped and the sun is coming up. I have gotten warm in the car and didn't want to get up, because I know it is cold outside. I think; what the hell am I doing going north? It's too damn cold to go north this time of year. Maybe I will go south to Pensacola. Yeah, that's it. I'm going to Pensacola and get a job on the beach, work, get a place to live until it warms up in the spring. I wasn't thinking too clearly when I left Miami. How quickly I had forgotten about Phil and I freezing to death just a few months earlier in Detroit. I'll call Kim, she'll understand. I pull myself together and head for a gas station to wash up. I get in the bathroom and strip down to my underwear, basically took a bath in the sink. Splashing soapy water on myself and then drying with paper towels. This became one of my traveling tricks in order to avoid becoming too fragrant. It took a while, and by the time I came out there is a woman standing there scowling at me, with her hands on the shoulders of a small boy standing in front of her with his legs crossed, squirming, holding his groin. He obviously had to pee badly and I am not helping matters. I smile sheepishly and scoot past them.

Soon enough, I am on 65 heading south to Florida. Never did call Kim. I make my way almost to Good Hope, Alabama. I like the name of this town… thinking, I had some good hope in me. It has warmed up quite a bit. In fact, it felt like sixty, and the sun is shining… I am not even in Florida yet. Man, this is going to be great. I catch a ride with this older fellow. He is country; dirty flannel shirt, khaki work pants, needs a shave, and I can smell him. He asks the usual questions, "Where you headed, where you from?" I give him the usual answers. He asked me, "Do ya have a girlfriend?" He has this peculiar way of glancing over at me. He would keep his head perfectly straight but slide his eyes my way when he spoke. It makes me feel uneasy. I thought oh crap; I hope he's not a creep of some kind. I told him, "She's in Minnesota," while I maintained a reserved demeanor.

"Why aintcha ya goin' ta Minnesota?"

"It's too cold up north this time of year," I said.

"If I 'ad a girlfriend up north I wouldn't care how cold it were. As long as I knew I could get warm when I git there." He smiles. Well, that made perfect sense to me. What was I doing going south when my girl was back north and I could, 'get warm when I got there.' Yeah, this guy made sense, he is absolutely right, so I tell him, "Let me out at the next exit."

"Why, I thought you were going to Florida?"

"Not anymore," I said. "You're right about going where my girl is, and she's back the other way, so let me out at the next exit."

He chuckles, then asked me if I want to get something to eat before I turn around… tries to convince me to go home with him so his wife can fix me something to eat. I thank him but decline. He gives me a few dollars when he let me out. I thank him again. My initial feelings about him were all wrong. He is really a good guy. I walk to the entrance ramp northbound, and I am on my way to Minnesota…again.

Yeah, I am out on the road with my purpose and direction as nebulous as the clouds in the sky. A little warmth, a fresh outlook, and hell, I didn't have to give it much thought at all. It is a feeling of complete freedom mixed with confusion, though the later does not bother me. In the words of, Bob Dylan, it is kind of a "No Direction Home" sort of philosophy. Of course, I change my mind, of course I am confused. I am searching, chasing or being chased; moving seemed to be my only solace, my only purpose. I am not about to let the lack of a plan keep me from feeling good. I am free! That's my plan, to be free and to enjoy my freedom. It's not complicated but its mine.

My next ride going back north is unmemorable, as are most of my rides this day. I catch one right after the other, and work my way up to Centralia, Illinois. I am less than five hundred miles from Jackson, Minnesota, according to my map and that is where Kim lives. I can do that in one day, with a little luck, no problem. My ride let me out into the night and it is cold as hell, easily in the thirties. There is old, hard snow on the ground, and as I walk, it crunches under my work boots. This crunching sound makes it seem even colder. I thought about when I had left home and just knew my work boots would make good traveling boots. I leave the highway and walk into the town of Centralia. Everything is closed. I am down to about six bucks… thought about a cheap motel but knew I didn't have enough money. I walk into the old downtown area, which is not much, maybe fifteen or twenty stores and businesses on either side of the street. Feel reluctant about sleeping out in the cold; it is far too bitter and getting colder or so it seems. No church, no mission, and I am becoming more worried with each passing minute.

There is an old red brick building with a white globe light and the word POLICE on it. I walk inside. Feeling desperate, I step up to a large looming desk. I have a question that I know is not going to go over well, but I have little fear of the consequences. The cop sitting behind the desk looked intimidating, but without any hesitation or stutter, I say, "Can you put me in a cell for the night. I'm not from here; I'm just passing through and I'm broke." He looked at me and scowled,

"Kid, this isn't a God damn hotel; get the hell out of here." He motioned with his thumb toward the door.

"Look, I'm not from here I'm just passing through and I'm broke. I'm freezing my ass off and I've got no place to go and no money for a hotel." I did my best attempt at a pitiful delivery. He stood up, leaned forward, put his hands on his desk, while straightening arms and without any sympathy in his voice, he said,

"I don't care; we're still not a hotel. MOVE ON!"

I responded, completely unaffected by what he had just said, I nodded toward the door I had just came in.

"If I break the plate glass window in the 'five and dime' across the street, would you put me in a cell; would you lock me up then?" I stood there looking him in the face, not blinking. He sighed, sat back down, picked up the phone, hit a button, and said,

"Come on down, I got one for ya."

A few feet away I hear a clanging noise, and in a few moments an old elevator door slid open and a stiff-legged jailer stepped out, dressed more like a nineteen-fifty's train conductor than a cop. He is all in black, with brass buttons straight up to his neck. He is wearing a black hat with a shiny plastic brim on the front. He has a big ring of keys in one hand and a Billy club hanging from his waist. The guy behind the desk says, "Put him on the second floor." The stiff-legged jailer must have had a fake leg, or lost the ability to bend it.

"This way," he said, almost ghoulish like. We ascended. Every foot or so the elevator moved, there would be a clang sound. *Clang...clang... clang.* It reminded me of when I was a kid and would go visit my great Aunt Francine, who lived in Manhattan. There was an elevator in her building that used to clang as it moved. It made me nervous, like there is something wrong with it. Only this one didn't seem to bother me... guess I am just glad to be getting out of the cold. He shows me to my cell and never said another word.

The next morning the jailer wakes me wearing the same outfit, holding a steel tray with scrambled eggs, hash browns, toast, and plastic fork on it. I thought this is better than a hotel. I ate, and they send me on my way. I walk down the street and decide to hitchhike around town and try bumming some money before I move on. The sun was out, so it seemed warmer, though it is still very cold. Sure enough, I get a ride with three young townies in their early twenties, smoking weed and just riding around in an old beat up '58 Ford four-door. I hear one of them say something about calling in sick to their job at a fiberglass plant because they are sick of itching all the time. Well, this isn't so bad, driving around with these guys— better than freezing to death. Then the guy driving mumbled something. Next thing I know, the guy riding in the passenger's seat said clearly,

"Do you want to give it a try?"

"I don't see why not; it's been plenty cold lately" The driver replies. All of a sudden off the road we go, spinning and sliding out onto this big, white, snow-covered field. I thought wow, these are my kind of fellows, not a cloud in the sky, three locals getting me high. Yeah, this was cool… so round and round we go, tires spinning, all three of them laughing.

"Whoooo… yeah that's it, cut it-cut-cut! Yeeeeeehaaaa…" With thoughts of my friend Phil back home rolling around my head, I ask the guy sitting next to me while trying my best not to slide off the seat, "Is this somebody's yard or just an open field?"

He laughed and says, "Man, this ain't a yard, this is a lake." Needless to say, I went from enjoying the moment to oh shit! Round and round we go, while the whole time they are laughing and my stomach begins to knot up; so much for enjoying the day. As we spin and they laugh, the thought of going through the ice and freezing to death was engulfing my thoughts. I look to see if my door was unlocked, thinking if we go through the ice I'll need to jump out and swim for it… When we finally did get off the lake and back on the road I was relieved to be on terra firma, though now thinking of how to get away from these whack jobs. If we had gone through the ice I wonder if I would have survived… or just gotten trapped in the car and drown with no I.D. on me. I would have been listed as a John Doe, my family never to hear from me again, with my mom left to wonder what happened to me. I really need to give her a call and let her know where I am.

Eventually I decide they are not so bad and we end up at the apartment of Jerry who was the driver. I hung out, smoking weed and watching TV. At one point they get a pizza and invite me to eat with them. I blew off going back out on the highway. I am enjoying the warmth of the indoors and am not in a hurry to get back out on the road; it is just too damn cold. I seem to hit it off with Roy, who is another of the guys from the car he invited me to stay at his place for the night. He says he lived with his mom, and that she would be cool with me staying there. He is a big oafish kind of fellow with shoulder-length, messy blond hair, and wore a brown suede jacket with a fur collar. He has a b-flat personality with no redeeming qualities, but he did like to laugh at my jokes and I like that. The fact that he invited me to stay at his house is a real Godsend. The news man said it is going to be in the teens again tonight and I didn't think the jail was going to be quite so accommodating a second time.

We leave the apartment and went over to his place, everything seems okay. Roy's little sister shows up with a couple of her little girlfriends, who are about fourteen or fifteen and immature for their age. They would look at me whisper to each other and giggle. Roy took me aside and informed me, "Hey man, I think my little sister likes you," he nudged me with his elbow. Now I am uncomfortable; the five of us are all in the same bedroom and his little sister is about fourteen and not cute by any stretch. I somehow got to sleep that night without having to make a love connection with Roy's horny sibling.

When I awake, I slip out before anyone else is up, and yes, it is still cold as hell. I thought about Kim in Minnesota… how nice it is going to be when I get there, how warm I will get, how we will hug and kiss. Walking toward the highway I was already feeling the bitter cold slicing in on me. I approach the highway; the wind was whipping in hard from the southwest. I thought if it were blowing from the opposite direction, it would be so much better; it would be blowing against my back. Well life isn't always the way you want it. Then I thought if I were going south the wind would be perfectly at my back… hmmm. Yeah, I'm afraid it is too cold and I am not up for it, so I cross the highway and stick out my thumb. I am going south once again. Kim will just have to wait. I remember my friend Glenn Jarred back in Miami talking about how great New Orleans is. He used to go there for his summer vacations and come back with stories for days… talking about Bourbon Street, the French Quarter, and people with odd accents. I thought, sounds good to me.

I catch a ride out of town and am on my way, when a stereotypical redneck picks me up and immediately began telling me about how the niggers are ruining everything. He says he belongs to the 'White Hats', apparently they were some sort of white supremacist group, a spin-off of the Ku Klux Klan or something. This made me uncomfortable; I am not into hating anyone, let alone an entire race. I also thought maybe he didn't like hippie-types either, and maybe he is thinking about him and his friends taking me out in the woods and lynching me. I think to myself, just act like you're interested in what he has to say. If you tell him how you really feel, he's not going to change his mind or like what I have to say. I'll just keep my mouth shut and get out the next chance I get. I think it was my Dad who once said, "Gene, some of the best things you've ever said was when you kept your big mouth shut." When the guy finally did let me out, he gives me a couple bucks; he is a charitable bigot.

Right off the Interstate I get something to eat at a convenience store, I strike up a conversation with an older gentleman in a pickup as he sat in his truck sipping a hot beverage. He says, "I'm going south on 67 a pretty good way and it runs right back into the Interstate if ya stay on it." I thought what the hell; its south and I liked the sound of that. Driving along, we talk and I tell him I am traveling and seeing the world. My pickup truck driver said he was fifty-nine and had never been out of Missouri. I thought my God that is unbelievable. How incredibly unadventurous can you be. It is completely baffling to me. When he let me out, we are in the country… the real country, the sticks.

He said we were in the Missouri foothills, and I assure you it is just that, no houses stores or any signs of civilization, just rolling hills as far as you can see and a highway running north and south. I watch the taillights of his pickup get smaller until they disappear down the only visible turn-off from the highway. The light of the day seems to quickly leave the sky as I stand on the side of a two-lane highway. In about a half hour of my being let out on the road, the night cloaks my world in black. I think maybe two cars pass by during that time and I am regretting my choice to take this highway. No traffic and the temperature dropping. For the first time in my life, the feeling of really being alone is beginning to overwhelm me. I think about my last ride and how he said he had never left home, and here I am far, far away from mine. Another half hour went by and not a car passed in either direction. My anxiety is getting the best of me. I give some thought to running to the other side of the highway if a car came from the south, just to catch a ride out of this desolate place.

As loneliness and despair seem to envelope me, I take deep breaths, letting the air out slowly. Where are the cars? Where are the people? What the hell? I am feeling desperate. Off in the distance, to the west, I can see a light— maybe a porch light or maybe just a lone street light. It was too far away to tell. I thought about walking in that direction, but didn't. The highway stretched out in both directions as far as I can see. To the east is an open field, rolling hills, patches of snow on the ground. I take out a cigarette and light it. I can feel my eyes tearing up. Looking around and seeing nothing and no one is intimidating as hell. Looking down at the pavement, I kick at a rock in disgust. With a cigarette in my right hand and my left hand a fist in my pocket, I stare down at my boots. I am scared, shivering and out of ideas. I remember sitting at the dining room table with my dad, taking the five bucks, and how cocky I was. I am not feeling so cocky now. No friends, no family, and my girl, five hundred miles to the north; it might as well be five thousand. I glance over at a ditch on the side of the highway and think about laying out my sleeping bag, crawling inside and curling up in a fetal position. I cannot feel sorrier for myself. Then it hit me like a cool crisp slap in the face. I had always been so gutsy, and here I am, like a sniveling child.

Wait a minute; I can't let this get to me. I've got to pull myself together… I've got no other choice, I can't curl up and die that's ridiculous. I'm going to stand tall, stick out my thumb, and get a ride the hell out of here. A car will come by at some point, this is a highway, God damn it!"

I closed my eyes and told myself be strong, be a man. When I opened my eyes, I seemed to be looking down at myself from a nearby hill, maybe 50 yards away. It is weird, but comfortable at the same time, to be looking at myself from a distance. As I gazed at myself, I am not cold, in fact I feel perfectly comfortable. I can see myself clearly on the side of the road, wearing my St. Bonaventure sweatshirt with my pack at my feet. I looked like a decent guy— not a threat— a guy whom I would give a ride to if I were driving. Now all I need is a car. From my vantage point up on the hill I can see off in the distance to the north, as well as to the south, where I am headed. Suddenly from the north, lights catch my eye. Yes, it is headlights, and they were headed my way. I had been on the side of that highway ready to shrivel up in a ball, and out of the blackness came a car, an angel. As it came closer I quickly became nervous. I thought I better get back down inside myself before the car gets to where I am standing or I will miss it.

At that moment, as if I were a blast of air, I shot down off the hill and back into my body. BAM! I was there. It was freaky. I stood there thinking about what had just happened… looked at my hands, my arms, to see if they were there; yeah it's me and I'm here. Then I remember, there is a car coming. I try not to look desperate… but at the same time I want to look like I need a ride. I stick out my thumb and stand tall and begin to pray, fast; "Hail Mary full of grace, the Lord is with thee, blessed art thou amongst women and blessed is the fruit of thy womb Jesus…" I hold my breath as the car zooms by… was it slowing down? I am almost too afraid to turn and look, my heart stopped and I turn to look. Yes! It is slowing down; I reach down, pick up my pack, and ran. I ran to that car like a terrified child runs to their mother. I get to the door, reached for the handle and was in the seat with the door closed behind me in one motion. I could not have cared less how far he was going or if he had a single eye in his forehead; I was taking this ride.

"Man, you, saved my life, I thought I was gonna die out there."

Unimpressed, he glanced at me and said, "I'm going about an hour and a half south of here." He pulled back on the highway and we were gone. I felt like I had been plucked from a black hole in space.

"Thanks," I said. "I felt like I was never going to get a ride. You're the only car I've seen in I don't know how long." He says nothing. I thought he must not be in the mood to talk. I of course was ecstatic and wanted to babble; but held my mouth in check. I noticed a couple packs of cigarettes on the dash, and pointing to them I ask if he minded if I bummed a smoke. He obliged.

He was in a black suit and was about forty… looked like a businessman… and seemed somber. After fifteen or twenty minutes of silence, I attempt to strike up a conversation; but before I had a chance to get out my next question, he said, "I don't mean to be rude, but I'm on my way back home from my wife's funeral and I'm really not in the mood to talk." Man… and a few moments ago I was feeling sorry for myself and this guy just buried his wife; ho-lee crap, life is a trip. I sat there thinking about what had just happened. I was so upset about being alone on the side of the highway. I decide I cannot let that happen again. I'm on the road and this is where I want to be. If I allow a tough situation to get to me, I might as well quit and go home now. I vow never again to let a bad situation get me down. I have got to remind myself; no matter how bad it is for me, it's probably worse for someone else. I am an adventurer and adventurers don't get down… they get going.

By the time funeral man let me out, it is nine or ten at night, and lucky for me I am back on the interstate. I walk over to a near by truck stop. I am right outside the town of Cape Girardeau, Missouri. Sitting there in the truck stop café drinking coffee, I strike up a conversation with the guy next to me. He is amazed I am seventeen and hitching around the country on my own… said he was driving his rig south and offered me a ride.

His name was Don Herrman and that's what it said on his dashboard. I thought about a childhood friend, John Sherman, and I wondered what he might be doing right now. Don is a nice guy, tall and thin, and not more than thirty, maybe thirty-five. He wore a denim jacket and jeans, and has a flattop haircut. We talk on and off through the night. I tell him about my friend Glenn who used to spend summers in New Orleans and had told me how much he enjoyed the place. Unlike Bart, the Mary Carter Paint driver, Don didn't care if I slept, so I did, leaning against my door. I began thinking about my friends back at the Fisheries. They were probably all sitting around getting stoned and drinking beer. Damn, how I missed all that. Maybe going back to the Fisheries might not be such a bad idea. I could work somewhere and have a good time until the spring when my traveling would not be hindered by the cold. I know Jeff would be fine with me moving back in with him; in fact, he would probably be glad to have me. Don and I stop to eat along the way, and he buys me a sandwich. Back on the highway, about ten miles outside Hammond, Louisiana he said, "Up here is where I take the exit for I-10 East, and since you're going to New Orleans this will be where you get out." By now it is about 2:30 in the morning and though it wasn't cold, I wasn't too happy about getting out on the Interstate. There is a certain amount of traffic, but there were no gas stations or businesses of any kind. I am not in the mood to stand in the dark hitching or more likely, looking for a place to lay out my sleeping bag on the side of the road. I said to Don, "So you're going I-10 East, how far?"

"Pascagoula, Mississippi."

"Yeah… how far is… where you just said?" He chuckles, then says, a little slower,

"Pas-ca-goul-a, it's about two hours east of here."

"You mind if I just keep riding with you? I've decided to go back to Florida."

"No, I don't mind; but what happened to New Orleans? You were talking about how much you wanted to see the city."

"I know; but I have been thinking about my friends back home and I think I'd rather go see them."

"Suit yaself," he said. A few minutes later Don took the exit for I-10 East. I am going home.

FREE LUCKY DOGS

We arrive in Pascagoula, four thirty a.m., and Don and I part company. I find a Diner and go in for whatever I can get for two dollars and change. It's a typical old eatery— linoleum floors, booths with tears in the upholstery, stale pastries in a round glass case on the counter with a knob on the top, so you could spin it. I think it's a requirement for the pastries to be stale; I've never had a fresh one. The stools are those stuck to the floor, cracking green naugahyde covered jobs, and running the length of the counter. There is a well-worn middle aged woman in a faded blue waitress outfit, complete with dirty white paper tiara sitting on top of her bouffant hair-do. She seems to be handling the place by herself. I put my butt on a stool at the end of the counter. I sat there pondering my situation while sipping a cup of the hot dirty dish water, though she called it coffee. She was not much conversation and the only other person in the place was a normal looking 40 something man, sitting in a booth, engrossed in a paperback. He was close enough for me to see the cover. Zane Grey. Huh, who is Zane Grey? So there I sat, not feeling bad and not feeling good. It seems odd in some respects when you're not directly connected to any place or anyone. I feel like getting up and going is really not something I need to do. Then again I obviously can't sit at this counter the rest of my life.

By about six o'clock in the morning I feel like I have over stayed my welcome. I leave a fifteen-cent tip; it is all I have left after paying for scrambled eggs, toast and coffee. When I step outside it is still dark. I begin to walk along; I will need to ask for a handout from my next ride. I come across a train station. As I approach, I notice something sticking out from under the walkway that ran along the outside of the building. On closer inspection I realize its shoes, shoes on people's feet. Apparently a number of homeless types are allowed to sleep under the boardwalk that runs the length of the train station. It's freaking me out. It reminded me of the war movies I'd seen with pictures of the executed prisoners laid out next to each other. I wanted to get away from there quick. Then from out of the shadows, two hobo-looking characters start following me. I begin to walk a little faster. They did as well. Oh shit, what's this about? They can't possibly think I've got money, look at me. Maybe they just want to kick my ass. I speed up. They keep up. I break into a trot. They start trotting. I can feel my heart thumping in my chest. I have to think of something and I have to think fast. Can I outrun them? Doesn't look like it. Can I hide? No, they are too close; I ran on. I ran around the corner of a building, stop, turn around, and get ready to face them. I took my pack, held it in front of me with both hands, and waited. Around the corner they came I startled them when they see me standing there. They looked at each other confused. I make the first move, slowly stepping toward them with my pack in my hands, holding it up in front of me, like it were a shield or a gift. I ask in the most sinister, low register voice I could muster, "Is this what you want?" I was looking them both in the face and slowly moving toward them.

"Is it?" I throw the pack at them and it fell to the ground at their feet. I pointed at it and moved closer,

"Pick it up… Go ahead… pick it up!" By now I was just a few feet from them both, loudly and menacingly saying, "PICK IT UP!!!" They back up, looked at each other turned, and left. Whew…that was close; I had bluffed my way out of whatever it was they had in mind. Yes, I was an actor, or a bullshit artist, according to my dad. At times it was a real lifesaver. Like just now.

I pick up my pack and head in the opposite direction. That is it for me. I decided from this point forward I would stand my ground, no matter what the outcome. Maybe I should carry a knife; it would at least be some kind of protection. If someone got in my face, I would not run; I would deal with it right then and there. I am on the road, on my own, and I needed to stand up for myself. No matter what the out come, at least I will be facing my fears like a man.

As I walk along, the sun came up. I find myself in front of a gas station, and it is starting to rain. There is this older fellow pumping gas. He had weathered skin; deep worry lines and a smile that showed his yellow teeth. I must have looked like I needed a friend, because he struck up a conversation with me. He had a thick southern accent. After some idle conversation, he said, "I'm a minister and I don't live fur'from here. I'm off in 'bout 'n' our. You can come by my place n' shower n' get sump'm ta' eat." I thought, if he's a minister, what is he doing pumping gas? Shoudn't he have a church…

He seemed decent enough though, so I decide to take a chance and come back when he got off. I sure would like to take a shower. I wander around Pascagoula for an hour, and when I get back to the station he is still there.

We walk a little ways and come to some small, old, wooden cabins. He says he is renting one. He reached in his pocket, pulled out three dollars, handed it to me, and said, "Why doncha' go to the store and getcher' self som'em to eat." Upon returning, I found him hanging out with one of his neighbors. They were sitting outside his cabin on an old picnic table rolling their own cigarettes. The minister is telling his neighbor about the Lord working in mysterious ways, while I ate my ham n cheese sanwich and hung out, listening. The minister was a great talker. He had all sorts of insights, which he dispensed along with his biblical quotes. I found myself thinking that this was a trip. It sounded so peculiar, hearing wisdom delivered with a heavy southern accent. Up to this point I had equated thick southern drawls with the not too intelligent types, like Li'l Abner and hillbillies, but the minister certainly gave me a reason to re-think that.

He is a nice guy, and after telling him about how I didn't get along with my folks and how I plan on going to head back to my friends; He tells me that going back and hanging out with my friends wasn't going to do me any good. He said, "ya need ta go ta N'alins n' get a job. There's plenty of work in restaurants down there, n' ya can rent a room down on Rampart Street. Ya oughta see what it's like bein' on your own. You'll prob'ly appreciate what it takes. From what ya've tol' me, ya really haven't done anythin' on ya own. Ya need ta' at leas' prove it to ya self that ya can." Of course I took a shot at debating him; but I was no match for his down-home southern logic. He made sense— and living on my own where I didn't know anyone and had to make my own way would prove to my folks I am not just a bum, a loser. I thought, I don't need to go back to the Fisheries, I'll go to New Orleans, or 'Na'lins', as the minister said. I'll get a job and my own place… maybe even send my folks a postcard telling them how great I am doing. Hell yes, that's exactly what I will do.

He gave me a few more dollars and tells me he'd say a prayer for me. I rambled on to the highway, caught a ride headed back in the direction I just came from. After a few miles down the highway I took a highway south and was in New Orleans by late afternoon. I am quite taken by the place. It has an old feel to it. The architecture seems European. Walking down one street, there is church after church. I thought, a religious city? I wandered down Tulane Avenue, where I came upon the Tulane Café… Walked in and asked the lady behind the counter for a cup of coffee. She is pleasant enough so I ask, “Do you need anybody to work. I’m a good worker and could use the job.” She smiles and says, “come back tomorrow mornin’ dawlin. Mike, the manager, will be in after eight.”

I stroll off, wandering the streets, and by nightfall find myself under an overpass, not far from the café. I undid the belt holding my pack together, rolled out my sleeping bag, crawled inside and passed out. Early the next morning I am awakened by some young kids, boys and girls, nine or ten years old, who apparently had come upon me on their way to school. One of them picked up my belt and swung it around over his head. I tried to get up but I was too weak— like I was paralyzed. I tried to speak, but nothing came out. The one with my belt and the others danced around me in a circle, giggling. I am scared, but could not seem to move. It’s weird. They all ran off together, laughing with the one kid still swinging my belt over his head. I thought, Damn, now what am I going to use to hold my pack together. When I did get up, my belt was lying right next to me. Guess I’d been dreaming, though it seemed so real.

I pull myself together, make my way over to the gas station next to the café, and clean myself up… walk next door to the café and found the manager. He is a sleepy-eyed, yellow-toothed, middle-aged, chain-smoking fellow… Wore a wrinkled white shirt, faded black slacks, and needs a shave. He hires me on the spot, and told me to get to work. I am a dishwasher, just like that. Later that day, about five o’clock, Mike gave me fifteen dollars and tells me to see this lady on South Robertson Street. He said, “She’s a nice lady that has rooms for rent, cheap. Tell her Mike from the Tulane Café sent you. Her name is Mrs. Zagorski.”

I make it to the address, knock on the front door of a large old house and a heavyset lady in her fifties greets me. I introduce myself to Mrs. Zagorski. She is wearing a faded old dress and a dingy white apron. She is from Lithuania, the old country, as she put it. She has a thick accent. She told me, “Yar dent iss nine dolla a week ‘ent I wash yar’ clos fo’ you too.” She gave me the key and says, “Yar’doom is out behine’ my house.” It’s a three-story frame house, right down in the city, in sharp contrast to the newer concrete and steel buildings on either side. The rooms she rents are rickety old affairs, about six of them, three on the bottom, three on top, in a rickety wood building separate from the house. There is a single shower and commode, shared by all six tenants. My room is on the first floor, about 10 x 12, smelled like old cypress, mildew, and Lysol. Reminded me of that church where I spent the night in Georgia.

It has one of those little gas space heaters, and though it really is not even cold, I find a match and lit it. I pull off my clothes and crawled in bed. The walls of my room were so old and thin the headlights of the cars pulling into the parking lot next door would shine through the cracks in the walls. I did not care; it felt like heaven to me. I am so proud… it is my first real place of my own. I have a job and a place to live. I am going to make it. I am feeling relieved to be off the road. I lay there staring at the flickering flame of the space heater and doze off.

The next morning Mrs. Zagorski wakes me, knocking on my door and told me, "Come up to da house. I have yar close ready." At her request, I had given her my clothes to wash. When I walked in her kitchen, there were my folded clothes, a cup of coffee, and a biscuit and jelly waiting for me. I sat there at her kitchen table thinking, if everyone in this town is like this, I am never leaving.

I thank her and took off for the café. By the end of a week I have fifty-five dollars, even after Mike took out the fifteen I owed him. I am making a buck twenty an hour, so I am doing much better than pan handling. When I get off that night, I took the bus home. Man this is living, I thought. Before I went to my place, I stop into a K&B drugstore and bought a little radio. On my way back home, I stop at a gas station to get a soft drink, strike up a conversation with the attendant… said his name was Jerry. We talk for a long while. He is a big rock and roll fan and seems to know a little something about all the popular bands on the radio. He tells me I need to listen to TUL, the Tulane University station, when I get home. I eventually went back to my room, turned on my new radio, tuned in TUL, and sure enough, they were playing Jethro Tull, and the song was one of my favorites:

In the shuffling madness, of the locomotive breath,
Runs the all-time loser, headlong to his death.

I lay back in my bed with a smile and doze off. In the middle of the night I awoke to car doors slamming and people in the parking lot next to my room arguing. I peeked out the window and saw two guys headed toward my building. I figured it was a couple of my neighbors, and I went back to sleep.

Next day I went to work and really enjoyed myself. Washing dishes never seemed so right. On my way home from work, I stop in a gas station at the corner of Tulane and Broad to get a coke, right across the street from the Parish Prison (that would later become relevant). There is an older guy, short, stocky, in grey coveralls, wearing a burgundy beret. He is under the hood of a nice looking Alfa Romeo sports car. I walk over to him and said, "Nice looking Alfa. What is it, a sixty-four?" He acted surprised, then in an accent that sounded Italian he asked,

"You know 'bout Alfas?"

"Not really, except this Giulietta is one of my favorites." Because of my dad and brother, I was a bit of a car enthusiast.

"You want a job? I need somebody to pump de gas."

"Maybe. How much does it pay?"

"I pay a dollar forty an hour, if you start tomorrow seven a.m." I thought for a moment

… the pay was better…

"I'll take it," I said. We shook hands and I walk off. Can you believe it; I just got another job and a raise. I am up to my old tricks. Maybe I should start a class on how to get a job. I knew Mike at the café would let me work at night, so I could easily have both jobs. Man, I have just got to call home and tell my folks what I'm up to. They won't believe it.

I show up at seven sharp the next day. The boss was Rosario Violo. He was Italian all right, full-blooded. The station was called Violo's Gulf. We get along pretty well. He works on cars, I pumped the gas, and Mike let me work at night at the café. One afternoon Violo told me,"I got a guy coming back to work, his name Angelo. He works for me before. Now he come back. but he don't go in the register… only you or me." I thought, okay, so he's hiring a guy he doesn't trust. He continued, "He's a good worker, but he got problems."

The next morning… "Hey bra' how ya doin'? I'm Angelo, but my friends all call me Angel." Now, this guy was a ball of energy. He was thin, muscular, a brown complexion and some gold teeth right up front. "I'm malado," he informed me, proudly. "Bra' this and bra' that, Whe'yat bra'?" He would run around all morning like a wild man, fixing flats, changing tires, pumping gas, then around lunch time he would take off. When he got back he would be completely lethargic, he would sprawl out in a chair, legs straight out and spread, arms limp on the arm rests, and his chin on his chest. He would look up at me barely able to lift his head, and with what sounded like a mouth full of marbles, he would say, "Meth… a …done bra', meth…" After a half hour or so, he would pull himself together and start back to work.

That evening Mr. Violo asked me, "You got a driver's license?" I said, "Sure." He didn't ask me if I had it on me. He said, "Good. Take my pick-up home and on your way into work tomorrow pick up some parts at the Fiat dealer on Canal St., just tell them you're there for Violo's."

I thought, hot shit! I got a truck. Angel asked me, "Bra', you need to give me a ride home tonight, okay 'bra?" I agreed.

At closing time, around six p.m. we take off. Two blocks down Broad Street, Angel said,

"Bra, pull over up here. I need to run in this store and get something. Leave your motor runnin'… I won't be long." In less then a minute, Angel came running up to the truck and jumped in yelling,

"GO, GO, GO!" I just sit there with a puzzled look; he became even more frantic and screamed,

"I just robbed the fuckin' store! GO! Motherfucker! GO!" I punch it, the tires squealed, my heart is racing, like the motor. I start screaming at Angel as we flew down Broad St. "Are you out of your mind, what the fuck did you just do?" I am pissed. As we slid sideways around a corner, my mind was about to explode. We are tearing down a side street; glancing in my rear view when I noticed Angel with his hand up to his mouth snickering. Completely pissed, I say, "I'm glad you think this is funny, you fuck wad!" My head is ringing, and I am thinking about how the hell this going to play out, would I be busted as an accomplice? Would Violo's truck be impounded? Then he reached over and slapped me on the back and says, "You can slow down 'bra, I was fuckin' wit'choo, I didn't rob nobody."

I said, "Holy shit, are you kidding me?" I was relieved, but still mad as hell, shaking my head in disgust; but relieved. After I got back to my room on South Robertson, I swore to myself I would never give Angelo a ride again… anywhere… ever.

I quickly settled into my life in New Orleans. I am making enough money at Violo's to quit my café job, though I would still go down there and hang out. At the station I was even working on the cars. Violo gave me a twenty-cent-an-hour raise, and man, I was proud. I am so cozy at my job, I felt like Violo really liked and trusted me. For fun, I began purposely giving tourists wrong directions, a tradition in New Orleans, according to Angelo. Anytime cute girls came in the station I would attempt to flirt. Though was never very good at it. There was a law office right next door and I befriended one of the young attorneys, Bobby. I would clean his car for a few dollars once a week; figured befriending a lawyer might not be a bad idea.

At night I would go down to Bourbon St. and hangout in front of the Far Out, a head shop that sold rolling papers, roach clips, rock band tee-shirts and incense. For some reason the freaks running the store didn't care if my street friends and I hung out in front. Maybe they figured we were part of their ambiance. More likely they just didn't give a shit; they were hippies, not businessmen. Though I wasn't a street kid anymore, now that I had a place, I would still hang out like I was. I would buy a bottle of Boone's Farm Strawberry Hill, sit in front of the Far Out, and offer sips of my wine to the girls who strolled by. That was my icebreaker.

On my way home from Bourbon St. one night, I decided to take the streetcar down St. Charles for the heck of it, something I occasionally like to do. Rolling along, I noticed this cute-looking college age girl sitting by herself. I thought, I need to make my move— but I wasn't sure how with out my bottle of wine. Guess I'll have to strike up a conversation when she gets off the street car. When she did get off, I got off as well; I walk up along side her and said, "Hi I'm Gene Martin and I just moved to this town. Do you by any chance know where Bourbon St. is from here?"

She smiled and said, "When you got on the street car you were about a block from it."

I sheepishly said, "Oh, I guess that was a pretty dumb line?" "Kinda," she said, still smiling.

"Well anyway, you looked like someone I wanted to meet, so hi, what's your name?"

"Amy."

"You live around here?"

"I live in a dorm, not far from hear," she said. I got the feeling she was enjoying my company.

"Dorm, huh. So you go to Tulane?"

"No, I go to Newcomb College. I'm a Newcomb bitch," she said proudly. I smiled.

So, after a short walk to her dorm, I got her number, and told her I would call her. I headed for a bus stop with a bounce in my step, thinking, *that was great*, and I didn't even have any wine. Yes, life is good.

One afternoon, I am working at the station when this young shorthaired straight looking dude, in his early twenties, rolled in. Straight in the sense that he didn't look like a freak. He looked clean-cut. He is well built with a chiseled chin, short hair, and pearly white teeth. He is driving a late-model convertible Delta Eighty-Eight. He struck up a conversation with me, and we sort of hit it off… said he was in town for Mardi Gras. Hell, I didn't even know what Mardi Gras was. Angel had told me about it; but that was about it. 'Clean-cut' then asked me with wide-eyed enthusiasm, "You like to party?"

"Sure," I said.

"Let's get together after you get off… I've got some orange sunshine." I thought,

Holy shit, this guy has acid? I said, eagerly, "Sure, I get off about six."

"I'll be back," he said. As he pulled away, I yelled, "Hey, what's your name?" But he was gone. I wondered if he really would come back or if he was just one of the many bullshitters.

At six o'clock up pulled the Delta. The guy's name was Greg and he was from Ohio; recently discharged from the Marines. I thought, this guy is an ex-Marine who trips… What's the world coming to? As we drove off, he plugged in an eight-track and it was The Who, blasting from the speakers, with Roger Daltry howling,

Out here in the fields,
I faught for my meals,
I get my back into my livinggg…

He handed me a lit joint. I was thinking, if this guy ain't gay or a psycho killer, I've struck gold! We take off for an adventure in the city, but first we went by my place so I can shower and change. I took him upstairs and introduced him to my neighbors, Harry and Ray, the same guys who woke me up yelling at each other my first night on south Robertson. I hardly knew them. Harry was a smallish, yet hard-looking, unattractive thirty-year-old ex-con-looking guy, with black hair on either side of his balding head, with a small tuft of hair right above his forehead. Ray was a nineteen-or-so-year-old street kid, with dirty brown shoulder-length hair and a small, unmemorable face. He always wore this green army fatigue, and never said much of anything. They made a dubious pair. They were sitting in their room watching their tiny portable black and white TV. I asked them, "Is it okay if Greg hangs out with you guys while I take a shower?" Harry nodded his approval and pointed to a chair.

About fifteen minutes later I am ready to go, and I tell Greg, "Leave your car here. We can walk to the French Quarter." As we head off to the Quarter, Greg said,"Your neighbors are kind of strange."

"Yeah, they are a bit peculiar." Greg went to give me a hit of orange sunshine. He said,"You want a half or a whole? It's pretty strong shit." Now up to this point in my life I had tripped some, and though I am not actually a seasoned tripper, I wanted to think of myself as one. I say," I'll take a whole hit, hell yeah." I'm no pussy, I thought, though later I would regret the choice.

It is the first night of Mardi Gras and the Quarter was more crowded then I had ever seen it. We start wandering around sipping on wine, chatting it up with people on the street. Greg turned out to be quite a chick magnet. Before I knew it, we were hanging with two nice-looking girls. Drinking and walking around with them, I was feeling really good.

Then the acid started to kick in, the walls started melting, and people's faces began to contort. I felt a little more loaded than I had in the past, and it was making me nervous. I thought, I need to pull myself together, and start acting like I'm having a good time. I forced a smile, but the melting walls and sidewalks were seriously messing with my mind. I look down and can not see my feet. They were sunk in the sidewalk as if the cement was just poured and I was glopping through it. It is freaking me out. I turn to Greg and said, "Man, I'm startin' to lose it. This acid is kicking my ass." Now that is a mistake, because it only made things worse. Greg said, "Just relax, you'll be all right. Here, have some wine. It'll take the edge off." I lean back against the building for support and try telling myself I would be all right.

At that moment I hear a strange noise, but I couldn't quite make out where it was coming from. I slowly swung my head around the corner. A parade was coming right at me. There is what looks like fifty guys with flaming batons, spinning, whirling and marching right at me. I am terrified, it is wild, loud, and flipping me out, I start to collapse and almost lose my balance. Greg catches me. He props me up against the wall and said, "You'll be okay man, just cool out for a minute." Feeling overwhelmed I said, "You can stay, but I gotta go." He then turned to the girls and said, "Hey, my friend isn't feeling too good. I need to get him back. We'll have to catch you later." We walk off, or I should say Greg walked. I stumble like a drunken blind man. I was lucky Greg is with me, because every time I try to focus my vision, my mind would screw with what I saw. Not sure I would never have made it home by myself… at least not for quite some time. Eventually Greg gets me back to my place.

This guy was an absolute gem of a dude. Here he is, his first night in N.O. and babysitting some guy he hardly knew. When we got back to my room he said, "Look, you just hang out. I'm gonna walk over to the store and get a quart of O.J. The vitamin C will make you feel better." Obviously concerned about leaving me alone, he said, "Maybe you shouldn't be by yourself right now. Let's go upstairs and see if your upstairs neighbors are home." We both climbed the stairs, Greg in front, I followed, watching my feet melting into each step. He knocked on Harry's door and it swung open. There was Harry, up on his knees, with his hands on Rays hips, steadily giving it to him from behind. They both looked up at us with these awkward grins. Their faces reminded me of the picture on the inside of the record cover from the album, *In the Court of the Crimson King*. It's a freaky picture, and both of them looked just like it. Greg whirled around and took me by the shoulders pinning me against the door, got right in my face and said, "Did you know these guys were fags? Are you a fag?!?!" Wide eyed and about to shit my pants, I was barely able to blurt out, "No… no, hell no." He reached around me and pulled the door shut, and we stumbled back down the stairs.

When we got in my room I collapsed on my bed, and Greg plopped down in my only chair. I was relieved to be back at my place and began to relax. We turned on the radio and listened to some music while for the next four hours we talked about how much we liked girls and how we couldn't understand how any guy could be gay… probably more a way for us to convince each other, as well as ourselves, we were heterosexual. By sunrise I passed out and Greg takes off.

At around noon, Greg came rapping on my door. He is with the same two girls we had met the night before. I couldn't believe this guy. They turned out to be schoolteachers from Chicago, down for Mardi Gras. He said, "Get dressed. We're going to a parade." I jumped up, feeling a little groggy, but pulled myself together.

We headed down to Canal Street to catch beads and doubloons. You hear a lot of: "Throw me somethin', Mister!" and, "Show us your tits!" There was at least one parade a day, and sometimes two, with around half a million people crammed into a ten or twelve square block area. The teachers partied with us most of the day and by night we are all pretty intoxicated. We ended up back at their motel room, but I am too drunk to take advantage of my teacher, though I later heard from Greg that he had a good time with his.

The weekend came to an end and I went back to work on Monday. Greg had whirled off with some people he ran into from his hometown, so he is no longer in the picture.

That night, I head down to the Quarter with a bottle of Boone's Farm in hand and parked my butt in front of the Far Out, once again. This street freak I was friendly with by the name of Marko showed up and wanted a hit off my wine. Marko was your classic street hippie— long hair, dirty jeans, jean jacket, and flannel shirt, with rarely brushed gray-teeth. He smells like a cross between Patchouli and B.O., mixed with cigarette breath. He is from Michigan and is nineteen years old. He would bum money while he had a pocket full of change, and bum cigarettes with a full pack in his pocket. I told him, "I'm waitin' for a good lookin' girl before I open this bottle." So, he sat there with me. He was challenging passers-by to arm wrestle. He would arm wrestle people for money and usually win. He would say to a likely candidate, "Hey, you look like a pretty stout fellow, wanna arm wrestle for a dollar?" And to my surprise, he would get takers.

This cute girl passed by alone. She has short, light brown hair, in sort of a Beatle haircut, a clear, tan face, and a great smile. She had a nice little shape and is wearing a jean jacket and some tight Levis with butterflies embroidered on her butt. I caught her eye and asked, "Hey, would you like to drink some wine?" She smiles, walks over, and sits down right next to me. I crack open the vintage bottle of Strawberry Hill and pass it to her; she takes a sip and says, "*Gracias.*"

Intrigued, I ask, "Where you from?" as I take a swig, I didn't take my eyes off her while passing Marko the bottle. She replys with a thick accent, "Santa Marta, Columbia." I take the bottle back from Marko and hand it back to her.

"My name is Gene. What's yours?"

"Edma"

"Eeedma?" I said very slowly.

She smiles and says, "Edma Elena Marquez."

I said,"Jeez, sounds like royalty." I was smitten…

At this point Harry, my upstairs neighbor walks up. I thought, this is awkward. I could hardly look at him, though he didn't seem to care about seeing me. Marko asked him for a cigarette. I thought about the fact that his being gay really didn't make him any less of a person, and just because I wasn't, didn't mean I needed to dislike him or his roommate, Ray. Harry shook his head no to Marko's request for spare change, and Marko challenged him to arm wrestle for a dollar. Harry accepted the challenge, so Edma and I stand to give them some room on the steps. Harry sits down and Marko got up and squatted down on the other side, so as to have a place for their elbows. They slowly locked hands, Harry smiling, looking Marko in the eyes, Marko blankly looking back at him. Marko then said, "Are you ready; this is for a dollar now." Harry nodded then, W*ham*! Marko threw Harry's arm almost flat— but not quite. Harry began to strain, still smiling, started pulling Marko's arm back upright. Marko looked a bit surprised. They began to sway back and forth, neither one getting the upper hand. Back and forth they went, both grunting and moaning. Finally Marko gives it a real heave and pins Harry's arm flat. This time the back of his hand clearly hit. Marko slowly rose to his feet, but as he did, Harry maintains his grip on Marko. Slightly annoyed, Marko said, "Ah, you lost man; you can let go now." Harry just smiled, still gripping Marko. Marko looked at me puzzled, and then back at Harry and said, with a stern delivery, "You can let go, motherfucker!" Harry, still sitting, began pulling Marko toward him. Edma and I looked on, both of us perplexed by Harry not letting go of his grip on Marko.

I spoke up. "Harry, what are you doing? It's over." He turns to look at me, smiling, giving me the creeps. That's when Marko put his right foot squarely on Harry's chest and shoved him, simultaneously yanking his hand away. Harry lost his grip, rolled off the steps, and on to the street.

I turned to Edma and said, "Lets go." Marko was standing there cursing at him as Edma and I take off.

That night, Edma and I walk around drinking wine and conversing as best we can. I didn't mind her lack of English skills. She didn't seem to mind my lack of Spanish. It was a classic romantic encounter, with New Orleans as the backdrop. Of course, at first, I am merely concerned with satisfying my libido, but as the night wore on it became truly special, to my mind anyway. Edma and I ended up back at my place, where we spent the night satisfying our primal urges.

The next morning, I have to work. I tell Edma, "You can sleep as late as you want, but I've got to go to work." She looked at me smiled and went back to sleep. The night before she had given me the address where she is staying with friends, so I didn't mind leaving her; I knew where to find her. All day at the station, I thought about her. I was love struck. After I get off work that evening, I am heading down my street and to my surprise, there is Edma sitting on the front steps of Mrs. Zagorski's, charming the pants off three old black men. I knew one of them, James E. Lowe. He was a gentleman in his sixties, who liked to wear an old, tattered tweed sport coat and lived in one of the rooms in the back of Zagorski's. I had sat around talking many an evening on the same steps, listening to stories of Old New Orleans and how the city used to be. James is a real good old dude. I am glad she is there and happy James is as well.

As I approach, smiling and happy to see Edma, they greet me. James spoke first. "How ya doin' son, we were keepin' ya girl comp'ny till ya got home." I thank him, took Edma's hand, and we walked on back to my room.

I ask her, "So what did you do all day? Would you like to walk down to the Quarter and get a cup of coffee at Café Du Monde?"

"Okay," she said smiling… always smiling. When we get to the café we get our coffee and found a table. We huddled close, and she draped her legs over my legs, almost sitting in my lap. She knew how to get cozy. We went off exploring the Quarter, drinking wine, wandering in and out of bars, shops, and side streets. At one point, we were strolling down a street when a guy came whizzing by on a tandem bicycle, almost knocking us down, ringing the bell on the handle bars and shouting, "Tour the Historic French Quarter… fifty cents!" As he flew by, I realized it was Marko. I thought, That guy is such a trip, always up to something. No wonder I like him…

For the next few days, Edma and I hang out and enjoy each other's company. She didn't spend every night with me. Some nights she went back to the house of her friends where she was staying in the Garden District. I didn't mind. I knew she was with me, and she made me feel good about our connection. Seeing the sights, drinking wine, we could not have cared less about the parades; we just liked hanging out together. I was really enjoying Edma, and had forgotten all about Kim in Minnesota. One morning when we awoke together, she smiled and said, "I need to tell you something." She paused. "I leave tonight, go to San Francisco." My heart sank. I am upset. I felt like I was dunked under water and gasping for breath.

"What? I thought you were here until the end of Mardi Gras."

"But something has happened to me," she replied hesitantly. She knew I was upset.

I said, "How are you going? Can I go with you?" She frowned, and slowly shook her head no.

"I'll be with my husband, Thomas." Now I was really freaking.

"You're married?" I sat up, she nodded her head yes, adding, "But we go to divorce, in San Francisco."

"Is he here in New Orleans?"

"He be here today"

Completely upset by this turn of events, my head was spinning. We got up and got dressed without a word. Finally, I asked her, "Are you going to live in San Francisco after the divorce?"

"I think so," she said.

"Well then, I'll come visit you there, maybe even get a place to live… if that's okay with you?"

"When will you come San Francisco?" she asked, smiling.

"It'll take me about three or four days to get there," I said. She looks surprised, and then smiled.

"I'll leave the end of this week." I said. She threw her arms around me and we kissed. We walked back to her friend's house without speaking, and she gave me the address in San Francisco. We said our goodbyes and I slowly walk off, wondering if I'd ever see her again. My heart was heavy. I walked along thinking that not long ago I was living a dream, and now I was being forced to wake up. I remind myself, I can hitch to San Francisco like I told her I would. I began walking a little quicker, with a spring in my step. I was going to California.

By the time I got back to my place, I am already late for work. I call Violo and tell him I am on my way. I had worked the whole thing out in my head. I would work the rest of the week and then take off. I could be in San Francisco by the following Tuesday. That night, I am back down on Bourbon partying in the street, making it a point to get good and drunk to forget my broken heart. I ran in to Marko who is working a Lucky Dog cart on the corner of Bourbon and Toulouse. Lucky Dogs are a French Quarter tradition; the hotdog-shaped carts on wheels are pushed around the Quarter by vendors. He gave me a dog and I gave him some of my wine. Marko was bitching about the guy he worked for… something about him not paying him the way he should. I said, "Screw him, quit if you don't like it. You don't need this crappy job."

All I wanted was for him to hang out with me. His eyes lit up, like he had a good one up his sleeve, and in usual Marko fashion, he did not disappoint. He says, "Check it out." Pulling out a piece of cardboard he wrote, using a black Magic Marker:

FREE LUCKY DOGS

He set the sign on the cart and we walk away laughing. We were drinking and carrying on like a couple of idiots, noticing people walking along, or should I say stumbling along, calling out names, then exchanging hugs, like they hadn't seen each other in years.

"Johnny, you bastard, I didn't know you were here." They would throw their arms around each other and hug, maybe trade swigs off their bottles and party on, so we started doing it to each other and than to anyone who caught our eye. Marko picked the wrong guy and a scuffle ensued. I tried to pull them apart and the next thing I know the cops had Marko, his scuffle partner, and me on our way to the cop car. During Mardi Gras the cops don't play around. They will arrest you for the smallest of infractions. As we were being driven to the jail, we passed by the corner of Toulouse and Bourbon. There was Marko's boss, holding the sign Marko had written, bent over looking down inside his Lucky Dog cart; we looked at each other and nearly busted a gut laughing.

We get to the jail and I thought, Happy fuckin' Mardi Gras. We are put in a cell with ten other revelers, and I sat wondering whom to call— Violo? Mike from the Tulane Café? Well that was moot; they never gave me my phone call. When the sun started coming up the next morning, I could see it shining through the window across the hall from our cell, but it quickly rose out of sight. I thought, Damn, was that what Bob Dylan was talking about when he sang, "There is, a house, in New Orleans, they call the rising sun." The fact is, it wasn't… seems House of the Rising Sun was written back at the turn of the century and it was simply the name of a brothel.

At about 8:30am a guard came to our cell and said, "Martin, step up." I jump to my feet and he opens the cell door and said,"Come with me."

As I walk off I heard Marko yell, "Hey man, what about me, he's my friend!" I walk downstairs, and there, to my surprise, is Bobby Sims, the lawyer from next door to Violo's Gas Station. He is signing some papers, then he said hi to me, and showed me where to sign. I said, "Man, I can't believe you are here, how did you even know I was in jail?"

"Angelo told me… said something about some friend of yours came by the station and told him you were in jail across the street at Parish Prison."

"Friend of mine?" I was baffled.

"Damn, that's unbelievable." I said. "What luck…"

Bobby then explained, "You were thrown in jail on a drunk and disorderly charge. You will have to appear in court. I'll let you know your court date."

I said to him, as we walked outside, "I'm not sure I can make it. I was planning on going to San Francisco." Bobby said, "Well, as long as you never step foot in Orleans Parish, don't worry about it."

I paused, and then said, "Thanks for getting me out Bobby. Do I owe you anything?"

"Don't worry about it." He shook my hand and walked off. "Good luck, Gene," he called over his shoulder.

"Thanks again, man," I said back. I walk over to the station and apologized to Violo about being late. He said nothing. Guess he was pissed.

After a couple days at work, I decide, why wait? I didn't need a week's pay. Two days would be plenty. That night I tell Mr. V. I need a thirty-dollar advance; he gave it to me, no questions asked. Next morning, I roll up my sleeping bag and pack my bare essentials. I bought a pocketknife and packed that as well, not sure what I would do with it if the need arose to defend myself. But I still thought it is a good idea to have it; remembering Pascagoula. I left my radio and a few other things I had acquired. I bade farewell to Mrs. Zagorski, and walked to the entrance ramp for I-10 West. I was on my way to San Francisco and my girl Edma.

I immediately thought about Kim and how I was supposed to go to Minnesota way back when. Then again, when I thought about it, I had been on my way to California before I even met Kim. Besides, Kim had probably met some other dude by now and I am nothing more than a memory— kind of like what she had become to me. I am all about Edma now. Edma and I were going to get a place, and it will be great.

IN LESS THAN FIVE MINUTES

I catch a ride to La Place, about 15 miles out of New Orleans, then it's on to Baton Rouge. Almost left the highway to go looking for an old friend I knew whom lives nearby; but didn't. I am going to San Francisco to be with my girl. Eventually I catch a ride with a military dude, passing through Louisiana on his way to Corpus Christi, Texas.

He turns out to be a very hip character, for being in the service. Began talking to me about Jimmy Hendrix and the fact that Jimmy was in the 101st Air borne, which is news to me. He has some other little tidbits of information I enjoyed. He also bought me dinner at a roadside restaurant. When he drops me off he makes sure it is at a truck stop, he is a real considerate guy, yet another Good Samaritan.

Out of Houston, a traveling salesman with a car full of 'Pet Rocks' (a gag gift that featured a rock in a box with a booklet that explained how to care for and train your rock) picks me up. After looking at one of the rocks, I express my opinion of what a nothing sort of thing it is; he responds by explaining.

"Hell, I could care less what people think *after* they buy it, so long as they buy it." Made sense to me; but the smart ass in me came out.

"I don't believe in keeping rocks in a box, they need to be free, free to roam, free to roll, if you had any compassion you'd set those rocks free." He smiles…he is going all the way to San Antonio and that was a long way. Texas; the endless expanse of desert landscape is relatively mundane, though I did see my first 'roadrunner,' as they ran across the open plain kicking up dust behind them. I was amazed at how much the cartoon from television resembled the real thing. The tumbleweed really tumbled, except for these moments, Texas is an exercise in shear boredom; we're talking thirteen or fourteen hours from one side of the state to the other. I hit El Paso in the middle of the night; I am cold and tired, looking for a place to sleep. Thought about a Motel 6, I had heard it was six bucks a night; but I wasn't in need of a soft bed and didn't think it was true anyway. A place on the ground would be fine for me. I came upon a public school and notice some hedges lining one of the walls. I slip in behind them and climb into my sleeping bag. I begin to dream of Edma and the grand life we are going to have in San Francisco. I will get a job and we will rent a little place...Yeah it is going to be great.

The next morning, I am wakened by the sun. There are a few people arriving to the school so I quickly scoot away before anyone notices me. My next few rides get me to Tucson, Arizona. Even though it was late February it was extremely hot. I am on an entrance ramp with a pack of cigarettes, no water and nothing to eat. Probably about 5 or 6 miles outside of the city, I am miserable, standing than sitting, than standing, smoking one cigarette after the other as the hours tick by. I am baffled by how few cars pass by. At one point I laid down using my pack for a pillow and would just stick my thumb up in the air, as the occasional car would pass by. I was completely parched and beleaguered. Then a car slowed down that I recognized; it was a State Trooper. He got out and slowly walks toward me, so I quickly get to my feet. He began.

"Got any I.D.?" I lost my license back in New Orleans, though I had a Library card with my name typed right on it, real legit, I thought. I said,

"I have is a Library card from New Orleans." He blankly looked at me from behind mirrored sunglasses.

"Let's see it." He was a tall intimidating dude. "How old are you?"

"Seventeen," I said, somewhat hesitantly.

"And you're from where?"

"Well I was living in New Orleans; but I'm actually from Miami, Florida."

He stood there looking at me, then at my library card flicking it up and down against his thumb; I could tell he wasn't sure what to make of me. He handed my library card back to me, than said,

"If some rough looking cowboys come by offering you a ride don't take it. We've had some trouble with you hitchhiking types getting taken out in the desert and getting beat up." He turned and walked back to his car and left. Now I really want a ride out of here and not in a pick-up with cowboys. I stood there thinking, this is not good. What am I suppose to do if some rednecks in a pick-up pull up and offer me a ride. "No thank you gentleman, a state trooper said you were going to take me out in the desert and beat the crap out of me, so I'll just wait right here for some nice people." I thought about how I would run off into the desert with them chasing me in their truck trying to run me down like a dog. I thought about the movie

Easy Rider, when the two rednecks in a pick-up shot Wyatt and Billy. A sense of angst begins to fill my gut.

At that moment a Volkswagen van drives up and pulls over with a freak at the wheel, halleluiah, I'd been saved! Yeah, even the driver was related to Jesus… in a way. He was a Jesus freak. He had all the standard hippie accoutrements, long hair, tie-dye, incense; except he didn't do drugs. He did Jesus. So after about a half hour of chit chat, laced with Jesus, I asked him.

"You mind if I crawl off in the back to catch a nap. I'm tired as… heck."

"Sure, help yourself."

As I made my way back, there are a guy and a girl and a small dog already in the back sleeping. I didn't know anyone else was even in the van. I assumed my Jesus freak must have saved them as well. When we get to Phoenix, our driver invited us to his retreat where he said we could shower, eat and kick back, I declined; but the two with the dog accepted. I bid them all a farewell and strutted off. I had no interest in Jesus. Funny considering I would ask God or Jesus for help anytime I got in a real jam. My next ride is with 'Mad Man Mark.' Or at least that's what I ended up naming him.

This guy is driving straight through from St Louis to L.A., or so he says. I have no reason to doubt him; he looks completely wigged out. His eyes are bugging out of his head, his hair was greasy, I'm not sure what color, an aroma that was a cross between cigarettes, B.O., fast food and mildew filled the car. His clothes look like he'd been in them a week, the Mustang he is driving has seen better days and the exhaust pipes are loud. No sooner do we reach cruising speed when in an agitated voice he asks,

"Can you drive?" I thought oh great, I just get picked up and he's pissed off.

"Sure."

"Here, slide under me and take the wheel." Now mind you we were doing at least seventy.

"Why don't you just pull over?" I said.

"Fuck that, just hop over me. I don't wanna waste time stopping." Next thing I know the guy is sliding out from under the wheel, leaning forward, so I slide under. No sooner do I get situated behind the wheel, and he begins rifling through the glove box.

"Where's my shit?" He says out loud, but obviously he wasn't asking me, he pulls out what looked like an eyeglass case and sat back in his seat, undoes his belt, pulls it from his pants and lays it in his lap. He opens the eyeglass case and takes out a small glass vile and a spoon, he carefully pours some of the powder from the vile into the spoon.

"Don't hit any bumps." He says pointedly; he flicks his lighter and begins cooking the powder with the flame under the spoon. Once it begins bubbling he sets it on the dash and takes out a syringe, sucking the cooked liquid up in to the rig. Setting the rig on the dash he takes his belt and ties off his arm, holding the end of the belt in his teeth, he puts his arm down to his side and began flicking the vein in the crook of his elbow with his middle finger. Next he picks up the syringe and through his clenched teeth says,

"Keep the car steady." I was already nervous to begin with, just looking at the guy, now he's about to shoot a load of something in his arm, I was shittin' in my pants nervous, and just as he's about to stick himself, BANG! We hit a bump.

"GOD DAMN IT!" He screams through clenched teeth,

"Sorry man, I can't help it if the road ain't perfect; why don't I pull over?" He ignored me, just looked down at his arm and shoved in the needle, his eyes rolled back in his head and he relaxed, he slowly turned his head in my direction and said in a very soft yet clear voice,

"Damn, I needed that." I was never so relieved, now I want out of this car. Though I did love to get high and trip, I thought shootin' dope up was just too much. I guess you could say that was where I drew the line, I said,

"Hey we're about out of gas; we better start looking for a station." Thought to myself, I'll lose this dude when we stop.

"Oh yeah." he says, in a real blasé sort of way. "Got any money?"

"No I sure don't." I did; but wasn't about to chip in.

"Well what good are ya?" He glances my way and smiles, then says,

"I'm just messin' with you, I've got money, pull over at the next exit, we'll get gas and I'll buy you something to eat if you want." I thought, maybe this guy might be all right for a little while longer.

After gassing up we drive through the night and have some normal conversation. We were getting close to L.A. winding through a mountain pass. As we pull up over the top of a rise, Mark tuned in the radio, a Neil Young song came on and it was, 'Everybody knows this is nowhere.' What a perfect song for the view, it's about 4 a.m. in the morning and we are coming down into a valley, it is beautiful. You can see car tail lights for miles; snaking down into the valley in front of us. There seems to be thousands of different colored lights strewn across the valley floor and we have a panoramic view. I almost feel like Neil had come up with this song title while driving down this highway, the closer we get to L.A., the better the music on the radio. The Doors, Hendrix, the 'Stones, one after the other, this is great after hearing a lot of crackling country for too many hours across the California desert. It feels like my old friends are welcoming us to the west coast. When we arrive in Hollywood, Mark is driving; I told him to just let me out any where. I am feeling good and ready to do some exploring. He said,

"You sure you want to just start walking; I got a place you can stay with my friends and me, get some rest if you want?"

"No thanks, I'm cool, I'm gonna do some walking around, then head for 'Frisco, at that he pulled over and let me out. Madman turned out to be not so bad after all. I still had about twenty bucks left of the thirty I started out with; things couldn't be better. I thanked him and headed down the road.

Walking down a brightly lit street; turns out to be Sunset Boulevard. There is a Jack in the Box fast food place, so I head for it. Before I get there, a long hair, maybe thirty, in a tee shirt and jeans walked up blowing on a harmonica. "Whaaaaa-ahhhhhh-ahaaaaa,

"The Moody Blues." he says, like I should be impressed. I just look at him and he does it again, "Whaaaaa-ahhhhhhh-whaaaaa."

"That's great," I tell him facetiously, walking away, hoping he'll go away. There is something about him I don't care for. I walk in the Jack in the Box, fast food place and he follows me in, walking up to the girl at the counter and ordering. The harmonica player is sort of flittering around in the dining area behind me.

"Can I help you sir?" she asked the harmonica man.

"No, no, I'm just waiting." I thought, oh great, just what I need, a moocher, who can't play harmonica. I get a breakfast 'Jack' and a coke and sat down. He plops down across from me.

"Hey; where you from?" Like he really wants to know, now when it comes to eating I don't like a beggar sitting across from me, just as I wouldn't do that to someone. I did have my considerate side. So I say,

"I'm trying to eat here, I don't have any money for you and I'm not giving you any of my food." At that point I think the girl at the counter put two and two together and said to harmonica man,

"Sir, if you're not going to order anything you'll have to leave." Obviously he knew arguing would do no good, without so much as a word he gets up and walks out.

When I walk outside he is waiting for me, now I'm starting to get pissed; but there wasn't much I can do, he is not a little dude so he is not going to be intimidated by me. I thought, if I tried to walk off he will probably just tag along, again my choices are few, so I walk and sure enough he follows. Agitated, I say,

"Man, what do you want?"

"I don't want a thing; you're the one who probably wants something."

"Oh, really; what do I want?"

"A place to go, a joint to smoke, you might even need a place to crash."

"Well that sounds all fine and dandy; but I'm in a hurry to get to Frisco, so no thanks."

"That's cool brother; but let me give you some advice; the locals don't like anyone referring to their town as 'Frisco; its San Francisco or San Fran'"

"Thanks, I'll keep that in mind." I started across the street, looking back I said,

"See ya."

"Yeah, good luck to ya brother." As I walked off I could hear him headed the other way, as the sound of his harmonica faded,

"Whaaaaaa-ahhhhhh-whaaaaaa..."

As I walked away I thought, hmmm, those three notes remind me of the intro to the Moody Blues song, 'Have You Heard?' funny.

By now the sun is coming up and I'm walking through Hollywood, the place is glitzy and grimy, dazzling and dirty. A lot of Chinese restaurants, pawn shops, night clubs and stars embossed in the sidewalks with names of famous actors in them, though half the names I never heard of. The people are all flavors, hippies, straights, tourists, foreigners, runaways and so on. After a while I decide to hitchhike to try and bum some money off the drivers, though nobody is picking me up. I wander around looking for an entrance ramp and finally found one; it's Highway 101 North and I am on my way, again. Would have liked to hang out in Hollywood to see what it is really like; but I had a girl to see.

I'm now into my second day out of New Orleans and still had at least a five or six hour trip to 'Frisco, I mean San Francisco. I wasted a good few hours wandering around Hollywood, so I need to get back on track. I caught a little sleep in Mad Man Mark's car; but not much, so I am tired. I catch a short ride and am let out in North Hollywood at the bottom of the exit ramp, the driver tells me the entrance ramp to get back on 101 is right across the street, only there are about ten assorted hitchhikers lined up. They all have packs of some kind so they are obviously on the road to somewhere. I heard not to get caught on the Interstate in California because the State Troopers will give you serious shit. Everyone is lined up along the ramp about four or five feet apart, a very organized bunch.

I walk up wondering which end of the line I'm supposed to get on. Then this mid twenty-year-old blonde motions to me to come over to where she was standing.

"Hi, where are you going?" she asked with a smile,

"San Francisco" I said a little perplexed at her friendliness.

"Great, I'm going to Santa Cruz, wanna hitch together?" Puzzled; but pleased, I said,

"Sure." Now this girl had a well-maintained appearance, a nice tan, a bit on the chunky side; but cute, she seems almost preppy, not hippie like at all; except she is hitchhiking and had a pack, she said,

"My name is Diane, what's yours?"

"Gene," At that moment a car pulled up with a college age couple in it, so we hop in the back seat and we were off, a little way down 101 she asked me,

"Have you ever been on the Pacific coast highway?"

"No, this is my first time to be in California."

"We'll head that way, you'll love it. The 101 will run right into the 'coast highway," she said smiling at me. I was quickly building an affinity for this girl. Normally I am not attracted to husky girls being a skinny guy myself; but she was enchanting and smelled good too. When the highway finally does hit the coast highway I notice the signs, U.S. 1. That reminded me of back home in Florida. I had walked down U.S. 1 many times back home and had no idea there was another U.S. 1 on the other side of the United States. All the memories, the restaurants I had worked at, The New England Oyster House, the Lum's restaurant, the Broadway Joe's hamburger joint my friend Glenn worked at. I mean U.S. 1 was the center of everything in Miami. I am feeling homesick again; I mentioned to Diane,

"Actually, now that I look at the signs, I have been on U.S.1 before; but it was on the other side of the country."

"Really?" She seemed interested.

"Yeah, Dixie Highway is on the east coast of Florida, though it's actually U.S. 1."

"Florida, is that where you're from?" She asked.

"Sort of, I was born in Miami and not long after my mom took me to New York where she was from. So I grew up in New York until about the seventh grade. Then my family moved to Miami; where I had been living until I left home about five or six months ago."

"So you left home to travel?" Diane asked; her inquisitive nature made me feel good; I liked her being interested in me.

"Something like that, I wanted to live my life on my own terms and traveling is something I do whenever I get the urge." This was true; though I left out the part about my dad, and being shown the door.

By now we are heading up the 'coast highway and the scenery is like an oil painting, the Pacific Ocean to our left and beautiful rugged terrain to the right. The highway meandered back and forth, hugging the coast; sheer cliffs dropped into a rocky coastline, while on the other side of the road the landscape went almost straight up to the sky. I am impressed; Diane and I caught a ride with a couple of California hipsters. They were two guys who wore cool looking sunglasses, expensive looking watches, driving a Mercedes and their body language said they didn't have a care in the world. They said they were on their way to Carmel. I thought; how appropriate, as if their world could not be any more fabulous, they were on their way to a town named after a creamy soft candy. Diane began chatting it up with them.

"Carmel, that's beautiful up there." She said; speaking like she is familiar with the area. Diane and the two fellows traded names of places they all seem to know. I forgot all about Edma and I am enjoying Diane's company. One of the guys asked Diane what she did for a living and she said she is a teacher at U.C.L.A. I thought, jeese, what is she doing hitchhiking; and what is she doing with a seventeen-year-old kid? But here she is and here I am, enjoying every aspect of the moment.

By the time they pop us out in Carmel it's late afternoon. Taking the coast highway may have been scenic; but it is also a longer slower route. We are standing on the side of the road, actually I am sitting on my pack and she is standing. Not many cars were coming by and it is beginning to get cool, I said,

"Hope someone picks us up soon, it's starting to get chilly." She smiled, looked over toward a clearing in the woods and said,

"I'm not worried, I've got a little tent in my pack and a down sleeping bag; we'll be fine, besides it won't drop below fifty." I looked up at her with an obviously surprised look on my face, at the thought of her offering to sleep with me. She leaned over and kissed me sweetly. I thought, what a trip, picked up by a college teacher and end up in her sleeping bag, my friends will surely accuse me of bullshitting when I tell them this tale; hell, I'm finding it hard to believe myself.

We then catch a ride with a couple of middle-aged hippie types. I am almost disappointed. Said they were going as far as Watsonville, not sure how far that is; but at this moment who cares. We hop in and they fire up the obligatory joint; Diane is not a pot smoker so I took her hits, we made small talk with them and by the time we reach their town we get to know them a little bit. His name is Ray and she is Sunshine, I had met a number of hippie girls who called themselves 'Sunshine' in Coconut Grove; which is a hippie haven back in Miami. Though judging by her age, this could be one of the original Sunshine's. Ray offered,

"Look, we have a small place; but you're welcome to spend the night on the floor, its better then being out in the cold." Glancing up in the rearview mirror he added,

"You'll probably have a tough time catching a ride now that it's dark, then again that's up to you." Diane and I looked at each other.

"Sounds good to me." I said to her quietly, to give her the option to decline. She said,

"Alright if it's not too much trouble."

We get to Ray and Sunshine's and they share a little homemade wine, Sunshine offered us some Zucchini bread she had made, chances are they grew their own weed as well. They had a cute little tri-colored mutt they called, 'Good Dog'. Their place was basically one big room with a separate kitchen and a bathroom. Sunshine said,

"We're pretty beat from driving so we're turning in, you can lay out your sleeping bags any where you like."

"The kitchen floor will be fine for us." Diane said.

"Sounds good to me." I said. Diane unpacked her sleeping bag and rolled it out in the kitchen; I began to unroll mine when she said,

"What are you doing, we can both use mine." We consummated our friendship and I slept like a baby.

Next morning after some hot herb tea, Ray brought us back to the highway and we are off, we are in Santa Cruz in no time. We get to Diane's house and her mom greeted us, Diane introduced me as her friend. She wanted me to hang out with her for the day and though I want to, I also want to see Edma. She eventually gave up trying to convince me and let me use her bathroom to get cleaned up, washed some of my clothes for me as well; she was a sweetheart. Diane borrowed her mom's car and gave me a ride out to the highway. She began to tear up when we said goodbye, she was just a warm-hearted girl and I would miss her. I thought about how lucky I was.

On the way to the highway Diane mentioned something called the 'switchboard'. She said there is a network of volunteers that had little offices set up in the towns along the highway, to find hitchhikers a place to spend the night. She said if you get into a town just call the operator and ask for the number to switchboard. Once you get them they'll tell you how to get to their office. She said they will call one of the people who volunteer to take in travelers. I thought, what a trip, California thinks of everything, what a state!

Catch my first ride of the day and the scenery was fabulous again, highway 9 is lined with evergreen forests, quaint little homes set back in the trees and the air is as crisp and clean as any air I ever inhaled. Winding up and down left and right the highway is a winding slow rolling coaster ride. Though I have seen some beautiful country in Tennessee and Kentucky this was different. The woods came right up to the highway and the trees seemed taller. Diane told me if I took highway 9, I wouldn't regret it and she is right; now I will have to recommend this road. Look at me; recommending highways 3,000 miles from home, I really am a traveling man, an adventurer. I am let out in front of a little country store and am hungry; I went in and was looking around, walked up to the counter and ask a guy who looks to be of College student age, standing on the other side of the counter,

"Hi, you got anything hot to eat?" The guy behind the counter says dryly,

"Tamales, fifty cents a piece."

"Tamales, what's a Tamale?"

"You've never heard of Tamales? Where you from?" He was amazed at my ignorance.

"Miami." I said, almost apologetically. He than said while wrinkling his face at me,

"Miami, you mean you guys don't have Tamales in Miami?" I responded,

"I guess I have heard of hot tamales; but never had one." He took a pair of tongs and fished this greasy looking thing out of a small steam table behind the counter. I buy a coke and walk out side. There is a planter made of logs outside the front of the store just wide enough to sit on, I began to partake of my first tamale. As I bite in to it I thought, this is tasty, except the insides were squirting out. So after a few bites and chewing like hell I just squeezed it and ate the filling. I went back in the store to buy some cigarettes,

"How did you like it?" the counter guy asked,

"It was pretty good, but tough as hell." He looked a little perplexed for a moment then said,

"Tough, what did you do, eat the husk?"

"What's the husk?" I asked.

"The husk is…" He then stopped turned around and fished out another Tamale, turned back around to the counter in front of me and set it on a paper plate, unwrapped the thick skin and pointed at the insides and said,

"That's what you eat, the outside is the husk." He slid the plate toward me,

"Here, this one's on me."

"Oh, jeese, thanks," I said.

After my Tamale experience I am back on the road, through the redwood forests I caught rides and am mesmerized. I keep thinking how great California is and no wonder so many people want to come here, then I realize, I must have left my St. Bonaventure sweat shirt in one of the rides I caught, I was pissed, real pissed, that is my lucky sweat shirt, I just knew rides would be harder to get. I mean, I had a lot of faith in that sweatshirt, I felt it was the reason I caught rides so quickly. It also was an immediate icebreaker, a number of people had heard of the school and those who had not; would ask about it. It is funny in a way because all I would say was my sister went to school there. Though that would lead to other subjects, like family and back home; I just knew it is going to be tougher without it. Also it was my warm coat, now if I get cold; all I have is flannel shirts. I wondered if my sister Patty would be wondering what happened to her sweatshirt. I thought funny how an article of clothing could mean so much.

It isn't long before I am strolling through San Francisco. The town is very cool; the buildings were old and full of character, it has a very unique vibe about it. The town seems to look European, like New Orleans or maybe a bigger version of New Orleans. The whole city is set on rolling hills. The people are about as eclectic a group as you could imagine. Everything from Asians to hippies, old wine-o's, runaways, business types and so on. After a few inquiries I find Edma's street, she is staying in the Haight Asbury area. As I walk down the street it begins to rain. I am nervous and exited; I am finally going to see Edma again; my Edma.

I walk up to the apartment or house or whatever it is and knock on the front door; my heart is in my throat. Some older longhaired guy with round rim glasses answered the door. I ask for Edma, with out a word to me he turned back into the apartment and called out,

"Edma, someone is here for you," he had a Latin accent, I thought, *was this the guy she was divorcing?* Edma came to the door and he walks away, she stepped out side and I hugged her, though she didn't hug me back. She is as beautiful as I had remembered her. Though, her demeanor was not one of happiness.

"Edma, what's wrong, it's me Gene, I've come all the way from New Orleans to be with you." She stood there looking awkward and uncomfortable, gazing at her feet with her hands behind her back.

"Edma, are you not happy I came, what's wrong?" I was getting upset.

"I stay with Richard." She said, still looking down.

"Richard; are you kidding, you said you were getting divorced?"

"I'm sorry, I stay with him, I'm sorry." She looked up at me for a moment than back down. She then said "We can be friends." Now I was pissed.

"Friends, friends? I don't wanna be friends…I don't fuck my friends! I immediately realized how that must have sounded, though I didn't try to explain. She didn't look up. There we were within a few inches of each other, yet it felt like she was miles away. Rain began to fall stronger, which seemed appropriate, because in my heart it was pouring. My anger turned to remorse and I said, "Oh well, if that's the way it is." I put my hand under her chin to lift her face to kiss her; but she turned and gave me her cheek. I am losing the love of my life, and the girl of my dreams. I said, "Bye Edma, I hope you'll be happy." I tried to say it like I meant it. I reached down picked up my pack, slung it over my shoulder, turned and walked away. I never looked back, it was over and I knew it.

As I walked away I thought, three and a half days and twenty four hundred miles to be spurned by the love of my life; in less than five minutes. What happened, what I was thinking; I hardly knew her. Yet I was willing to chase her hundreds of miles across the country. I had a pocket full of wishes and a spirit that was willing to chase them anywhere. The dreamer, the wisher, the wandering soul, passionately confused; while in my heart I just knew I was always doing the right thing. I clung to my dreams like a spider clings to a strand of web, no matter how hard you try to shake the spider off, no matter how obvious it is that the web has been destroyed, the spider will not let go. You would have to step on him if you wanted him to release his grip. So you could say Edma just stepped on me.

I began thinking about my friends back home. I always thought of my friends when I was feeling bad on the road; I thought about my family as well. But my friends seem to hold a place closest to my heart. At that moment it hit me, its time to go back to Miami, back to my friends. I wiped my eyes took a deep breath and threw my pack high on my shoulder. I had this way of walking when I wanted to feel good about myself, it was a kind of strut, subtle but distinctive. It is basically me imitating the way my friend Gene Jarred walks, it is a brisk long stride that says, I know where I'm going and I'm not to be fooled with. Yeah, he has a great walk; I know it is probably bullshit to anyone else, but I still like to think of it because it makes me feel good, gave me solace. I can picture him walking. As a matter of fact I can see him walking right at this moment, right now.

"A REAL GOOD GUY"

On my way out of San Francisco I catch a ride with an Asian dude, a nice guy, a young businessman headed for Palo Alto. The traffic is heavy, but we make it by dark. Though I had a little money, while disembarking I hit him up for a couple bucks and he obliges. I remember my fiend Marko back in New Orleans would say, "Just because you have something, like money or cigarettes doesn't mean you can't ask. It's always good to stock up for leaner times." The sun is setting as I stand at the entrance ramp. Decide to take off walking back toward the business area, but there is not too much to see in Palo Alto. Meet some young dudes and bum a cigarette in front of a Shoney's restaurant. I say young, because they were not over sixteen, but I can tell they are cool—long hair, used hippie speak, and one of them even smells of patchouli. Tell them how I am traveling just to see the world. They like my story. They invite me to go with them to their brother's house. Said it would be cool for me to hang out there. When we get there I am not surprised to arrive at your standard looking hippie haven; needs a paint job, yard needs mowing, a beat up Volkswagen bus out front, and several wind chimes dangling around the front porch. I could hear the Steve Miller Band as we approached:

Kow kow calculator, was a very smooth operator,
Had himself a pet alligator, kept him in a chrome elevator.

I wondered, just what is that song about anyway? After a quick knock at the door we walk in and I am introduced.

"Hey, Tim, this is Gene from New Orleans, he needs a place to crash. Can he hang out here?" His brother shook my hand. I thought this guy is cool. He has very long hair past his shoulders in a ponytail, with a short beard, probably in his twenties. I could smell weed burning. He invites us into the living room where a few freaks are hanging out, getting stoned. We all sat and partook of the weed, while two very large speakers sitting on the floor delivered some great sound. Before long, I almost feel like I am back at the Fisheries. I feel good. Out of one of the backrooms came a guy who is a bit older than any of the other people there. I did not like the vibe I get from him. He appears menacing, sinister; dark piercing eyes, a huge tattoo on one of his arms that looks like it is attempting to hide a huge scar, and his head is bald, yet he has a ponytail. He has to be thirty-five. He immediately focused on me and started asking me questions, too many questions. I feel uncomfortable. Eventually I stand and say I am going to walk down to the nearby convenience store. The creepy dude offered to give me a ride, but I say, "That's cool, I'd rather walk."

After stepping away from the house, I simply kept on going, I am not about to go back there. I am beginning to trust my instincts, as opposed to ignoring them and just going with the flow. Walking along, looking for a place to crash. I come upon a hill with some bushes on top and thought it looked secluded. Making my way through the brush up the hill, at the top I crouch down behind the bushes, unroll my sleeping bag and climb in. The temperature is cool, but not cold. I start thinking about Edma again. I thought about Diane. Oh yeah, and Kim. I wondered if she ever thinks of me. Feeling lonely and forlorn, melancholy feelings get the better of me. I want a girl to love and care about, who in turn will care about me. I thought about my first serious girlfriend, Natalie Kleiner. I thought about how much we cared for each other, how we were going to be married when we were old enough. I was fifteen at the time; she was sixteen. It was the first time I ever told a girl, I love you, and she in turn told me. I want desperately to have that feeling again. As I lay there languishing in self-pity, I doze off.

When I awake the sun is up and shining. Rolling over on my back and looking up to see a blue sky, a new day. That is all I can see because I am surrounded by tall brush. As I lay there staring at the sky I thought about how free I was and how this day was mine, all mine. I crawl out of my bag and begin to roll up my belongings while doing an inventory. Three flannel shirts, a couple of tee-shirts, socks etc. and no St. Bonaventure jacket. While pulling myself together I realize there are people talking very close by. Peeking out from the bushes I am surprised to see kids everywhere. There were droves of teenagers getting out of Yellow buses, while others were standing in small groups talking. I slipped back into my hide out. Apparently I had gone to sleep on a hill directly across the street from a big public high school. I sat there and think, guess I can wait until they go to class. It will be kind of embarrassing to walk down off this hill with my pack. They will know I slept up here. I thought, Embarrassing? They don't know me from Mahatma Gandhi. Screw this…I stand, brush myself off, through my pack over my shoulder, and walk down the hill like I am coming home from the Hundred Years War. Not only do they not snicker or point, but their eyes get wide and they back up as I approach they make a path for me. I think to myself, they're in awe. The truth is, I probably just look like a teenage hobo and smell like an old hamper; but I don't care. I am proud to be doing what I am doing; I am the adventurer I always wanted to be.

I find a gas station and clean up best I can. When I hit the street, I look at the map I had gotten from the station. I thought, I'm glad these road maps are free. At a gas station in Detroit they tried charging me thirty cents for one. What bullshit. Decided to take 101 south; though I did think about taking a look for Diane in Santa Cruz, but I nix the idea. I find the entrance ramp and stick out my thumb. Not long after, a dude on a chopper—a Harley Davidson—pulls over. It is't anything special, but it is a chopper and he is going south. He has to yell over the loud exhaust pipes, "Hop on and lean back… and hold your pack in front of you." I did as he instructed, and we are off. He isn't wearing a helmet, so I figure I wasn't breaking any law either.

"How far are you going?" I hollered.

"Forty miles," he yelled back.

"Sounds good to me."

"What's that?"

"SOUNDS GOOD." He nodded his head, like he heard me. As we fly down the highway, I begin to tell myself how I, will have a chopper someday, and see the country in style. Forty miles later he popped me off.

I walk over and stand at the entrance ramp; but there is little traffic coming on the highway. I read the graffiti written in black Magic Marker on the back of the Highway 101 sign.

'No cars, no hope,
no money, no dope,
get a rope!'

How pathetic I think, and it's not even that funny. After an hour or so has passed with maybe half a dozen cars coming by I thought, Hell, this is the middle of nowhere. State Troopers aren't going to care if I'm on the side of the Interstate. Up the entrance ramp and out on the highway I walk. I didn't venture far from the entrance ramp though. Figure I would just stand there, discreetly, although, how does one hitchhike discreetly…?

Ten minutes later, up pulls a California Highway Patrol. The officer got out and nonchalantly walked over, and with a somewhat disgusted look on his face, he said, "Let's see some I.D." I awkwardly respond, "I've got a library card."

"A library card, huh." He took it from me, and scrutinized it. "Are you from New Orleans?"

"No, my folks live in Miami, Florida." I said almost bragging.

"Miami huh, How old are you?"

"Seventeen," I told him, indignantly, like I had every right in the world to be out on my own.

"Your parents know you're in California?" he asked, with his tone telling me he was not going to believe my answer.

"Well, they know I'm traveling, but they don't know exactly where I am." He handed me my library card back and said, "You know your parents phone number?" Somewhat surprised at this question, I gave him a quizzical look; but said, "Sure."

"Turn around and put your hands on your head," He patted me down. Luckily, my pocket knife was in my pack and for some reason he didn't check it.

"Get in my car. Were gonna make a phone call." I walked to his car and got in. He drives down the highway about a mile, took the exit, and pulls up to a gas station. He got out and then let me out of the back seat. He walked up to the pay phone and dialed, and I heard him say, "This is California Highway Patrol and I will need to make a long distance call, my code is…" He then motioned me over and asked me," What's the number?" I told him and he relayed it to the operator. I thought, my mom last saw me at the Fisheries, now she's gonna get a call from a state trooper in California— Holy shit! Moments later I heard him say, "Hello Ma'am, this is The California Highway Patrol. Is this Mrs. Martin?" He continued, "No there's no real problem. I have a young man here by the name of Gene Martin, says he has your permission to be hitchhiking in California." There was a pause, then, "No, he's not in any trouble; but I was a little concerned when he told me all he had for I.D. was a library card and that he was only seventeen." Another pause, then, "All right mam', that's all I need to know, thank you. What's that? Yes Ma'am I'll tell him. Good bye." He hung up, then said, "Your mother wants you to call her, collect if need be." I say nothing. He followed with, "Stay off the Interstate. It's the law in California. You're not to go past the freeway entrance sign, got it?" I acknowledge him; he walks back to his car, and drives away. I thought, I guess the locals weren't kidding when they told me to stay off the Interstate. And I'll bet that phone call freaked my mom out; I really do need to call her…

My next few rides are nothing special, eventually I find myself leaving the coast and heading inland. The guy who picked me up outside L.A. was the quiet type; luckily he had the radio on a rock station, so the ride is enjoyable. A song came on that I recognized, the name of the group was, America. I was not really a fan, but when I looked up at the freeway signs and noticed it saying Ventura Freeway, it hit me.

"Hey," I said, "This song is *Ventura Highway* I'd always thought the song was called, *Venture A Highway*, like venture down the road." The quiet man glanced over at me and nodded fane admiration, with this look of, wow; you're a regular Sherlock Holmes, although he said nothing.

When he let me out I am back in Hollywood. It is just turning dark out and I am hitching at a well lit entrance ramp, so I thought I might just get lucky. A big, black Oldsmobile pulled up and I open the door and hop in without saying anything or glancing at the driver, which is not like me because usually I would ask, "How far you going?" or something like that. I would size up the person I was about to get a ride with, possibly turn the ride down if I got the wrong vibe. The moment I shut my door I knew something is not good. An overwhelming smell of cheap perfume, was so thick in the air I could taste it, and the driver is not a woman. I am immediately uncomfortable.

As we take off down the highway the electric locks click down. I glance over at the driver and ask, "How far you going? Are you taking I-10 East or West?" I am trying not to appear nervous. He is a tall, thin guy, maybe twenty-seven, twenty eight and wore a black silky shirt and black slacks. He has a pasty white complexion and thin eyebrows.

He said, "I could probably go either way." I thought, hmm, whatever that means. He continues, "Been on the road long?" he asked politely.

"A week or so," I dryly respond.

"You ever get picked up by a guy who wants to take you home?" My heart started to pound in my chest, I could feel a peach seed in my throat and I didn't answer. He went on, "What would you think about going home with me?"

My pack was on my lap and I began to work my hand into it searching for my pocket knife. My adrenalin was surging in me like ocean waves hitting a sea wall. I could see a slight smirk on his face as he cut his eyes my way.

"No thanks," I said with an obvious disdain in my voice, like he was offering me a liverwurst sandwich. "That really wouldn't interest me." I said trying to maintain and not show fear. My right hand found my knife and I began to ease it out.

He said, "Why don't we go have a drink somewhere?" At that point my heart felt like a piece of throbbing gristle in my chest and if my mouth were any drier it would have stuck closed. I thought quickly; if I acted the least bit intimidated or panicky he would have the advantage. I needed to act like I was in control and capable of anything. I slowly took my hand from my pack and very slowly yet deliberately set my knife on my pack in front of me holding it in my fist. With my left hand I opened the blade. Holding the knife in front of me in plain sight, I looked at the blade and said, in the softest, most ominous voice I could create, "No, I don't think so; as a matter of fact I want this car to stop so I can get out…right now." Not taking my eyes off the knife in front of me, not even glancing his way, as if I was about to do something he would regret. He swerved the car to the shoulder and slammed on the brakes, the lock clicked up and I got out. He tore off before I had a chance to thank him for the ride, or close the door. Damn, that was close. Or it least it felt close. Don't know if I really could have stabbed him; just glad I didn't have to find out.

I walk to the next exit and made it without getting caught. Across the street is the entrance ramp, and I decide, the next car that pulls over I think I'll take a whiff, before I get in. There is a Texaco station across the street, I walk over and buy a coke and a honey bun. I sit outside and think about what had just happened. I decide I did the right thing, though it might have been a little melodramatic. Maybe if I just asked him, he would have let me out. At the time I didn't think he would. As I pondered what had just happened it is exhilarating and at the same time it scared the shit out of me.

I decide I am not going to get picked up tonight, so I crawl off in the bushes and go to sleep. After the last encounter, the adrenaline rush had really worn me out, and I quickly fell asleep. The next day I was up and back on the road. A guy and girl picked me up. They had Georgia tags on their car, and I thought, *Damn, what luck.* My elation was short-lived, as I found they were only going as far as Joshua Tree Park, about a hundred miles. It is just as well… they were a couple of hicks and I got the feeling they would have been pretty boring to talk to. It was funny… I had become so confident in my ability to get a ride, if I get in a car that I find uncomfortable or even just too slow, I would tell them to let me out. Because I just knew I could catch a faster ride. After they let me out, I had some uneventful rides until I hit Phoenix.

In Phoenix I was picked up by an Army captain, a real serious character. I felt a little uncomfortable, like I was in a car with a cop. He was my dad's age and sat behind the wheel at attention. I was dirty, wearing a flannel shirt and blue jeans, and my thick dark brown hair hung almost to my collar. I was on the road traveling by thumb. He was pressed and starched and at the other end of the pendulum from me. I thought about telling him how I almost joined the Army, but was tripping on acid so it didn't work out. I smiled to myself. We made small talk, though it seemed phony on both our parts. We are outside Tucson when we passed four hippies hitchhiking— two guys, two girls— and the captain asked me, "Think we should give them a ride?" Surprised, I said "sure, why not?" He pulled over and backed up.

This crew is a hoot; scruffy, talkative, and on their way to Mardi Gras. That's right, my New Orleans. I remembered the fact that Mardi Gras went on for two weeks, so it is still going strong. They started out in Santa Cruz. I felt like these were my people, though I am still surprised about this Army captain picking hippies up to begin with, me included. I thought of hippies and the military being polar opposites. The two guys and one of the girls hopped in the back seat and the other girl hopped up front between the captain and me. Luckily, he had a nice big four-door Ford and we were not too crowded.

The girl who was up front was a bubbly, cute twenty-year-old. She introduced herself to the captain. "Hi my name is Jennifer, what's yours?" She looked at the captain. He smiled and said, "Captain William T. North, but you can call me Bill." Then Jennifer said, "All right, Captain Bill, in the back is Charlie, Angie, and Pete. We got wine, anybody want some? Charlie, pass me the wine." The wine came up front and Jennifer offered some to the captain. It was a bag of wine you hold up in front of you and squeeze it to shoot a stream of wine into your mouth, or that's the idea. Captain Bill said politely, "No thanks, I've got my own." At that he reached under his seat and pulled out a pint of Jack Daniels, undid the cap and took a swig. Jennifer reached for his bottle and said, "Let me try some of that." She took a belt off the bottle and let out a, "Whoooooa! Hell, yeah!!!"

One of the guys in the back yelled, "Turn up the radio!"

Radio plays that forgotten song'
Brenda Lee comin' on strong,

The song was *Radar Love.* I was becoming a little anxious; one of the guys in the backseat said, "Hey, Captain Bill, mind if we smoke?" The captain replied, "Go ahead, I don't care."

By now Jennifer was wearing the captain's hat… I mean his dress uniform hat. I thought, Holy shit, these people are either crazy or got balls like coconuts. Jennifer began dancing in her seat, clapping her hands to *Jumpin Jack Flash it's a gas, gas, gas…*

At that moment I smelled weed. Oh my God, I thought. When he said smoke he was talking about weed? I was terrified. However, Captain Bill didn't seem to care. From the back seat I heard, "Anybody want some mushroom tea?"

That was it; it was too much for me. I said, "Hey, you can let me out at the next exit?" Jennifer acting surprised said, "I thought you were going to Florida?"

"I am, but I got a friend that lives near here and I'm gonna stop and see him." At that point the car slowed down, pulled over and they let me out. Off they zoomed in a cloud of smoke and booze. That was just too crazy, I was more of what you might call a conservative hippie, if that's not too much of an oxymoron; maybe I was just a chicken shit.

A Toyota pulled over and a Mexican-looking guy on the small side was driving. I asked, "How far ya going?" He said in a latino accent, "El Paso"

I got in. *Ahhh, peaceful and normal,* I thought. We glided down the highway making small talk. He was a pleasant fellow, small and somewhat effeminate. He asked me about being on the road and seemed genuinely interested. I felt comfortable enough to tell him about the various thrills as well as the fears I had about the road. He was obviously comfortable with me because at one point he told me he was gay and had to keep it a secret because of the small town he lived in. By the time we reached El Paso it was dark. I had really enjoyed talking to the guy. He had many of the same concerns and worries about life that I had. He was not that different at all. When he let me out, I thought about the fact that he was a decent dude who was simply gay and not a pervert at all. I thought about how I needed to reassess my belief that gay meant pervert. I guess everyone did not have to be straight to be normal. I walk along looking for something to eat and found a Burger King. I bought as much as I could for three bucks. After eating I walk off to find a place to sleep and ended up under an overpass.

Next day I caught a ride to Van Horn, Texas and then onto Highway 90 West, instead of staying on Interstate 10, simply because the car I was in was going that way. I moved across West Texas with relative ease. People in West Texas were Generally friendly. I made it to a small town outside San Antonio by the name of Castroville and get a little bogged down. After an hour or so of standing in one place on the side of the highway, three girls in a flatbed truck came by and hollered something out the window at me. I didn't think much of it until they came back by. This time they yelled and whistled; I started to get a little uneasy. When they came by a third time they slowed down, yelled, and this time I could understand them.

"Hey good lookin', you wanna to party?" They giggled and laughed as they drove by. I wasn't sure if I wanted to party with three West Texas girls in a flatbed. I just looked at them like I didn't understand a thing they said, not wanting to encourage them. I was not sure if I had what it takes to handle a trio of country girls. I could just see myself ending up somewhere in the sticks, only to be confronted by their moonshine-powered, overall-wearing brothers.

Standing on the side of the road hitch-hiking was a kind of mind dance. There I was, hoping for a car to pull over, and at the same time hoping the car that pulled over did not have someone in it with an idea for my demise. The cars passing by held drivers that were saying things to themselves things like, 'Should I give that guy a ride, or would that be a mistake?' As a car would come by and I would attempt to catch the driver's eye and convey in a matter of seconds that I was a safe, normal guy who needed a ride. The driver, in turn, would look right at me and drive on by, almost indignantly, or see me looking, catch my eye, then quickly look straight ahead, as if fighting the urge to pull over because it's considered wrong to pick up a hitchhiker. It was funny to stand on the side of the road, watching and draw conclusions about people I knew absolutely nothing about. I found pleasure in doing it . . . like it was part of my job as a hitchhiker... as a philosopher... to ponder each and every passer-by. But all that went out the window when three girls in a truck drove by and hollered at me. Because all I felt was uneasy, defenseless, and exposed.

A young guy in a pickup pulled over, and I was thankful to be out of there. It was a trip to think about how quickly things can change on the road. I mean you could instantly go from scared to glad to scared again, all within a few seconds; then again, that was part of the thrill. The young dude in the pickup was B-flat, with not much to say, though he did take me all the way to San Antonio.

Wandering through the city of San Antonio, I happened to pass the Greyhound station, thinking how I hated buses. As I walked by, a girl sitting on her pack and wearing a Cal State sweatshirt and jeans spoke up. "Hey, where you headed?" I was a little surprised, she seemed too sophisticated to be hanging at a bus station, and I answered, "Why do you wanna know?"

"Well," she began, "I was hitching with my boyfriend to Mardi gras and we had an argument and he dumped me. He told me to take a bus. I don't really wanna spend the money on a ticket."

"Mardi gras huh; so he dumped you while traveling with you?" Must have been a hell of an argument?"

"Not really," she said. "He's always been kind of a hothead."

"Where did you start out from?" I asked her.

"Santa Cruz, California." Surprised and smiling, I said, "I ran in to some people from Santa Cruz not too far back, down I-10."

She jumped to her feet, "Really? What were their names?"

"Let's see, there was… Jennifer,"

"Jennifer Michaels?" She came closer, wide-eyed and all beside herself.

"I didn't get her last name."

"Who was she with? Who was she with?" she said real fast, flittering in front of me like a bird flapping its wings. Before I had a chance to answer she asked,"Was Charlie, Charlie Costanza with her?"

"Yeah I believe, some guy named Charlie was with her." Though to be honest I didn't remember. I just wanted to tell her what she wanted to hear. Then she said,

"There were about twenty of us from Santa Cruz that were gonna meet up in New Orleans. We were all hitchhiking, in groups of three or four."

I said, "Well if you wanna hitch with me, come on, I'll pass by New Orleans. What's your name?"

"My name is Jennifer Sargent, but let's gets something straight. . . I'm not sleeping with you. I just can't take the chance on hitching alone and I don't want to take the bus.

"All right, whatever," I said.

"I do have some money and I can buy you something to eat along the way," she said.

"Yeah, great, let's go before the sun goes down." And we walked off together.

On our way to I 10 East, I introduced myself. She, of course, couldn't believe I was seventeen. I got that a lot. She said, "You seem older… though now that I look at you… do you even shave?" She smiled.

We found the entrance ramp and caught a ride after about fifteen or twenty minutes with a fairly young couple from East Texas.

"We're on our way to Crowley, Louisiana for a family reunion. This is Candace and I'm Morris."

"I'm Gene and this is Jennifer. We're on our way to New Orleans." "Carnival huh," Morris asked. I thought *carnival?* I remembered that was how the locals referred to Mardi gras. We were in the back seat of their beat up old Dodge Dart. I thought, Crowley, that's a good… and Jennifer piped up, "How far is it to Crowley?"

"About six hours. We'll get there around midnight," Morris answered. Jennifer and I looked at each other and nodded our approval.

Candace, Morris's significant other, then asked, "Are you two married?"

"No," Jennifer replied. "Just traveling companions," Jennifer and Candace began to chat it up about a lot of nothing, while I took the opportunity to doze off.

It wasn't long before I felt an elbow poking me. Jennifer said, "We're stopping. Do you want something to eat? I'm buying." It was a gas station with a Sonic Drive-in next door. "Yeah, but I need to use the bathroom. I'll take a chili cheese dog, some fries and a coke."

When we got rolling again I noticed we were near Houston. I said to Jennifer, "When we get to Crowley we'll need to find a place to spend the night. I've never had much luck catching a ride late at night." Morris, who obviously had his ears peeled, or it was just an amazing coincidence, said,

"When we get to Crowley you're welcome to spend the night at Maw Maws." That's how he said it too, "Maw Maw's." He glanced in the rearview as he spoke; I looked at Jennifer and said,

"I guess that would work.Thanks."

Three hours later we hit Crowley, piled out of the Dart and into the house. Candace introduced us to their Maw Maw and she offered us all something to eat. She was a fat lady in her fifties, with a thick Louisiana accent— a very nice country lady with a motherly demeanor. She plopped some what I thought was rice on a plate, and handed it to Jennifer, then handed me a plate. It turned out to be Jambalaya. I'd, had it in New Orleans, but it wasn't this good. It had chicken, sausage, rice, and I'm not sure what else—but by God it was good. I gobbled it up, thanked her and headed for a place to roll out my sleeping bag. Morris said, "There's plenty of room in the living room." I thanked him and rolled out my bag. Jennifer asked to use the bathroom and then came out in what looked like an oversized football jersey. She lay down on the couch and pulled her sleeping bag over her like a blanket. I said good night and so did she.

Of course I had to take a shot so I said, "Is that couch comfortable?" She replied, without any hesitation, "Don't even think about it." Well, I did think about it, but I went to sleep anyway.

In the morning, bright and early, kids were giggling and running around in their BVD's, and Morris walked in.

"You awake?"

"I am now," I said smiling, trying not to seem too annoyed. Jennifer was opening her eyes as well.

Morris asked, "You wanna go fishin'?"

"Fishin'? I don't think so. We need to get back on the road," I said.

"Ah come on, we'll fish a little and in less than an hour my cousin has got to make a run to Baton Rouge. He'll have you there before noon." I looked over at Jennifer and she shrugged, like, "I guess so." She got up and headed for the bathroom. I pulled myself together and asked Morris,

"Mind if I take a quick shower?"

"No, go ahead," he said. "We got bacon and eggs in the kitchen and then we'll go fishin'." At that point Jennifer came out of the bathroom. I slipped in and took all of a three minute shower. When I walked in the kitchen, there were Candace, Morris, Maw Maw, Jennifer, and some scruffy looking fellow. Morris introduced him: "Gene, this is Lester." The scruffy dude held out his hand, we shook..

"My name's Lester but I ain't lazy, h'yelk,h'yelk." I thought Holy crap, look at this guy, why are his eyes so close together and his lips and nose so small? He kind of freaked me out.

I wasn't real excited about going out in the woods with these guys. but it turned out to be cool. We drove about ten minutes and ended up on the side of a creek. They handed me a pole and a cricket and I was fishin'. Lester fired up a joint and Morris cracked open a beer. *Wow,* I thought, these guys really know how to enjoy themselves. I had left Jennifer back at Maw Maws. She was helping with something in the kitchen and also wanted to take a shower.

Forty-five minutes later this guy showed up at the fishin' spot in an old pick-up and wearing overalls.

"Who needs a ride to Baton Rouge?"

I stood up and said,"That would be me." I bade Morris and Lester farewell and thanked them for everything. I was off with "overall man." He introduced himself as Vince. We got back to Maw Maw's and found Jennifer waiting on the front porch. I walked up with Vince and introduced him to Jennifer, then went in the house, got my stuff, and said thanks and goodbye to Maw Maw. She was great— invited us back any time, and I think she meant it

Moments later we were on our way. Vince told us a couple fishing stories and a few other tales just as mundane. I did enjoy hearing about the alligators and crabs that will eat anything.

"Yeah," he said, "If a man's body were throw'd in the *buy-o*, it don' take long fer the gators to eat it up, bones and all. 'N whatever they don' eat the crabs will."

"Well," I said, "that's good to know; in case I ever need to dispose of a body." Sarcasm; I did take pleasure in it.

When we finally got to Baton Rouge, Vince droppd us right downtown. We thanked him and waved goodbye.

I told Jennifer,"Look, I'm not going to New Orleans. I keep going straight down I-10; but I'll hitch with you and wait until a car stops that looks safe and is going all the way to New Orleans." She got this worried, puzzled look and asked, "How are you gonna do that?"

"Well," I said, "I'm gonna stand at this entrance ramp with you and when someone pulls over we'll ask if they're going all the way to New Orleans." She gives me this, look of doubt, at that point a car pulled off and I hustled up and opened the door asking, "Are you going all the way to New Orleans?" He had a kind of a hippie look to him, so I decided he was okay.

"Metairie," he said. I turned to Jennifer and said, "That's not far from the city. You should take it."

Jennifer asked me, "Is that close to the French Quarter?"

"Close enough," I said, as I held the door for her.

"You can catch a bus into the city from Metairie." I gave her a hug goodbye. She said, "You've been a real good guy about this. I won't forget you." I swung the door shut and in a moment she was gone. I thought to myself, 'Won't forget me?'

Life Story

I'm thinking about going to look for my friends Timmy and Mick Shedagar, but want to get back home. I find a two-lane highway and head out of Baton Rouge and make it to a town called Hammond. My next few rides get me down I -10 East and four hours later I am in Pensacola. A young Air Force dude, maybe twenty, picks me up. His hair, is military short, he's wearing a clean button-down shirt and new blue jeans, and is driving a pretty nice Ford Grand Torino. My first thought is that he is a strait-laced dork.

He says, "My name is Steve." He sticks out his hand and I shake it. "Gene."

"Where you going, Gene?"

"Miami."

"Miami, huh? Well, I'm headed over to St. Augustine. Ever been there?" he asks with a hint of enthusiasm.

"No, can't say I have."

"Wanna go?"

"Sounds good to me; it's in the right direction."

"Gotta go by a friend's before we leave. Is that okay?"

"Yeah, that's fine by me."

We came off the highway into a Pensacola suburb, pull up to a nondescript house and he invites me to come in with him. At the front door we knock, and from the other side of the door we hear, "It's open." We walk in; a couple of military types sitting in the living room, smoking a joint, watching some T V game show. Steve said hi to them and turned to step into the kitchen. There is a cute looking girl in a tee shirt and shorts with rollers in her hair, sitting cross-legged on the kitchen counter, doing her nails, smoking a cigarette. She was probably in her early twenties. Steve introduced me: "Connie this is Gene, Gene, Connie." I nodded, trying desperately not to stare at her crotch, which seemed to be staring at me.

He asks her, “When is Bret getting home? From the looks of your hair, probably no time soon.”

“What’s that suppose to mean?” She reacted indignantly.

“Well, I know you well enough to know you never let him see you in rollers.”

She smiled coyly. “What do you need Bret for?”

“I wanna buy ten hits.”

“The brown?” she asked. Steve looked at me,

“Wanna do some mescaline?”

“Sure,” I said. He looked back at Connie, “So, when do you expect him?”

“I don’t expect him for a while, but if you wanna buy ten hits its right here.” She reached in the kitchen cabinet behind her and pulled out a Tupperware container, popped it open, and counted out ten hits.

“Twenty bucks,” she said. Steve handed her the twenty, and we left.

We get in his car and headed east on I-10. Steve gave me a hit and took one himself. As the mesc’ started to kick in, the tracers from the lights started, and that funny feeling washed over me, like I was, warm yet at the same time chilly.

Steve said, “Talk to me so I can stay focused. It’s gonna be a long drive, and my radio doesn’t work.”

“Talk to you, about what? I can’t just talk; I have to have something to talk about.”

“Tell me a story,” he said.

“What kind of a story?”

“A hitchhiking story; I’m sure you’ve got plenty of those.”

It was funny… I loved to tell stories, but when someone said, “Tell me a story,” I became speechless. He said, “How about your life story?”

Surprised, I said, “My life story? What do you care about my life story?” This was a funny request from a stranger.

“I don’t, but if we just drive and listen to the hum of the motor, I’m afraid I’ll hallucinate too much.”

“Okay, I’ll try,” I said.

“My father, Benny Lucci, was born in 1898, in Bologna, Italy.”

“Wait, your father was born in 1898?” Steve interrupted. “You mean your grandfather?”

“No, I mean my father. He was fifty-six years old when I was born in 1954.”

“Damn”, he said, “That’s a trip.”

"Yeah, so anyway, my mother, Marie Marsh, was born in 1925 and was twenty-nine when I was born. Steve interrupted again. "Wait, so your dad was... twenty-six, twenty-seven years older than your mom? Wow."

"Yeah, anyway, we lived in Coral Gables, Florida at the time. After a few years in Florida, my parents split up. My mother left my dad and took me to Brooklyn to live with her mother. My dad stayed in Florida and lived in an apartment by himself. He was a chef at one of the big hotels on Miami Beach."

"In 1956 shortly after my mother and father split up, he was killed."

"Really, how did that happen?"

"Apparently, he met two young street kids on his way from work, a young guy and a girl. He invited them up to his apartment for something to eat. At some point in the evening, the guy decided to jump my dad and rob him. There was a struggle, during which the guy punched my dad in the throat. He died from a crushed esophagus."

"Damn," Steve said. What a way to go."

"Yeah, to this day I'm not even sure where he's buried. The perpetrator ended up doing seven years in the penitentiary and his girlfriend received probation."

"Seven years?" Steve said, disgusted.

"Yeah, the only memory I have of him is, well. . . not even a memory. It's a black and white photograph of my dad, mom, and me. It has 1956 written on the back."

"My mom and I hung out at my grandmother's apartment... 156 Prospect Park West, Brooklyn, New York."

I still remember the address. My favorite uncle, Uncle Buddy, also lived there. I really liked him a lot. He took me to Yankee stadium, where I got to see Mickey Mantle, Roger Maris, Joe Peppitone..."

"No, shit?" Steve was impressed.

"Yeah, it was pretty incredible all right. My Uncle Buddy was a great guy. Although, according to my mom, he did time in Leavenworth penitentiary, 'making little ones out of big ones,' as she put it."

"Really? What was that about?"

"He apparently beat up an officer while he was in the army."

"Anyway, I liked him and I spent a lot of time with him. My mom would take us to Manhattan— my Great Aunt Frances lived there. Or we would go to Kearny, New Jersey to my Aunt Peg's. I had another Aunt Frances— her husband was my Uncle Justin. My mom would drop me off with their family, out on Long Island. My mom had a tendency to drop me off frequently with various relatives. I did an awful lot of crying as a small child. My oldest memories are of crying incessantly while looking in to the faces of worried adults. They would pass me around from person to person trying desperately to get me to stop."

"Unhappy childhood, huh?" Steve asked.

"I guess so. My Aunt Frances had a story about my mom dropping me off with her on Long Island. At some point I began crying—I mean really screaming and carrying on, according to her. After a long time trying to get me to quit, she finally became so concerned that she told her kids to come with her out to the front yard. She figured that way her neighbors would be able to see that they weren't in the house beating me. Funny huh?"

"Yeah, funny," Steve said.

"Are you feeling that mesc' yet?" I asked Steve.

"Hell, yeah. Are you?"

"Yeah, I am. So anyway, when I wasn't being dropped off with various relatives, we would hotel hop; that's when I began to notice my mother had a drinking problem. I was about four years old at the time. We hung out in hotel rooms while my mom drank until she passed out. It's not a fond memory, but I did like it better than being dropped off at a relatives. I guess when you're a kid you would rather be with a drunk mom than a sober relative. Eventually, my mom met and married a man by the name of Jack Dial. He took us in and my mom set up house in his home in Bayport, Long Island. I was about six by then."

"New York, huh. Did you like it?" Steve asked,

"For the most part. So when I first met Jack Dial, I'd call him Uncle Jack. Later on my mom said I should call him 'Dad.' It felt a little awkward, but eventually I did. Jack was in his late fifties, a Cuban cigar-smoking alcoholic, about five eight, thirty or forty pounds overweight, with gray hair he combed over the top of his baldhead. He was nice at first, but it wasn't long before he got mean and started getting physical.

Anyway, a short time after we moved to Bayport, my mom said, "I have a surprise for you." We drove across Long Island to a place I'd never been to before, pulled up into the driveway, and my mom got out of the car. This two-year-old little girl came running up to her. My mom scooped her up in her arms, turned to me, and said, "'Gene, this is your little sister, Judy.'"

"Sister?' I said, a little surprised, to say the least."

"Yes, your sister,"

"What, you didn't know you had a sister?" Steve interjected.

"No, I actually had no idea."

"I later found out that after my dad was killed in Miami, she met this guy, Judy's father, who she intended to marry, but never did. Judy was born with a number of medical complications and after a lengthy hospital stay; she ended up in a foster home. Not sure why, probably had something to do with my mom's drinking and her lack of income. That's where she was when we picked her up."

Steve was a little baffled by this and said, "That's kind of funny, I mean your mom keeping your sister a secret, for what— a year or so?"

"Yeah, it was funny all right; but Judy turned out to be really a neat little kid. She liked to sing and dance, and it was easy to make her laugh. She was small for her age, so it would astound everyone when this peanut of a kid would stand there and sing her heart out."

"So there was our new little family unit: my mom, Jack, Judy, and me. They put me in Catholic School at St. Lawrence. Judy stayed home with my mom. Jack would go to work every day in Queens. He was an electrical engineer. I had an almost normal childhood for… I'd say about six months… maybe a year. My mom had quit drinking, or at least kept it to a minimum. I would come home after school and play with the neighborhood kids. My mom would come outside with a pitcher of Kool-Aid and Dixie cups, wearing a pastel colored sundress, with an apron, and her hair would be pinned up behind her ears. She would be smiling and happy, asking my little friends where they lived and what grade they were in. She was actually a very pretty woman when she was fixed up and sober. It was something right out of a 'Leave It To Beaver' episode. My friends used to say, 'Your Mom's pretty,' or 'Your Mom's really nice.' So I was especially proud of that. On Saturdays, Jack would load us into his brand new 1961 Impala and take us to the park for a picnic. Well, turned out it was too good to be true, and grim reality was just around the corner."

"First came the endless chores he'd have me do… raking the leaves, sweeping the driveway. Jack would say, 'No, you can't go play with your friends; you've got chores to do. And when you finish that, I've got something else for you to do.' Now being six or seven years old, I would of course whine and moan, but I soon found out Jack liked to hit, and hit me he did, while saying things like, 'You ungrateful little shit. You and your mother would still be scrounging around somewhere if it wasn't for me.'" At first, he wouldn't let my mother see him belting me around. Then, as time went by and the bourbon would kick in, he'd just haul off and whack me any old time. I never saw him hit my mom, though he was mean to everyone once he got a little drunk.

"Yeah," Steve said. "I had a friend in my neighborhood that grew up like that."

"Oh, I know it wasn't unique," I said. "I knew of a couple other kids who came to school with bruises. One time I broke my arm, falling out of a tree. Jack told me after I got home from the hospital, 'If you ever climb a tree again, you better not let me catch you. Broken arm, huh? I'll break your neck.'"

Steve then asked, "So, he was mad at you for breaking your arm?"

"Well, he was mad he had to pay the doctor's bill. He couldn't have cared less about my arm. So, for the next few years, I remember an alcoholic, abusive, fear-laden existence, along with the ever-present smell of cigars. He never did hit Judy for some reason. I often wondered about that.

"Now, during the Jack Dial years it wasn't all misery. We did have some good times when Jack was away at work. My mom and I would play endless games of Crazy Eights and Go Fish, while Judy would amuse herself on the kitchen floor nearby. I'd be hoping Jack would never come home."

"Jack also would take me bar hopping with him on road trips down Montauk Highway. By then I was about seven. We would stop off at bar after bar. Jack would buy me a little bag of Wise potatoes chips and a Coke, give me a hand full of Nickels, and tell me to go play the juke box. So, I would play my favorites, mostly Elvis, some Gene Vincent and the Shouts. Jack would holler over at me from his barstool, 'Put on that nigger music and show the man how you can dance.'"

"Wait… nigger music?" Steve asked, taken aback.

"Yeah, apparently Jack thought Elvis was black. Then one day, as luck would have it, I was fooling around in a tree and fell out, breaking that same arm again. Only this time my mom lied for me and told Jack I was running and tripped in a hole in the back yard."

"Did he whip you for it?" Steve asked.

"No, by this time his health was failing and he just cursed at me. Not long after that, around 1962, my wish finally came true. My mom told me Jack was in the hospital. I couldn't have been happier. I was hoping for dead, but the hospital was the next best thing. I knew he had been sick lately, but I had no idea he was that bad off. My mom was not so happy. Either she really liked the jerk or she foresaw the unpleasant future. We would go to the hospital from time to time to visit him, but mostly my mom would visit alone, while Judy and I would hang outside and wait in the car."

"What was wrong with him?" Steve asked.

"I don't really remember, but he was not at all well. I remember one visit in particular. One sunny afternoon we drove out to see Jack. When we got there, my mom said, "You stay out here and watch your sister." After a while, I became bored and got out of the car. I was poking around in the ground nearby when I found some earthworms. I began carefully pulling them out of the ground and putting them in my pocket."

"You were putting worms in your pocket… you're kidding me, right?" Steve asked.

"I was a funny kid; what can I say. So anyway, my mom finally came back to the car and said, "You and Judy come with me; we're going up to visit your dad." I thought, my dad, hell, Frankenstein is more like it. When we got up to his room he was lying on his back in bed. His hair was white and what was left of it was going in a few different directions. His breathing was slow, and he was just sort of staring into space. My mom picked up my little sister and leaned her over so she could give Jack a kiss, then she turned to me and said, 'Give your dad a kiss, Gene.' I stood there just looking at him disdainfully. The sheet was pure white and was draped over him right up to his neck very neatly… not a wrinkle. You could easily make out the shape of his fat stomach. His arms were outside the sheets and one of them had a tube running to it. He slowly turned his head toward me, though nothing else moved. My mom, encouraging me, said, 'Go ahead give your dad a hug Gene.' Then for some reason I remembered the worms in my pocket. Reaching in I felt them squirming. I gathered them up in one hand and carefully took them from my pocket so as not to hurt them. They were now in a ball, all intertwined. I noticed my mom was distracted for the moment with Judy; I took the ball of worms and politely placed them on the middle of Jacks stomach, stepping back. It reminded me of the Medusa.

"Oh, you're shittin' me?" Steve said, laughing and slapping the steering wheel. "You gotta be bullshitting!"

"No, I am not and it was beautiful. Jack opened his eyes, looked at the worms and moaned. He had this perplexed look but was obviously too weak to do anything about it. When my mom looked up, she screamed bloody murder. 'WHAT ARE YOU DOING? GET THOSE THINGS OFF OF HIM! WHAT IS WRONG WITH YOU!?!' I then very slowly, savoring every moment, picked up the wriggling ball, walked over to the nearby commode, and flushed my friends away. Around and around they swirled, and then they were gone. I remember wishing I could have thanked each one of them individually."

Steve said, "Man that was sweet revenge if I have ever heard of it." Again, he slapped the steering wheel.

"Yeah, it was; my mom gave me grief all the way back downstairs and out to the car; but I didn't mind. I couldn't have been prouder. I can truly say, looking back on my early childhood, that it was one of my most memorable moments. It ranks right up there with going to Yankee Stadium with my uncle Buddy or the visit to the Statue of Liberty with my mom and my aunt Peg."

"Not long after that, Jack died, and things were just fine at first—endless games of cards with my mom, playing with the neighborhood kids after school. My chores were reduced to taking out the garbage. I did not miss Jack one little bit."

"We started having a babysitter from across the street, who my mom would get from time to time to watch Judy and me. Her name was Donna or Darla. At any rate, she was about thirteen and kind of cute. She would come over and pretty much sit in a lounge chair on our glassed-in front porch reading. She would be lounging in her shorts, and I think it was the first awakening of my libido. One day I was sitting next to her talking, when I asked her if I could rub her legs." Steve interrupted, "Wait a minute; how old were you?"

"Eight, I think."

"Damn, I was scared to death of girls when I was eight."

"Yeah, well, I did tell her she had to promise she wouldn't tell any of my friends.

"That's funny," Steve said.

"Well anyway, she did let me rub her legs, and I was thrilled. I just loved my babysitter."

"I would have too." Steve said.

"Then things started to change at our house. My mom began to drink again. She would drink beer with Uncle Rex from down the street. He was not my really my uncle, but that was what my mom said to call him. Rex was a very cool guy in my opinion because he wore mirrored sunglasses and was a Mechanic. He had long, slicked-back hair, and would speak to me like I was a person, not a kid. Uncle Rex became my mom's boyfriend, I guess. They would hang out together and Rex would even take Judy, me, and my mom on little outings. Over time, my mom began to drink more and see Rex less. I'm not sure if one had to do with the other."

"She sold Jack's Impala and bought a beat up old 1952 Chevy. Money was starting to run out. Without Jack's income, we were not doing well. Now it was public school for me; paying for Catholic school was just not feasible. That was a welcome change… I never did like being terrorized by the nuns. They were way too strict and corporal punishment was standard practice. I remember one time in the second grade; I was too scared to ask to go to the bathroom that I pissed in my pants, sitting at my desk."

"Next there were the bill collectors, harassing phone calls, the persistent knocking on the front door, as Judy, my mom, and I would hide behind the couch."

"Your mom you and your sister would crouch behind furniture?" Steve asked.

"It was a little weird; but I didn't really mind. My mom would make out like it was a game of hide and seek. Dinners got a little low-end as well. We were eating a lot of cereal and bread and gravy. As long as Jack was out of the picture, I would have been happy to eat mud pies.

"My mom started sending me to Rick's Delicatessen with a list of items that included a six pack of beer. Eventually she would send me to get just beer. At one point, I started telling her that the beer wasn't good for her and that she shouldn't be drinking it. She got really pissed. I started crying and she slapped me. Things were breaking down between us. We always had a very loving and warm relationship, but that seemed to be fading away. I was hurting a lot, because I knew how nice, loving, and considerate she could be. When I did go to the store, I think Rick noticed I was upset, and he became concerned. At one point he said, "I haven't seen your mom in quite some time. How is she?'

"She's all right," I'd tell him; but he didn't believe me."

"Well, this will be the last time I let you have beer without her. You tell her I said you're not old enough to buy beer. She needs to come in herself."

"When I told my mom, she accused me of lying. That was really bad, because, of course, I was telling her the truth. She was calling me a liar, which she never had done before. Up until then, I told her everything, no matter what, because she always understood. All that went away."

"Why didn't she just buy her own beer when she went to the store?" Steve asked.

"Because she sat around in her bathrobe all day and didn't go anywhere. She was rapidly deteriorating. Oh yeah, did I mention she was epileptic as well, and on medication."

"Man, what a mess," Steve said.

"Yeah, it was a mess all right. It was around May of 1963 and I was just out of school for the summer. Instead of looking forward to three months of fun, I was spending my time wondering how to get my mom to stop drinking. She started having groceries delivered along with her beer. That took care of the Rick's Deli problem. She would spend the day in her bathrobe walking around the house like a zombie, drinking beer; and when she wasn't doing that, she slept. No matter how I tried to encourage her to play cards with me or fix herself up, it didn't seem to matter. It was as if she had given up on life and no amount of coaxing was going to change her."

"One evening my little sister and I were home alone with our mother. Mom was in her room, while my sister and I were watching TV in the living room. Mom came into the living room in her pajamas and her bathrobe and staggered to the couch. She looked ragged as she melted into the cushions and passed out. I went over to check on her and she looked as pale as a white porcelain statue. I shook her shoulder and asked her if she was okay. When she didn't respond I decided she was sleeping and went back to watching TV. I told myself she was fine and just not feeling good. I thought if I acted like everything was fine, it would be. A little while later I heard her cough so I went over to her and saw she had thrown up in her sleep. I cleaned her up the best I could, though the puke was in her hair and on the cushions and I was very upset and tried to wake her, but she wouldn't wake up."

Steve interrupted, "Oh, man, were you freaking out or what?"

I was freaking out all right; I didn't know what to do. I sat there looking at her trying to see if she was breathing, again telling myself she was all right. The thought of her not being all right was nagging at my eight-year-old brain. I went back to watching TV with my sister because I didn't know what else to do, but kept going back and forth between the TV and my Mom, checking to see if she was okay though I didn't really know what I was checking for or how to check. My sister Judy noticed my nervous demeanor and asked, "What's wrong with Mom?"

"Nothing… she's just not feeling good. After all, I thought to myself she had done this before. When I next checked her, I couldn't tell if she was breathing at all, so I felt her wrist for a pulse, like I had seen people do on TV— but I didn't know what I was doing; in my heart there was a distressing fear that something was really wrong this time. I had to fight my fear in order not to become overwhelmed. I stood there looking at my mom shaking her shoulder; panic and confusion began rising within me. I said, "Mom Mom! Are you okay?"

"You were really in a spot," Steve said. "Yeah I was; there was a knock at the front door. I ran to answer it, and was relieved to see Uncle Rex.

ncle Rex, I said, there's something wrong with my mom. He rushed by me over to my mom and put his hand on her neck. I peered over his shoulder. Voicing my fear, I ask him, is she gonna be okay? By now I am crying."

"He told me, just go over there and watch TV with your sister. I'll call someone. Not five minutes later, an ambulance and the cops pulled up to our house, and the ambulance guys began feverishly working on her."

"Two of the cops were standing there looking around our living room and I overheard one of them say, "Christ, just look at this place." As I recall, it was pretty messy. There were open cereal boxes, candy wrappers, dirty dishes, a half-eaten loaf of bread, topless peanut butter and jelly jars, a pitcher of Kool-Aid, and the sugar canister toppled over— in the middle of the living room rug. It was obvious we were two kids without much supervision. My little sister had stains all over the front of her pajamas and I'm sure I didn't look much better. I felt embarrassed, so I started trying to clean up. I knelt down next to the sugar canister and tried to push the sugar back inside with my cupped hand and I could feel tears run down my cheek. One of the cops noticed and came over to me. He squatted down and asked, what's your name?"

"Gene," I said, though I didn't look up. He put his hand on my shoulder, and said with the warmest voice he could muster, "Why don't you and your sister come outside?"

I tried wiping the snot and tears from my face with my sleeve, but noticed I have something sticky on it... grape jelly I think, which made me, feel even worse. I remember feeling that my life as I knew it was over and I was not sure what the future would hold for Judy and me. It was a hollow feeling, as if someone had taken an ice cream scoop to my insides and left a big empty space—and there was nothing I could do to make that feeling go away. I walked over to Judy and took her hand. "Let's go outside Judy."

Gripping my hand, she looked up at me and asked, "Are we in trouble?" I remember looking down at her and thinking she has no idea what is happening. But then neither did I

"No, we're not in trouble... but we need to go outside". We left with the cop and never went back to that house again." Steve asked, "So your mom died?" "Yeah she must have died right there on the couch, because they didn't rush her into the ambulance as I recall." "Damn that was bad. What happened to you and your sister?"

"The cops took Judy and me to the police station, where they asked me if we had any relatives they could call. I told them our Aunt Frances and Uncle Justin lived near by, but I wasn't sure where. I told them the nuns at St. Lawrence Church knew me and maybe they knew how to get in touch with our aunt and uncle. The cops must have called the church, because two nuns showed up and sat with us until my aunt and uncle came and took us home with them."

Verbalizing this part of my past to Steve made me feel gloomy, but at the same time relieved. I had been walking around with a tremendous amount of guilt and hurt for many years for not having saved my mom. I also was mad at her for becoming the mess that she was, which in my mind, was the reason she died, leaving Judy and me behind. Articulating that I had stood by, while my mother slowly and methodically killed her self, made me realize it was not quite as simple as that. I began to understand that I was only eight and she was the adult, and therefore I was as much a victim of her alcoholism as she, herself, was. Still the self-blame within me was real. I tried telling myself it was not my fault. Going down the highway, I gazed out the passenger window into the darkness and felt like crying, but I did not, I could not. I had many fond memories of my birth mother, and I would call on these memories to ward off remorse, shame, and guilt. Drugs and adventure were also a distraction I counted on. Steve broke the silence and asked, "So, what then?"

"The next day Uncle Justin called me in to the living room. Aunt Frances was sitting nearby with very red eyes and Judy was sitting on her lap. He sat me down on his knee and he was visibly upset. I had an idea what he was about to tell me, so I tried to make it easier on him and spoke first: 'I know; my mom isn't coming back.' He stiffened his lips and shook his head no. I told him, 'I understand.' I felt sad, but didn't want to show it."

"My Aunt Frances said we would be staying with them. I turned to my uncle and asked if it would be okay if I went back to Johnny's room."

"Who was Johnny?" Steve asked.

"Johnny was my older cousin, my Uncle Justin's son, who later became my brother."

Steve, keeping track of my tale, then asked, "So you and your sister ended up with your aunt and uncle?"

"You got it. They later adopted us."

"Really? Where are they now?"

"In Miami."

"Oh, so that's why you're going to Miami?" Steve said.

"Yeah, sort of,"

"You hungry?" Steve asked.

"Yeah, I guess."

"Let's get a burger."

We had been driving for about two hours and it was almost eight o'clock at night. We were right outside Tallahassee when we pulled off the Interstate and into a What-A-Burger. We got burgers and gassed up and were back on the road.

"So where were we?" Steve asked.

"What, you want me to keep going?" I said, surprised.

"Why not, we've still got a way to go," he said.

"All right, but I can't believe you find this stuff interesting. So then came West Sayville and the Martins."

"Wait, West Sayville, the Martins?"

"The Martins were my aunt and uncle and West Sayville was where they lived. There was my Aunt Frances, Uncle Justin, and their three kids. The oldest was Maggie, who was about twenty. She was an artist and was away at college. Patty was about seventeen and a senior at St. Lawrence High School. They also had a son— that was Johnny— who was about twelve, and in the seventh grade at Sayville Junior High. Judy and I spent the summer becoming a part of the Martins."

"Myself… I quickly assimilated with the neighborhood kids, and there were a bunch of them. Across the street were the Rikers— Tommy, Willy, Steven, Bobby, Kathy, and Ronnie. Down the block were the O'Ryan's— Pat and his three sisters. Over on Brook St. were the Doyle's— Kenny and his three brothers and sister. Next to them were the Nuval's— Tommy and Jedi. Next to them were the Cones— John and Judy and numerous others I can't remember at the moment."

"That's enough," Steve said.

"Are you getting sick of this?"

"No, no, not at all. Keep going."

"Johnny, my cousin, and I were friends at first, but soon became like typical brothers. We played with each other half the time and fought the other half. He was a little introverted and I was the opposite. He played guitar and had a fish tank; I played sports and had a big mouth. He was two years older, so we weren't exactly compatible. I do remember one proud moment when he and some guys got together and started a band called 'Shades of Sin'. He was in the eighth grade by this time and they played at his junior high in the gym. They only knew maybe three or four songs, but that didn't matter because all the kids wanted to hear was *Wipe Out* by the Ventures. so, they played it over and over again. Man, I thought that was great.

"My best friend at the time was a guy named John Sherman, 'Sherman the German' I called him. He had a brother named Tommy, who was also my friend. John and I used to do all the things kids our age did—play sports, ride bikes, talk about girls. We also did things kids shouldn't do— like vandalizing, stealing, and various other forms of mischief. I was doing that kind of stupid stuff with most of my friends. I had this 'screw it' attitude. Because my real parents were dead, I told myself I had a right to do stupid shit— like it was expected of me."

"I can see how you might think that," Steve said understandingly. "Do you still feel like that?"

"Yeah, somewhat, but I'm also starting to see it's a poor excuse for acting how I do; so, at any rate, back to my childhood. I remember Pat O'Ryan and me coming home from school one day, when we came upon a lady looking down a storm drain in front of her house. We walked up, and she said her cat had gotten in there and she didn't know how to get it out. Willy and I told her we could help. I slid down in the storm drain and got the cat. Pat gave me his hand and pulled me back up. The lady was so grateful she told us wait right there, went back in her house with her cat, and came back with a dollar for each of us. At that, a light bulb went off in our heads. We went down the street where we knew another lady with a cat lived. We found Mrs. Brown's cat, caught it, and tossed it down the drain right in front of her house. We went up to the door and knocked. A lady answered and I told her, 'Lady, I think your cat's in the storm drain in front of your house.' She looked puzzled and said, 'Really? Show me.' We went to the drain and showed her, and she was visibly upset. We, of course, offered to get it out. She said that would be wonderful.

"My daughter will be so grateful." So Pat and I did our trick. After we handed the cat to her, she said, 'Thanks a lot, boys' and turned and walked back in the house. Pat and I looked at each other and wondered what went wrong."

"So much for your con game…" Steve said.

"Yeah, we were pissed."

"So, over the next three years, life just seemed to roll along. Judy and I lived the life I had always wanted— an Ozzie and Harriet sort of life with all the trimmings… while secretly I was being a Dennis the Menace with a mean streak."

"There was this kid who lived across the street from John Sherman, Willy Mack. Willy and I, who were both about twelve at the time, joined the Bayport Drum and Bugle Corps. We wanted to play the snare drum. Practice was early Saturday evenings at the West Sayville firehouse, or at least I think that's where it was. We would skip practice and wander around town getting into various mischief. One evening— I'm not sure which of us thought of it—but we broke into a Boat Store/Hobby Shop. It so happens that this boat store was connected to a hobby shop, which sold H.O. slot cars. You know the kind— real small, but real fast. My brother, Johnny— I say brother because my aunt and uncle had adopted Judy and me by this time— had a set of slot cars in our basement."

"Yeah, I had a friend who had those when we were kids," Steve said.

I continued. "Willy Mack and I stole a bunch of those cars along with some track and accessories. It was a Saturday night, so we hid our booty in the woods nearby. Early Sunday morning before church, we rode down there on our bikes and hauled the stuff back to the basement of my house. That afternoon we set it all up. Now, my brother Johnny was curious about where all the new slot cars and track came from, but I think I gave him a couple of slot cars to keep him from being too curious."

"When my mom and dad inquired about all the new track and slot cars, I simply told them Willy Mack and John Sherman had brought their slot cars and track over to our house because we had so much room in our basement. Now, this was plausible. Johnny and I did have slot cars already set up down there, and we did have a huge table that our dad had built for a train set. We simply took the train table and made it into a slot car track. My folks had no reason to believe anything was amiss. Then Willy and I got greedy."

"That will do it every time," Steve said.

"Yeah, and it did us in. Like I said, we broke in on a Saturday night, and went back for our stash on Sunday morning. Well, that Sunday afternoon, while Willy and I were setting up more tracks in my basement, we decided to go back to the Boat Shop/Hobby Shop. Right then, Willy O'Ryan from down the street came by and was admiring our setup.

He asked, "Damn, where did all this come from?" Willy Mack and I looked at each other and smiled. Willy O'Ryan picked up one of the boxes and saw the label from the Boat Shop/Hobby Shop, looked at us and said, "What'd you do, steal it?" We burst out laughing,

"'You did," he said. 'You stole it from that place on Sunrise Highway!' Like a big shot I said, 'You didn't hear that from us.' He shook his head and left.

"That afternoon Willy Mack and I got the bright idea to go back to the scene of our crime to get more. So that evening, around dusk, we went back. When we got there, we noticed the back door was already slightly open. Now, we knew we had closed it when we left, so we were hesitant about going back in. As we were lurking outside, who should pop out the back door of the place but Pat O'Ryan, Bobby Riker, and two or three other neighborhood kids. We couldn't believe it! Willy and I looked at each other and ran up and confronted them as they came out, their arms full stolen goods"

We said, "Hey, what are you guys doing? This is our deal."

"Not anymore," they said. "Besides, there's plenty for everyone." And they ran off laughing. Willy Mack and I just stood there looking at each other, dumbfounded."

"Now your ass was cooked —the whole neighborhood knew," Steve interjected.

"Yeah, but we were too stupid to know it. Willy and I decided to grab an outboard motor… each."

"An outboard motor each; you really were juvenile delinquents." Steve said.

"Yeah, we were. We were hauling the motors home on our shoulders when we ran into two teenagers."

"Don't tell me, they turned your asses in."

"Not quite. They made us give them the motors."

"How old were you again?"

"Twelve."

"Jesus Christ, that is nuts!"

"Yeah, it was all right. The problem was, they were stopped by the cops before they had a chance to stash the motors."

"Then, they ratted on you," Steve said.

"You got it."

"Needless to say, my folks were not too happy. By the time the smoke cleared, my dad whipped my ass with a stick and my mom told me to not leave the yard and to have no friend's over until further notice. I even had to appear in juvenile court, where the judge said if he saw us again we would need to bring a toothbrush. Not long after that, my folks sold their house and moved the family out of New York and down to Miami."

"Shit, that was kind of drastic wasn't it?"

"Yeah, but they had been thinking about moving, and I think this incident with me just sped the idea up. They picked a house in the boondocks, out in West Miami, with the hope that I would be too far from anything and anybody to get in trouble."

"Did it work?" Steve asked.

"Yeah, I guess it did."

By that time, we were right outside St. Augustine. It was about midnight, and Steve was looking for a place to park... said he was going to sleep in the back seat of his car and told me I was welcome to sleep in the front. I took him up on it.

The next day, after saying thanks and so long to my Air Force buddy, I took off for the highway. It had been therapeutic telling my childhood story. It brought back a lot of memories, bad and good.

My next several rides were pretty ordinary and relatively consistent, so I made it all the way down to Miami by dusk. I was in downtown Miami, wandering around, when I ran into two street girls. I say street girls because that's how they described themselves. They were both about seventeen and one was kind of cute. So I tagged along with them to see what would happen. It felt funny being so close to my old neighborhood, yet not even trying to get there.

Then a cop pulled up, and I thought, Oh crap, how's this gonna turn out? Next thing I knew, the cute one leaned on the passenger side of the cop car, chatting it up with the cops.

"So, what are you pigs doing over here? I've never seen you on this beat before." I thought, did she just say what I think she said; this chick is nuts! I gotta get out of here. Moments later they pulled away, without as much as a look at me; but I couldn't take being around these two chicks anymore, so I beat it out of there. I walked a long way before I gave up and called my mom to see how she would react to my being back in town. The phone rang and she answered.

"Mom, it's Gene."

"Gene? Where are you, are you all right?" by her voice I could tell she was shaken by my call.

"Yeah, I'm fine, Mom, I'm on Bird Rd. and Southwest 27th. I was wondering..."

"I'll be right there," she said, and then hung up.

I had thought about going to the Fisheries, but it was about time I visited my folks. It had been almost five months since I left the house. I was happy the way Mom responded to my being in town. Ten minutes later, she pulled up, and was really glad to see me. She was crying as she got out of the car and hugged me. We got back to the house and she fixed me something to eat. My dad was away on a trip. Johnny, my brother, was somewhere with our cousin, John Marsh. My sister Judy was there, and happy to see me. It felt good to be home.

My mom asked me what my plans were, and I told her I was thinking about joining the service. She smiled, as if to say, that's a nice idea I know you won't follow through on. That night, I slept better than I had in months. The next day I had a big breakfast and started perusing the newspaper for jobs. I talked with my mom about my sojourn across the country. To some degree, I think she was impressed by my ability to make my own way, but at the same time I could tell she wished I would settle down and pick a direction. That evening I hooked up with my buddy Paul Collins. He came and got me in his little tan-colored Volkswagen beetle… said he'd sold his Olds. We went directly to the Fisheries and the guys greeted me like a returning hero. Glenn, Phil, Jeff, Don, Matt, and more were all hanging out— not to mention a few people I had never seen before. Guess I'd been gone a while. The Fisheries was still happening, and crazy as ever, although Paul had moved back home. We all decided to get some beer and head out to Key Biscayne to party on the beach. It was great being with the old gang again, and I had stories to tell.

Paul mentioned he was thinking about going to Louisiana to see Timmy and Mick Shedagar. I liked the idea; I liked the idea a lot. Louisiana was a great place in my eyes. I asked Paul, "How would you feel about me going with you?"

"Sure," he said, smiling.

"When did you want to leave; I'm broke at the moment. I was planning on getting a job tomorrow or the next day," I said excitedly.

"Don't worry, I've got enough money for both of us to go, and you can always get a job there," he said.

"Sounds like you're ready to go."

"How does day after tomorrow sound?"

"Hell, yes… let's do it."

The rest of the evening was spent cavorting with my friends. Nothing much had changed, except that Glenn, Paul, and Phil were living back with their folks. I was not about to do that. I had no interest in moving back home. So, it was either get a job and move out ASAP or take off with Paul. When I got back home that night it was late, but there was no confrontation with my mom.

The next day I told my mom I was going to get a copy of my driver's license, which is what I did. I spent the day struggling with how to tell her I was taking off with Paul, because I knew she would not be happy to hear it. I didn't want to hurt her, but I did want to go. Eventually I thought, I'm on my own, what's the difference if I move out and live across town or in another state; I'll just tell her. It was kind of funny to me in a way . . . my dad was getting home that evening from his trip, and I would be saying hi and bye to him. Now the thought of that made me feel good. Like he said, I was welcome to visit...

Disneyland

The next day, Paul picked me up at my house. I bade my folk's farewell and we drove straight through to Baton Rouge. On the way there I thought about what I was doing and how I really had no plan for my life. For the first time ever, this sort of bothered me, but not enough to make me do anything different. I thought to myself, maybe Baton Rouge will be just what I am looking for. Where I will find my calling, if I had a calling? Fifteen hours later, we arrived at Timmy's house. Timmy lived with his mother and brother. They had lived in Miami; that's where Paul and I knew them from. No sooner had we arrived, when the four of us decided to get an apartment together. Paul, Timmy, Mick, and I all moved into a two-bedroom apartment. Paul and I got jobs, Paul at a gas station and I at a restaurant. Timmy and Mick were already employed.

I had met Timmy in the eighth grade at Cutler Ridge Junior High back in Miami. We were in the same phys. ed. class. One day, our coach decided it was wrestling day. Timmy and I were about the same weight, so the coach told us to take the center of the mat. Then, for the fun of it, I guess, he decided to blindfold us. We wrestled for a good four or five minutes, going at it like a couple of wild mongooses, while the class sat around the outside of the mat cheering us on. Though neither one of us pinned the other; we became fast friends after that.

By now Timmy had become a great character; a long-haired, beer drinking, non-dope smoking hippie. He drove a '64 Ford station wagon with red, white, and blue curtains, which sort of made it, look kind of cool. He is a small, muscular dude, always in a good mood; smiling or laughing. Mick, his brother, was a great guy as well, up for anything, cared about everybody, and liked to drink and party with the best of them. Between these two and their friends, we had a blast— going to bars, sneaking in concerts, staying up all night playing cards and listening to Frank Zappa's Live At The Fillmore and Alice Cooper's Killer.

So living in Baton Rouge is easy and fun for both Paul and me. Paul got a job at a gas station and I got a job at a restaurant as a prep cook. About two or three weeks had gone by, and one day Paul got the bright idea to steal a pair of jeans from a nearby department store— Dillard's. I try talking him out of it, but to no avail. He used that classic ploy of slipping on a new pair of jeans and then putting on his old ones over them. He is caught, and the store called the cops and had him thrown in jail.

Then without even taking the time to find out how long Paul would be in jail; I decide I will help Paul by hitchhiking back to Miami. I will go to Paul's house and get the title to his car, hitchhike back, sell the car, and get Paul out. Yeah, that's it, I'll go to Homestead and ask Paul's mom for the title to Paul's car. Surely, she would want Paul to get out of jail. Mick took me to the entrance ramp on the outskirts of Baton Rouge and I was gone; down Interstate 12 East.

I was completely confident in my hitchhiking skills and didn't think twice about doing it. The trip to Miami was just a succession of rides that came fast and furious. Seventeen hours later, I am in Perrine, South Florida, standing in front of Food Spot. I called Paul's Mom from a pay phone, "Mrs. Collingsworth, this is Gene, Gene Martin. I need the title to Paul's car, he's…." Before I had a chance to finish the sentence, she hung up on me. I stood there thinking, Damn, now what do? I decided to go to the Fisheries and see what was happening. Jeffrey Joe, Don Stein, Glenn, and various other teenagers were hanging out. Paul Sanchez was there, along with Art Markowitz, Bob's older brother.

Then, after telling everyone about the Paul story, Phil, Art, and I went out by the pond in the front of the Fisheries and had a heart-to-heart. We discovered that all three of us had been thinking the same thing. I began by saying, "I have about had it with knocking around the country, basically going nowhere fast. I need to do something with my life, and I'm sick of doing drugs every day."

Paul chimed in and said, "Yeah, I'm screwed if I don't learn a trade. I damn sure am not going to college, and working at a car wash the rest of my life would really suck."

That's when Art said, "Hell, I've been thinking about joining the Navy so I can go to college for free when I get out."

Reacting positively, Phil and I perked up, looked at each other, and I said, "I've been thinking about joining, and now that Vietnam is about done, this would probably be a good time."

"Besides, how dangerous could it be floating around in a boat?" Art asks.

"Exactly," I said.

At that moment we all agreed we would go down to the recruiting office the next day. It was obvious that all three of us were on the same page before the subject even came up. Even partying can get old. It was just a matter of vocalizing what was already in our heads; we were all looking for a change, and the Navy would be our ticket.

The next day, when we went to the recruiting office, the recruiter told us everything we wanted to hear. He made it sound like we would be putting on a uniform and going to Disneyland. He said we could join on the "buddy system" and do our four-year hitch together. We came out of his office telling each other how great this is going to be. We were stoned, tripping, or both. We told our friends what we were doing, and partied like it was our last days on earth. Two nights later, Paul showed up at the Fisheries. I was there having a grand old time and had forgotten all about him.

I said, "Paul, what happened, man? They let you out and you drove back?" He looked at me like I was a jerk and said with half a smile. "Yeah, pretty much," he said.

"Did your mom tell you I called her trying to get the title to your car?"

"Yeah, she told me." I was a little embarrassed and felt awkward about not having stayed in Louisiana to help Paul, but then again, I was an idiot teenager. It seemed that Paul understood, so he held no ill will as far as I could tell; probably because he is an idiot teenager too. We are kindred spirits or kindred idiots.

When I told my mom my plans to join, she was thrilled. She said, "Gene, I think this will really be good for you. You're just messing around at this point in your life and this will give you some direction." I was so proud. I thought now I am really going to get my life together, in the Navy.

The Navy?

Next stop, Orlando Naval Station. They loaded us on a bus early in the morning and drove us to boot camp— Art Markowitz, Phil Sanchez, and me. No sooner did we arrive, than we found out Phil was in a different company from Art and me. We were pissed, but there wasn't anything we could do about it. Art and I hardly spoke in boot camp. For some reason we really didn't care for each other to begin with. We had a love/ hate friendship. I think we just hung out together because we had the same friends.

One thing I found interesting about boot camp was just how many of the guys in my company of a hundred and twenty were obviously away from home for the first time. From experience, I knew when you first leave home it can be kind of heavy; but to be bused to a Navy base and thrown in with a hundred and twenty other young guys you don't know from Adam can be daunting. Sixty bunks were lined up in one big room where we all were expected to sleep together. After lights out the first night I could hear guys whimpering in their pillows; it was almost surreal... I could not believe a guy could allow himself to be heard doing that. Did they not have enough self-respect to keep that feeling hidden? I thought, maybe they were kidding; then I heard in an annoyed tone, "Hey man, are you crying?" The kid in the top bunk next to mine is asking the guy below him. The guy in the bottom bunk was embarrassed, but tried to stiffen his upper lip, responding,

"Shut-up, I am not; I've just got a runny nose." His top bunkmate came right back with, "You fuckin' baby, quitcha cryin' and go to sleep."

I felt bad for the kid. I thought about my first night away from home in the back of Don Stein's car, and how unnerving it had been for me. I thought about saying something to him, something to let him know everything would be okay; but I didn't. Not to mention I didn't want to hear one of the other guys retort, "who the hell are you... the camp counselor?" So, I kept my thoughts to myself.

Boot camp was going to last ten weeks. I already missed Phil, and felt bad for him having to be on his own. In boot camp we did a whole lot of marching. I am not exaggerating when I say we marched to all three meals—there and back. When we were not marching, we were running and exercising. We took a few classes on lifesaving and what different ships looked like. It was a lot of nonsense in my opinion. If one of us would screw up, either by not paying attention or not having our locker squared away, we would be invited to a "grass party." A grass party was a select group of screw-ups meeting outside the barracks after dinner on the grass and exercising for sixty minutes; and yes, I was invited more than once. I began to have regrets about joining the Navy. I started thinking; why did I do this? What a stupid idea. It is not at all what I expected, although I'm not sure what exactly I did expect. I am quite happy when boot camp was over. My folks came to my graduation and were proud of their son, the Navy man.

I am able to spend a little time with them, about three days; then it was off to Memphis for more training. That's right—Memphis. What the Navy is doing in Memphis was beyond me. I thought the Navy meant oceans—but apparently not. Phil ended up in Memphis and Art is sent somewhere else. That is okay with me. Phil is the one I am really friends with anyway. Evenings, we would hang out on the patio between the barracks and drink beer. There is a coke machine that had been converted to a beer machine, and that is very cool. A can of beer was a quarter, which meant you could get drunk for a couple dollars. We spent two weeks in Memphis, then off to San Diego, California, where Phil and I are both assigned to the USS Kitty Hawk, an aircraft carrier. We were a little concerned though, because we had been expecting to go to a school somewhere. We were supposed to be learning a trade, but when we asked the officer in charge in Memphis, his response was, "Look fellas, we're not here for you, you're here for us. So do what you're told and keep your mouths shut and you'll be okay. Now get out of here and STOP WASTING MY TIME!"

When we get to San Diego, the Kitty Hawk was still at sea, so they stick us in some barracks and had us do yard work and other menial tasks around the base until our ship came in. Christ, I thought, when my ship comes in, how poetic. We had no idea what we were in for; but the fun is about to begin and poetry was not a part of it. Phil and I immediately became the celebrity pair. Since we knew each other from home and the majority of the guys were there on their own, we had a decided advantage. We hooked up with some very cool black dudes—there was 'Squirrel', this short, happy-go-lucky guy from North Carolina; Baked Bean, a short, stocky dude from Florida who could play the hell out of basketball; Joe Ray, "Bro Joe," from Georgia; "Fat Fred," who really wasn't fat at all, just huge; Wendell from Memphis, who grew up above a pool hall, so he could shoot the hell out of a pool table all day long; and Danny, from I can't remember where, very cool as well. Now these guys were all very good-hearted characters; they liked to drink beer and get stoned, listen to music, and talk about girls.

We would take the shuttle ferry across the harbor and end up right in downtown San Diego. On payday weekends, Phil and I, along with our newfound friends, would go into downtown San Diego and eat in nice restaurants, then blow our money in bars. We were paid once a month, so we would have money for two or three days, and then be broke for twenty-seven. Phil and I heard about a place called "O.B.," which was short for "Ocean Beach." It was your basic hippie beach, where you could buy weed, acid, or your drug of choice. Phil and I got the idea one day to buy twenty hits of Orange Sunshine. Thinking we could sell some and trip on the rest. When we got back to the barracks, he and I each took a hit, then we decided to turn our friends on to a half hit each, figuring that would be plenty for their first time. I went off to the PX to buy beer with Danny and Squirrel and left the rest of our crew at the barracks, listening to Sly and the Family Stone on a portable eight-track player in Phil's' cubicle. I am having a great time watching Danny and Squirrel get off for their first time on LSD and telling them what to expect as we walk along. After buying the beer, we got a little sidetracked looking at the lights in the harbor reflecting on the water. It is fantastic, and Danny and Squirrel were freaking, to say the least. By the time we get back to the barracks, things had changed drastically.

When we arrive, we know something is up? Danny turned to me, concerned, and said, "Looks like the power is out." I, too, felt apprehensive and said, "Yeah, all the lights are out and it's eerily quiet— but I know there are at least twenty guys in there." When we stepped inside the barracks, there is the watch, the guy who is supposed to be on guard, standing in the barracks entrance with about four or five other guys, peering around the doorway that led to where the sleeping quarters were— the "cubes" for short. They looked like they were scared out of their wits. Some were in their boxer shorts, others just in pants and socks. When they turned and noticed us, one of our barrack mates rushed up to me with this wild look in his eyes and said, "Gene! Gene! Your friend Phil is going nuts! He's been breaking light bulbs out of the light fixtures with a broom handle and won't let anyone in the barracks!" Another guy, quivering in his socks, just as upset said, "Yeah, and he's got some kind of machine that's making an ear-splitting sound, and he says it's gonna bloody our ear drums if we don't leave him alone."

Then Squirrel, noticeably surprised by what he is looking at, calls me over to the window. Looking out, he said, "Hey, Gene, you gotta see this." I looked over his shoulder and a few spotlights were shining on the grounds behind the barracks. There, laid out in various locations on the grass, were about eight or nine guys. Wendell was lying on his stomach staring at a Jimmy Hendrix poster. Fat Fred was on his back, gazing at the sky and laughing. All of them were acting peculiar in one way or another. It is like looking at a bunch of tripped-out hippies on the lawn. The only problem is, they were not hippies; they were enlisted Navy men. Phil apparently had everyone in the barracks tripping.

Then suddenly we heard a *CARAASHHH*! I thought, God damn, is that one of those light bulbs those guys were accusing Phil of breaking? I told the group of guys at the entrance to the barracks, "Just stay here a minute, I'm going to talk to Phil."

As I walk down the center of the barracks in the dark toward the cubicle where they said Phil is; broken fluorescent light bulbs crunched beneath my shoes. I thought, Damn, Phil has completely lost it. When I get to where he is, he is sitting at his desk, with a little lamp barely lighting the desktop. Dressed in a T-shirt and boxers, and sweating like a pig, he looks up at me with this very strange smile and peering through glazed-over eyes. I said, very matter-of-factly,

"Hey, man, what's going on?" He replied nonchalantly,

"Oh, nothin' much."

He turned back around to his desk and started doing something— I couldn't see what. I sat down on my bunk, and said, "Looks like you've got everybody freakin' out." Then a piercing, high- pitched tone came from Phil's desk. I got up and stepped a little closer. He had a half a glass of water and is rubbing his finger around the rim, making an incredibly annoying sound that filled the air. It's an old trick and really nothing special, but when you're tripping, it's something that could completely mess with your head. He turned to me and said, "No... Not you too."

"Not me too, what? What does that mean?"

"Marty, don't start with me." He is smiling, but agitated.

I thought, Christ, he's fried and so is half the barracks. I try to think of how to quell the situation, but I am tripping as well, and not exactly thinking clearly. It is moments like this I would think, *c*rap, why can't I just trip and enjoy myself. Now I have to smooth this shit over and keep it from getting any worse. It is in my nature to fix shit; I take a certain pride in smoothing things over. I tell Phil,

"Get dressed. We're going down to the harbor. There's an incredible light show… you gotta see it."

"Light show?" he responds, intrigued.

I knew that would get his attention. I walk back down to where the flipped-out bunch of guys are waiting at the entrance to the barracks, and tell them to get a broom and sweep up the broken light bulbs. I said,

"Phil is done, so you can all go back to whatever it was you were doing." I then told the watch,

"You better get back behind the desk; you never know who might come by." Once again, all is well. Phil and I walk out of the barracks as if nothing happened, right past the other sailors, who were sweeping up glass, leaving the watch sitting behind his desk, now looking like he is on watch. There were still quite a few guys out behind the barracks on the grass, but I couldn't fix everything. We meandered down to the harbor, and like I told Phil, the lights were shimmering on the water. Danny, Squirrel, and Baked Bean followed us and sat down. After a while, we decided to go to the movie on base. They were showing *A Clockwork Orange*. There we were, the five of us, tripping our asses off and going to a movie. It turned out to be one of the most psychedelic movies ever made. We were all blown away. At one point while, the star, Malcolm McDowell, was put in a straight jacket with his eyes wired open. Squirrel let out a blood-curdling scream. I looked over my shoulder and he was sitting there with his head cocked back, shaking it from side to side, with his mouth wide open, howling like an animal. Even though I could tell he was not in pain, he was freaking me out. Shortly after this, we all agree the movie is just too much for us, and we get the hell out of there.

The next day everybody went about their business like it is just another day. We were all anticipating the arrival of our ship, as if that would be some sort of final destination, the culmination to our journey into the U.S. Navy. When the ship finally did come in a few days later, we are amazed. It is enormous. It is an aircraft carrier, a small airport on a boat. It is old and funky, with all sorts of strange smells— claustrophobic, and not very clean. Of course, we soon find out about cleanliness; that is one of the first duties we got after boarding— cleaning.

After a short time aboard the ship, Jim Stroud and I decide to hitchhike up to L.A. on a weekend pass. Jim is a great character from Ohio who turned me on to the James Gang, a great band, and Ten Years After, another great band. Jim was a good harmonica player and he taught me some harp as well. So, Jim and I took off for "bright lights, big city." We had an easy time getting rides out of San Diego. It is daytime, and we look young and non-threatening. By the time we made it to Venice Beach, it is the afternoon. Venice Beach is a gas, with girls in bikinis walking down the sidewalk or roller-skating, sidewalk musicians, and hotdog stands. We were digging it. We tried striking up a conversation or two with the girls, but to no avail. We were obviously military by our haircuts, and these girls were not impressed. At least that's how we rationalized our striking out. I turn to Jim and said, "Look man, these girls ain't having a thing to do with us. Let's hitch down the coast and see what else is going on." He agreed and we headed for the highway.

We get a couple rides into the night, and the next thing we knew, a late model El Dorado pulled over and gave us a ride. Turned out to be this very well-dressed middle-aged hipster wearing a Rolex, who said he is a retired movie producer. His name is Vic, and he was on his way to his beach house in San Clemente. He had long, stylish, silver hair, and really looked the part of a Hollywood mogul. Jim sat up front and I sat in the back. The guy is great, telling us stories about different actors, which ones were assholes and which ones were cool. Right outside San Clemente he said, "You guys are welcome to stay at my beach house. Tomorrow I have to go to San Diego anyway, I'll give you a ride back early in the morning. Jim looked over the back seat and said, "What do you think Marty? We'll be back in no time."

Jim obviously liked the idea, so I said, "I guess so, sounds good to me." A few miles later we pull up to the producer's beach house. It was plush. Obviously, the dude had money. We went inside and plopped down in the sunken living room. He offered us beer, then handed Stroud a huge joint and said, "Light it up."

So, there we were, drinking Heinekens, smoking weed, and watching some cheesy porno flick. Jim and I looked at each other and laughed. After an hour or so, I said to our host. "I'm really beat. Where can I sleep?" He said, "Take any bedroom down the hallway."

I told him and Jim goodnight and wandered off. I am dozing off, when Jim shoots in the room and shut the door behind him, jumping in the twin bed next to mine.

"What the hell are you doing man; you act like you're being chased by a ghost"

"Shut up; shut up," he said in a hushed voice. "I'll tell you in a minute."

Then I heard the garage door open and a car start up and pull out. Jim jumped out of bed and flipped on the light and yelled,

"The dude's a fag and he's going to get some friends to come back and party with us!" I throw off my blanket and sit up telling Jim,

"Look man, not all gay people are perv's, quit freakin out on me."

"I know all gays ain't perv's, but I'm tellin you this guy ain't cool and I'm getting the hell out of here!" At that point he convinced me and I took off out the house with him. As we passed through the living room, we notice a big gun, probably a .357 or a 44, just lying on the coffee table. Now I too am freaking, we run out the front door and down the street, until we made our way back to the little downtown area. Out of breath, we walk up to a "pizza by the slice" joint and asked the guy behind the counter how to get to the highway. He told us, in what seemed like an effeminate voice, Jim and I look at other and took off running again.

When we get to the outskirts of the business district, we saw a car that looked like it could be an El Dorado heading our way, so we jumped into some nearby bushes. Sure enough, it was our buddy. He slowed down as he passed where we were, and said, "Hey you guys come on out, we won't bite! We just wanna party." Stroud and I jumped up and ran further back into the brush. We came to some railroad tracks and decided to lie down in the ditch that ran alongside the tracks. Now, for the next what seemed like forever, a pick-up truck with about three guys in it, and our buddy Vic, in his El Dorado, rode up and down the highway parallel to the tracks yelling, "Hey you guys, come on out. Don't ya wanna go swimmin?" and "Whoooooohaaa... Come on fellows, it's time to party!"

We lay there like a couple of scared rabbits, trembling in the cool damp air, until we finally doze off.

When the sun woke us, we take off for the highway, stuck out our thumbs. We catch a ride pretty quickly with a young dude in an old BMW. After getting out of the BMW, Jim voiced his feeling that the guy seemed gay as well. I then try telling him my story about the cool gay dude I met in New Mexico but he was having no part of it. By then I agree to quit hitching and buy bus tickets back to San Diego, as much as I hate buses. When we did make it back to the base, we told our tale to our buddies, who told us what chicken shits we were for not kicking their asses. Yeah, right...I thought.

About a week later, this other character, a barrack-mate of ours, "Fast Eddie," said to Stroud and me, "You guys were wasting your time going to L.A.; if you want chicks, you need to go to Tijuana." I had heard Tijuana was a great place to party, and it is only about a half hour, south of our base. Eddie was a big-time bullshit artist from St. Louis, so we were hesitant to believe anything he said. Hmmm, now that sounds familiar. Eventually he convinced about four of us to go with him to Tijuana. The next evening we are off— Fat Fred, Danny, Stroud, and me, along with Eddie, pile in Eddie's junker of a car he bought for a hundred and fifty bucks, a few days earlier and headed south. Phil blew the idea off. He didn't care for Eddie. When we get to the border, Eddie said, "I'm leaving my car on the U.S. side and we can walk into Tijuana. There are too many thieves in that town. They'll steal my car for sure." We weren't too happy about this idea, but Eddie was our guide, so he parked and we headed for the border on foot.

We walked across a long footbridge that wound down past a bunch of cardboard boxes on either side of the road. Eventually, I noticed people in among the boxes. Eddie said that is where they lived. Next thing we knew, a bunch of little kids came running up to us yelling, "Neeko, neeko, neeko." "What the hell does 'neeko' mean?" I asked Eddie. "Nickel," he said. "They want us to give them a nickel— but don't, 'cause they'll follow us like stray puppies the rest of the night."

After a short walk, we made our way into the town of Tijuana, and I use the term town loosely. It was a ramshackle mess, with colored lights strung high and haphazardly across the main drag. The main street is a dirt road; the buildings are all made of stone, wood, or a combination of both. The town is old and dusty but crowded with tourists and locals alike. The Christmas lights, along with the Mexican and American rock music coming out of the bars, gave the place a party atmosphere. I thought, this is Mexico's version of Bourbon Street. Mexican dudes standing in front of the various stores and bars tried to coax us in. We rambled into a bar, and Eddie ordered us all beer and shots of Tequila. It was a dank old place, with funky colored lighting and an American rock song coming over the speakers:

Ooooh witchy woman, she got the look in her eyyyye…

Eddie said something in Spanish to the bartender, and the next thing we knew, a bevy of rough-looking young women came over and crowded in our booth with us. Some of them were actually not so young, either. Eddie's girl was actually kind of cute, and the others were not so bad after a few more beers. Next thing I knew, we are being led to the back of the bar, where the extra-curricular activities take place. The only problem was, my hook-up was not at all cute, and no amount of *cerveza* was going to make her attractive. So, when we started to head to the back, I acted like I was getting another beer, then ditched my date and slipped back out on the street.

I wander around in front of the bar and had all kinds of characters trying to sell me or take me or whatever me. I was really enjoying myself, when this one dude came up and said, "Hey *cabrone*, you want some marijuana?"

I thought, *now we're talking.* I said, "Yeah, what have you got?"

He gestured for me to follow him. We went around a corner into an alley and he pulled out what looked like a twenty-two revolver and shoved it at me saying, "Gimme your fuckin' money *pinchy cabrone."* He didn't have to ask twice. I reached in my pocket and pulled out some crumpled bills. In an instant, he snatched the money and was gone. I stood there thinking, well, I guess I got screwed after all. I walked back out to the main drag and stood around looking like a lost puppy. Then Fred came out of the bar with a stupid smirk.

"What happened? Didn't you get a girl?"

"I didn't want the heifer they set me up with, so I came out here and was gonna buy some weed from this dude and got robbed."

He started laughing. "You got robbed?" I just looked at him disgusted.

When the rest of the guys came out, Fred, of course, had to tell them. Eddy then said,

"I'll show you how to get some weed. Come on."

We walked over to a cab, and Eddie spoke to him in Spanish. We all got in and went tearing off down the street. When we get maybe half a mile from town, a cop came whipping up behind us, siren blaring, in this thing that looked worse than Eddy's jalopy. We pulled over, with two wild-eyed blaring lights flashing on what looked like a '64 Chevy Impala and Mexicans with guns yelling some Spanish that only Eddie could understand. So, he translated. "They want us up against the fence."

We complied, and then the cops yelled, "*Dinero, dinero*!"

I said, "Wait a minute— are we being robbed by the police?"

"That's what it looks like," Eddie said, completely disgusted.

"I've already been robbed tonight." "*Ki-a-tae cabrone*!" the so-called police yelled at me. In the meantime, the rest of the guys started digging for money. The cops snatched the money and were gone. The cab driver took off too, so we had to walk all the way back.

We bitched and moaned as we walked along… but what the hell were we going to do about it in another country? We walked all the way back to the border and crossed like a pack of whipped dogs. At least everyone except me had a story about a Mexican hooker, for what that is worth. I thought to myself, Christ, I've been enlisted about four or five months now and this sure don't seem anything like the Navy I was expecting… this sucks!

SEVEN DAYS

A few nights later, I am sitting on a catwalk of our ship smoking a joint with Fat Fred, looking out at the lights of San Diego across the bay when I think about taking off for a little while. I have been in the Navy a while and had become completely disenchanted with the whole thing. I think about how I had told everyone I will be learning a trade, and when I get out, I will get a great job and have the G.I. Bill to help me go to college, or whatever I want. Now it all seems like a distant dream to me; a bullshit story. I am feeling sorry for myself and can't seem to see any good in the Navy at all. I thought about Timmy and Mick Shedagar in Louisiana, and how simple it would be for me to hitchhike there and hang out for a few days. I tell Fred, "Hey man, I'm gonna split and go see some friends of mine."

Fred said, "Wait a minute man, you can't just take off… you'll be AWOL; you'll do brig time if they catch ya fool."

In a dejected tone I say, "Fred, at this point, I don't really give a shit. I'm so disgusted I just don't care." I think to myself, there are two kinds of young men. There are those who have the ability to think and plan for the future, and then there are the guys like me, who say, what can I have, now?

I hop down off the catwalk, stroll down to the ferry, and wave so long to Fred. I climb on the ferry with one other guy and the ferry pilot, and I am on my way across the bay. Looking back to where Fred and I were, all I can see is a tiny orange glow from the joint he is still smoking. I can tell each time he takes another drag the speck of light would momentarily brighten. Like a firefly on a summer night, the tiny beacon came and went, until it faded from view. I get to the interstate about midnight and figure, what the hell; I'll just stand here at the entrance ramp until I catch a ride. I have nothing else to do and I am not tired, so I didn't care how fruitless it is to hitch at night. Then a pick-up truck pulls over, and I am surprised and glad to be on my way to Louisiana, or at least headed in that direction. It's September, so the temperature was not a problem. All I had was the clothes on my back— a pair of jeans, a shirt, and brown polyester Levi's-style jacket. I had my wallet and my Navy I.D. and planned on telling whoever asked, I am on leave.

The guy in the pick-up is all right and gave me a good long ride. By sun-up, I make it to the California/Arizona border. Next, a little Latino-looking fellow picked me up. Pedro was his name, and he was pleasant enough. He tells me all about growing up with his eight brothers and sisters, the pet goat that lived with them and gave them milk, and about his relatives living in cardboard boxes in Tijuana. I thought, I saw those boxes not long ago. He gave me some change and let me out on the outskirts of a place called Gila Bend, Arizona.

I am standing at an entrance ramp in the desert, when up walked this very young looking dude, maybe sixteen at the most. He had long dark hair, wore a jean jacket and dirty black pants, and had a nervous demeanor. He had an accent, but I wasn't sure of the origin. He introduced himself in a forced upbeat tone, "Hi, I'm Robert. What's your name?"

"Gene," I answered. I then said, "Where are you from? You seem a little young to be on the road."

He replied resentfully, "I'm fifteen years old, and I'm from Calgary, Canada."

I said, a bit taken aback. "Holy shit… Calgary, Canada. That's a hell of a long way from here for a fifteen-year-old."

"Yeah, I ran away from home about a week ago."

"Why? Didn't get along with your folks?"

"Stepdad… He was a real asshole."

"Yeah, I had one of those, I didn't like much either." Now it was the runaway and I… when up walks this late-twenty-something-year-old with a backpack. He is dressed like a professional hiker, wearing expensive-looking hiking boots, thick socks, khaki shorts, a new flannel shirt, and a real nice looking, fully loaded backpack. His hair was in one of those long style cuts, and he has a healthy-looking tan. He is eating something that looked like rabbit food from a plastic bag. I spoke first and said, "Hey man, welcome to our lonely entrance ramp." I stuck out my hand for him to shake, and he shook it— the hippie shake.

"I'm Gene and this is Robert." He was cool, I was cool, and everything was cool. He said, while offering me some trail mix, "Lonely huh? I take that to mean not much traffic."

"You got that right," I said.

Turns out, "trail mix" was an accountant on vacation, and his idea of a good time was hitchhiking around the country. His name is Troy. Now, I am impressed with this, because I, too, put a lot of value on hitching as a learning experience. But I was bothered by how upper-crust he seemed. There is nothing really low-rent about him, and that rubbed me the wrong way. I feel like the road is for hippies and hobo's, oh and awol sailers and he is none of the above.

After a while, it became clear we were getting nowhere fast. There are hardly any cars coming by. We all agree that I had been there first, so I should get the first ride—but there are no rides. A car passed by about every five or ten minutes and just gave us the "I'm looking straight ahead and I don't see you" routine. From off in the distance, we heard a train, Troy asked, "Either of you ever hopped a train?" Both the runaway and I shook our heads no. He then said, "Well, neither have I, but if this train passes by slow enough, I'm jumping it." The runaway and I both nodded in agreement and we all moved a little closer to the tracks. As the train approached, we saw it was going pretty slow, though it was deceiving as to just how slow. Once the locomotive got far enough past us, we began trotting toward the boxcars. An open boxcar came into view and we all started running like thieves. We were running at a pretty fast pace, barely keeping up with the empty boxcar. Like I said the speed was deceiving All at once, 'trail mix' threw his pack in the open car, and then leaped in behind it. I jumped in behind him, almost not making it. I looked back at the runaway and he was desperately running alongside the train, looking terrified and sweats streaming down the side of his face. I reached out to him and yelled for him to grab my hand. He tried but couldn't. Then Troy said, "Hold on to my belt; I'll pull him in." He pointed to his waist; I grabbed his belt and he hung himself out of the boxcar as I held onto the edge of the door with one hand and Troy's belt with the other. By now the kid was sweating bullets, and I thought, He ain't gonna make it... When all at once the accountant yelled, "Pull us in!" I pulled and fell back in the boxcar, while Troy was able to drag Robert in. It was pretty hairy, but exciting. Panting like an out-of-breath marathon runner, Robert thanked us for not leaving him behind. I said, "You can thank Troy. It was his idea to hang out the door, 'cause I thought you for sure were not gonna make it." Robert nodded his head like he understood.

There we are, three guys in a boxcar rolling across the desert. The boxcar is empty and had hard wood floors. There is a slight smell of some kind of farm animal, although I think the smell is actually coming from a few cars up the line. The boxcar rocked rhythmically, and the sound of the steel wheels on the metal tracks was loud but became almost soothing as time went by. After about twenty minutes, the train began to pick up speed… I would say it is going maybe thirty miles an hour. Slow, but it is better than no ride at all. It felt like a scene from The Grapes of Wrath as we rolled past the barren lands at sundown.

I thought, just what the hell were Grapes of Wrath? We rocked and clanked, lying on or backs side by side with our hands clasped behind our heads, gazing out the open door of the boxcar at the orange sunset. I thought, Hmm, orange sunshine. I got a kick out of how the runaway seemed to pay close attention to whatever Troy or I said. As if he is desperate for knowledge. Yeah, he is young and scared, but pretty ballsy, in my opinion. As the sky turned to night, the full moon came out and illuminated the desert like a spot light at a concert; I couldn't believe how bright it was. The stars seemed to completely fill the sky, from horizon to horizon. It is magnificent.

The train began to slow down as we approach what looks like shanty shacks made of scrap plywood. We slow to a crawl passing these shacks, and the next thing we knew, people were walking up to the train, holding up watermelon. I thought, why are these people giving us watermelon? I mean, they wandered toward us like zombies with smiles, holding up the watermelon. Talk about strange. As we pulled away, they waved and I said, "man, that was a trip. They looked destitute as hell and they were giving us their watermelon."

The accountant said, "They were migrant workers and that was a migrant camp. That's how poor people are out here; they don't have much, but what they do have they share."

I said, "Damn, I've never seen anything like that." The train picked up speed and rolled on. It was almost as if the engineer thought we needed some refreshments.

Once we get back up to speed, our runaway friend began babbling incessantly. He wouldn't shut up. Maybe he was so anxious he felt the need to babble. He really got on my nerves. The next time the train slowed down I thought, Hell, I feel like walking. So, without so much as a goodbye, I jumped. I heard the kid call to me, sounding upset, "Hey, what are you doing, where are you going?" I called back, "See ya!" I loved doing that. Back home I would be hanging out with whomever, then without any warning I would just stand up and say, "see ya," and walk off. I'm not sure why, but I've never have liked long goodbyes, even short ones, as far back as I can remember. My friend Timmy Shedagar gave me the nickname, "the duffer" for doing just that. I walk along with the train and eventually it left me behind. I figure I'd just follow the tracks until I saw a highway, then I'd start hitching again.

Eventually, I did come to a highway. I have been walking for hours along the tracks, so I am happy to finally come to a road. The train was fun, but the pavement is where I felt I belong. It is my security blanket, the link to my soul. In the course of my journeys, I have woven my peace of mind into the highway. Occasionally I would reach down and touch the pavement from time to time. As if I was paying homage to the highway. The road would be warm or cold, smooth or rough; but it was always there and went on forever. I would tell myself that no matter where I go, I am connected to everyone by the road beneath my feet.

I continued to walk along. It is still dark, except for the brightly shining moon. I noticed snakes lying along the shoulder of the road. Passing them, I told myself I must be hallucinating from lack of sleep; either that or I was having a flashback. I walked a little closer to get a better look; I hear a rattle. Holy shit, I'm not, hallucinating! There are snakes on side of the highway, about every twenty or thirty feet— and yea some were rattlesnakes. God damn, what the hell are they doing on the side of the road? This was a virtual nightmare, because they were on both sides of the highway. I had to walk along in the middle of the road to feel safe. They didn't seem to venture much past the shoulder. Next thing I notice are cowboys— big, giant cowboys with rifles resting on their shoulders, and their hands draped across the barrel and the stock. They were wearing cowboy hats, white shirts, and tan slacks, and of course cowboy boots. They were standing just off the highway, about every fifty feet. As I walk down the highway they never moved, but their eyes are following me the whole time. My God, what kind of place is this? Right then, the sound of a car coming up behind caught my attention. I turned and stuck out my thumb, making sure not to get too close to the snakes. I prayed, Dear God, please let this guy pick me up, I'll never do anything wrong again, I swear I'll be as good as I… The car slowed to a stop, and I jumped in. He was an older fellow, headed to Texas, and I was once again saved. The sun was starting to come up and I noticed the cowboys weren't cowboys at all, but power line poles. I thought, were those really snakes I saw and heard? I turned to the dude who had just picked me up and asked, "Hey, have you ever heard of snakes on the side of the road, just lying there, rattling?"

"Hell yeah," he said. "They come out of the desert at night and warm themselves on the pavement." I said, "Christ, they scared the hell out of me. I'd never seen that before."

He laughed, and then said, "Hey, you want breakfast?"

I said, "Yeah, but I'm broke."

"I'll get you and me some breakfast; just follow my lead." I didn't like the sound of this, though the guy was at least sixty-something, so how dangerous could his idea be? We came to a roadside café and he pulled up. We walked into what looked like your typical diner in the desert, nothing fancy, but it worked. Booths lined the front windows, and a few tables were scattered about. Behind a counter stood a waitress, thirty-five to fifty-five years old — there was no way of telling her age, but she was weathered. She wore a pastel dress, an apron, and yes the obligatory paper head gear.

We strolled up to the counter and each of us took a stool. My new friend, who had just acquired a thick southern melodious drawl, began,

"Excuse me ma'am, but my name is Reverend Duncan Montgomery n' I'm from Dry Prong, Looziana… and this here is my nephew." He nodded my way, and then continued. "His dear mother, my sister, sent me to California to bring him back home. Only trouble is, the congregation gave me barely enough funds to get out there and get back, and with the grace of the good lord, we will make it; but at the moment our stomachs are so empty they hurt, and we would be more than willing to do any kind of work in order for us to partake in some meager nourishment."

Oh my God, I thought, this guy must be kidding if he thinks this will work. Without flinching, the waitress took the pencil from behind her ear, wet the tip on her tongue as she picked her ticket book up, and in a blasé almost sorry-she-was-asking sort of tone said, "What'll ya have?"

I thought, Wow, this guy is good. We chowed down on bacon and eggs, hash browns, toast, and coffee. At the end of our meal, the reverend stood up, rubbing his stomach and said, "Now what can we do for you, fair lady?" She waved her hand in a manner that said, "don't even worry about it."

"You're too kind, dear lady. Bless you, and the congregation thanks you, I'm sure." When we got back out to his car, I had to ask, "You really a reverend?" He replied,

"You really my nephew?"

We got as far as the outskirts of El Paso and we parted company. It is the middle of the day, and it is hot. I walk up to the entrance ramp and stuck out my thumb. After maybe twenty minutes, a young dude, college type, picks me up. He is cool… Smoked a joint with me. As we cruise through El Paso, we are coming up over a small rise in the highway, and who should be walking along the side of the highway? It is my young runaway hitchhiking buddy, from Calgary. I said, "Hey, look at that, I know that guy."

"Friend of yours; should I pick him up?"

"No, he's just someone I met on the road. I'd rather you didn't."

"Bad news, huh?"

"No, more like, annoying news."

"Hmm, okay, if you say so."

After a number of unmemorable rides across Texas, I hit San Antonio, again. I recalled passing through San Antonio less than a year before, when I went out to California, hoping to be with my girl Edma. As a matter of fact, I-10 was becoming an old friend. Coming out of San Antonio, I catch a ride with a young guy by the name of Brad, an elementary school teacher. He's asking me a lot of questions— a concerned big brother type. So, I oblige his curiosity with the truth. "I am hitchhiking to a friend's place in Baton Rouge because I was sick of the Navy," I said. "I'll probably spend a couple of days there and hitchhike back." He is amazed that I felt I could just get out on the highway and go thousands of miles, just like that. I explained to him how it is no big deal, and that all kinds of people hitchhike all the time. In Houston, he gives me a few bucks and wished me luck. He even gives me his phone number in case I need a place to stay on my way back.

In Houston, a scraggly looking hippie type picked me up in an old beat-up Chevy van. He had to be twenty-eight or so and looked rough. He had tangled black hair and had on a well-worn flannel shirt, jeans, and a dirty jean jacket. Though he had the right uniform, I didn't like the vibe I am getting. It is dark, and from what I can make of his face, it is not a happy one. As he drove, he leaned forward with his elbows resting on the steering wheel. I can tell by his demeanor that he is full of himself, though I am not impressed. He said he is going all the way to Baton Rouge.

I said, "Today's my lucky day. That's where I'm headed. How far is it, anyway?"

"Oh, about five hours or so, depending on the traffic." As we drove along, he babbled about the things he'd done and places he'd been, but I couldn't have cared less. I pretended to be sleepy, and lucky for me, he let me sleep.

We were not far from B.R. when quiet time was over. He spoke up. "Hey, you up for making some money?" To that I replied, "It must be two in the morning. How are we gonna make money?"

"It's three-thirty and I know how we can make some easy money come four-thirty."

"Oh, yeah? How's that?" I can tell I am not going to like his idea.

"There's this construction site just on the other side of the old Mississippi River Bridge, and I used to work for this guy there."

"So, he's gonna hire us?"

"No, stupid, he ain't gonna hire us; we're gonna rob him."

"Rob him?" I said, with a lump in my throat.

Yeah man, it'll be easy. You see at about four a. m. he arrives at the job and goes in this little trailer he keeps at the jobsite. I know he keeps a few thousand bucks on him, and he'll be there by himself."

"So, you're gonna what, knock him out?"

"Hell no, I'm gonna stick this in his face." At that moment he pulled a snub-nose revolver from his belt. I thought, Oh shit, now I'm in trouble.

He said, "Come on man, are you in?"

"No, I don't think so. I'm not into robbing people."

"Come on, you chicken shit. It'll be no sweat."

The whole time I am thinking, I hope he doesn't try that gun out on me. I sat there not saying a word. Then, without warning, he whipped the van off to the side of the highway and stopped.

"Get out. I know someone who is up to the job." He didn't have to ask me twice, I get out, and he tore off into the night.

As his taillights fade, I walk toward Baton Rouge. He had let me out on the west side of the old Mississippi River Bridge. I walk along thinking, *Damn… that was not cool.* It was a friendly reminder of just how dangerous hitchhiking can be.

Very few cars were passing by, so I decide to just keep walking and not even bother to hitch. When I get to the bridge, it looks a little tight for walking across; but with no real traffic to speak of, I figure I'd take my chances. There is about a 12-inch-wide piece of concrete running along the edge of the roadway, maybe six inches high. The cars and trucks that pass by were doing seventy, and were close enough to rock me, so it is a little tricky keeping my balance. I know it is illegal, but I do it anyway. I guess after just turning down an armed robbery, jaywalking across a bridge didn't seem so dangerous. At the same time, with each rush of wind from a car or semi, I made sure to steady myself by grabbing the cold, rusty metal structure. When I reach the halfway point, I look out at the river and saw a gigantic barge, slowly moving upstream. It looks to be almost as big as my ship, the Kitty Hawk, but not quite. I wonder if anyone on that huge thing was hiding somewhere smoking a joint. When I look out toward Baton Rouge, there were lights strewn across the tops of buildings. Only as I got closer, I realize it is not buildings, but refineries. Then the smell of oil and smoke fill my senses. Yep, this is an oil town all right.

I get to the other side without being seen by a cop and walk along, feeling pretty lucky. I made it to a twenty-four-hour greasy spoon and walked in for a cup of coffee. I sat there pondering my adventure and waiting for the sun to come up so I could hit on my friends, Timmy and Mick. I knew the Shedagers would be glad to see me… surprised too, considering that the last they heard, I was in the Navy, far away. At the first sign of light, I walk outside to a pay phone and call their house. Mick answered the phone. I said, "Hey, what's going on?"

"Who is this… Gene?"

"You got it."

"Where are you?"

"I'm at the Waffle House on Airline Highway, near the old bridge."

"You're bullshittin' me."

"No, I'm not. Come get me." Within fifteen minutes he pulled up smiling from ear to ear.

"How ya doin', ya crazy bastid?"

"Pretty good. I just got in from San Diego." We headed for his mom's house, where he and Timmy lived.

There is Timmy, happy as hell to see me. He said, "Hey man, you still owe me for half a month's rent from the last time you were here." He smiled, facetiously. I smiled back and said, "I'll pay you back… someday."

"Ah, hell forget about it man. We had such a good time it was worth it."

"You still with Allison?" I asked.

"Oh yeah. We'll probably see her tonight."

That day I just wander around with Mick and saw a few of his friends. In the evening we went to a little bar in a shopping center. I believe it is called Stumps, named after the owner. We had a good time drinking beer and bullshitting. I spent the night at Timmy and Mick's, and his mom didn't ask a thing. Nice lady. The next evening we went to a concert at a place called Independence Hall. We didn't want to pay to see Vince Vance and the Valliant's, but we thought it would be fun to try and sneak in. We ran around on the roof, looking for a way in, to no avail. Eventually we just gave up and went to drink at a burger joint that served cheap draft beer.

While I am in Baton Rouge, I thought I'd go by and see my friend Johnny Vassy. I wanted to tell him how I'd been screwed by the Navy. Johnny didn't take shit from anyone, and in a way, I admired that. We had worked together as cooks at a restaurant in Baton Rouge the last time I was there. Maybe I felt the need to have my ego fed. He was pretty much a southern redneck, but he did like to get high. Mick dropped me off at Johnny's apartment, while he was off to see a girl. When I got to Johnny's, he is surprised to see me. Johnny was a great guy if he liked you, not so great if he didn't. He was a few years older than me. Physically he was not impressive— average height and weight, but the way that he carried himself said he was ready and willing to scrap with anyone. At times, I wish I could be like him, but that just wasn't me. When I called him on the phone, he said he was living with his girlfriend and they'd just had a kid, Chloe, so I knew what to expect. When I arrived at Johnny's, he invited me to hang out with him in front of his apartment.

"I would invite you in, but the baby's sleepin' and I don't wanna wake her."

I said, "That's cool. Got any beer?"

Johnny responded, "Shit smell?" then said, "Wait here, I'll get you one. Bud all right?"

"Hell, I don't care, long as its cold."

I sat down on the sidewalk in front of his apartment waiting for Johnny when I noticed two guys across the parking lot, standing and talking. Next thing I knew, they came over to where I was sitting.

"Hey, man, what's up. You a friend of Johnny's?"

"Yeah." They plopped down on the parking bump in front of me.

"My name's Mike and this is Lenny." I shook their hands. They were drinking beer, but didn't seem drunk. They were pretty normal looking dudes, kind of redneck and hippie at the same time. They looked to be nineteen or twenty. Mike, the talkative one, asked me, "Known Johnny long?"

"For a while. I guess."

"He's cool ain't he?"

"No, not really." Mike gave his friend Lenny a quizzical look, then looked back at me and said, "No really, he's cool ain't he?"

"No, like I said, he ain't." Now I knew what he was getting at. He wanted to know if Johnny smoked weed, but when he asked me, what came to my mind was how Johnny would very easily get in arguments with perfect strangers over nothing. A lot of times he would be in a fist fight before anyone knew what happened. So the first thing that came to my mind was no, Johnny ain't cool, not cool at all. At that moment, Johnny walked out of his apartment and handed me a beer. He was barefoot, wearing a pair of Levi's, and shirtless. He sat down next to me, looked at Mike and Lenny, and said, "How you slugs doin'?" then took a big swig of beer.

"Oh, we're all right." Then Mike asked, "How's your baby doin?"

"She's fine. She's the love of my life," Johnny said. I could tell he was a proud daddy.

"What about your wife? How's she?" Mike inquired.

"My wife?" Johnny seemed bothered by the question,

"Marcia, she's not my wife, she's my girlfriend. What do you wanna know about her for?"

I thought, Oh shit, here we go.

Mike then said, "I'm just asking, man. I don't mean nothin' by it." Johnny responded in a real matter of fact way, "Yeah ya do...you'd like to fuck her, wouldn't ya?"

"No, man, I was just asking, just to ask," Mike nervously responded. "I mean she's good lookin', but that's not what I was thinkin'."

"Yeah, that's exactly what you were thinkin'," Johnny said. "You're probably hopin' for me not be around some night so you can hit on her." By this time, Mike was looking real nervous. He could sense Johnny was starting to percolate. Then, the phone in Johnny's apartment rang. He got up to go answer it. I noticed Mike mumble something to his buddy, who had been sitting there quietly the whole time. Then they stood up. That's when I said, "I told ya he wasn't cool." Mike gave me a half-smile and acknowledged me with a nod, he then said, "We'll see ya later."

"Yeah, later"

When Johnny came back out from the phone call, he asked, "What happened to my neighbors?"

"They left. Said they'd see ya later."

"Yeah, they needed to leave." Johnny said.

We sat there for the next hour or so, shootin' the shit. I told him a few Navy stories and he told me about his new job, working on oil rigs offshore. After a while, Marcia showed up, and Mike gave me a ride back to Timmy's. I never did get his opinion on my being shafted by the Navy.

The next morning, I bade the Shedagers farewell, and Mick once again dropped me off at an entrance ramp. Two and half days of Baton Rouge was all I needed; it is time to go back to San Diego. The rides back to California were a blurr... all I know is, I was back in at my base about thirty-six hours later, turning myself into the officer on duty. He referred me to the commanding officer, who gave me thirty days restriction to the base.

I thought, Not bad for seven days AWOL. Could have been worse. When I was sitting around shooting the shit with some Navy buddies telling them the story, one of them told me,

"Hell, seven days don't mean shit. You gotta be gone at least thirty if you really wanna get kicked out." I thought, Kicked out… hell, that's not a bad idea…

Triumph TR 4

Here I am, doing important things like raking leaves and picking up trash. Not that I expect anything more. Phil would walk by from time to time shaking his head. About two and a half weeks into my restriction, the USS Kitty Hawk arrived, and we were told to pack and board. We are excited, and at the same time curious about an aircraft carrier the size of an ocean liner. Phil and I were in the same squad, so we had bunks near each other, and that's cool, because we are both a little intimidated. The Kitty Hawk is not an ocean liner by any means. It is a no-frills warship, dark gray and down in the passageways not well lit, so it is creepy. It is simply an airport out to sea. As for creature comforts, there are none.

We try to acclimate ourselves to this new situation, but it isn't working. We have such high hopes for school and training, and it just isn't coming to fruition. Once we get settled on the ship, we leave port and head for San Francisco. It is a one-day journey up the coast, where we stop and go into dry dock. Now this is not good, not good at all. Dry dock meant this humongous ship would be lifted out of the water and worked on. One of the main tasks is chipping paint, which is extremely boring and a dirty-ass job we all hated, especially Phil. Things turned bad in a short amount of time. There are about thirty guys in our squad. Each of us is given a needle gun, and told to start chipping. This is a tedious task. First, the needle gun is powered by air, so it had a long hose that was attached to a compressor and a real pain in the ass to maneuver. Second, it is so loud; so you had to wear earmuffs, along with goggles and gloves. You had to make sure your collar was up and tight, so as not to let paint chips get down your back and chest because they would itch like hell. The ship was about an eighth of a mile long, so the job seemed daunting, considering we were chipping about three, maybe four-square feet an hour. Phil and I would look at this every morning and become more and more pissed off. We would talk at night. "Is this what we joined the Navy for?" Phil would ask rhetorically.

"Hell, no," I said, just as disgusted.

"I never would have joined if they had told me I was gonna learn how to chip paint," Phil responded. "Hell, no, this suck, and I ain't gonna do it any more."

"I don't think you can quit, Phil."

"Watch me," he said.

The next morning, we were all on deck being handed our tools when Phil refused to get a paint chipper. Our squad leader was this crusty old lifer, who looked like he'd had a bad accident. His face was badly scarred, right across his mouth, and he had a speech impediment. He was an E-4 and Phil and I were E-2s. He called Phil over and said, "Thanchez, get a gun and thtart chippin'," Phil just ignored him. The squad leader walked over to him and said, "HEY THAILER, DIDGE YOU HEAR ME!?!?!"

Phil turned to him and said, "Get away from me, prop face.

Now it is bad enough that he is not following orders, but to call the guy "prop face?"...He wanted to go to the brig, and he got his wish.

They let him out after twenty-four hours and told him he'd better shape up. After that Phil and I got the idea to buy 100 hits of Purple Microdot acid to sell and make money, and maybe go AWOL on the profits. I decide I am gonna buy a car, a sports car. I had seen a 1964 Triumph TR4 for sale in a car lot in San Francisco for $1,500. I had already asked the salesman about it. I told Phil, "All I need is ten percent down and they'll sell me the car."

"Marty, you're nuts. They're not gonna let you drive away in that car for a hundred and fifty dollars."

I told him, "The salesman said that's all I need. Since I'm in the Navy, I've got a steady job, as far as their concerned."

"I still say you're nuts."

"Okay, tomorrow I'll prove it. Can you loan me fifty? I'm short."

His response, "Oh shit, I should have known..."

The next day I get off duty around 4 p.m. By the way, Phil is chipping paint again. Take a bus over to the car lot. After talking to the salesman for about forty-five minutes, I drove away in my 1964 TR 4. When I get back to the base, Phil and our friend Wendell are standing in front of the recreation hall. I pull up and am smiling like a Cheshire cat.

"You son of a bitch, you did it," Phil said. Wendell has a big smile as well; he is a man of few words.

"You're damn right I did. I told you I would." I am feeling like a million bucks.

"You've told me a lot of things, Marty," Phil said, while checking out every inch of the car. It is a nice burgundy with a black convertible top, wire wheels, and a decent interior, an absolutely, super cool looking; two-seater, sports car. Believe me, it is easily one of the coolest cars you could own in 1972. It had chick magnet written all over it.

"Let's go over to Oakland and see if we can score that acid."

We went back to the ship and Phil got cleaned up, then it was off to Oakland, by way of the Golden Gate Bridge. The car drove nicely and it handled well. We were really enjoying my new purchase. We crossed the Golden Gate feeling pure joy. The four-cylinder motor was purring like a kitten.

When we arrived at Danny's, he said he is having a party and we could hang out if we want, while we wait for the dude with the acid. That was cool by us. Danny was a good guy. He even offered us a hit of some blue mescaline he had for his party. We gladly accepted, and people started coming over. It was a mix of guys and girls, including some very fine-looking black chicks. Then it dawned on me that I was the only white dude, besides Phil, at this shindig. I start feeling a little uneasy— probably the mesc' messing with my head, because everyone was cool to me. I notice Phil just chatting it up with some girl in the corner. At that point the mesc' started to really kick in and I felt like I needed some air. I go downstairs to my car, got in, and just sat there.

Next thing I knew, a race riot was breaking out behind me while I sat in my car. There were cops and German shepherd dogs, the Black Panthers marching down the street, tear gas and water cannons. I am scared out of my mind. I scrunch down in my seat, hoping no one will notice me, and just sit there. All this is happening in my rearview mirrors and I didn't want to turn around for fear of being noticed. Finally, I get up enough courage to look behind me, and saw that no one is there. I mean it is a completely quiet urban street. I couldn't believe it— the mesc' was screwing with my mind that bad— a very "bad trip," as they say. When I turn back around in my seat, my mind just shot off into space. It is a clear night and I could see myself as an embryo floating and slowly tumbling in space. It's freaking me out, so I quickly try to look at something in the car. Everything is a blur; I simply couldn't focus.

When I looked up in the sky again, there I am as an embryo floating; slowly tumbling, and then another embryo appeared. It is my mother and we were both floating through space, attached by an umbilical cord. Now that freaked me out again, so I try again to look at something in the car. I thought if I can look at something and focus, I would be able to calm myself down. I can feel the gearshift knob in my right hand, and I can feel the raised numbers on the top of the knob. It is the 1, 2, 3, 4, R, showing the shift pattern. I squeeze the knob and lean over so my eyes are just a few inches from the shifter, and it finally comes into focus. I tell myself this is reality; this is what shifts my car. I think to myself, I am in a car, my car, and I immediately begin to calm down.

Once again, as I ease my grip on the shift knob and sat back in my seat, the view of my embryo in outer space came back; but this time it didn't freak me out. Then I see my dad, my brother, and my sisters, all as embryos attached to each other by umbilical cords and floating, slowly tumbling through space. This seemed to go on for hours; it is bizarre and soothing at the same time. I knew better than to look in my rearview mirrors, because that is not a good scene at all.

Then the passenger door opened and Phil looked in at me and said, smiling,

"Marty, what the hell are you doing down here? Are you okay?" I looked at him and his face was a little distorted, I then said, "Man you wouldn't believe it…I saw a race riot, embryos floating, and my whole family attached by umbilical cords."

He starts laughing and shaking his head and says, "Jesus Christ man, how many hits did Danny give you? I haven't hallucinated at all. Do you want me to drive?" Relieved to see him, I responded, "Yeah, you better. How long have I been down here?"

"I don't know… forty-five minutes or so."

"Damn," I said. "Is that all? My ass is sore as hell and my back is stiff as shit. Did you get the acid?" I asked.

"Yeah, I got it."

"A hundred?"

"Purple Microdot," Phil said.

"We can make a couple of hundred if we don't eat too many," I said.

"If we're lucky," Phil said, forever the cynic.

When we get back to the ship, we both agree not to hide the acid in our lockers. We found a place below deck in the bulkhead (the wall of the ship). That evening, when I am coming down off the mescaline, I thought about how I flipped out at Danny's. I decide right then and there I am going to be more careful about what I put in my mouth. I damn sure didn't want to go through that again. When I wake up the next morning, yesterday is a distant memory. We need to try the Purple Microdot; we tripped pretty much every day for the next month or so. Chipping paint, going to the mess hall, playing cards in the evening— all while tripping our asses off. We walk around with stupid smiles on our faces and our pupils were the size of dimes. When I think back, I can't imagine how our superior officers didn't notice we were on something. Or maybe they did and just didn't care.

As for our selling and turning a profit, I think we sold about ten or fifteen hits and ate the rest. Our profit went out the window. When the acid ran out, I get another bright idea.

Phil and I both had enough of the Navy, and after doing a little research, we decided on a plan we'd been thinking about. The Navy had a policy of kicking anyone out who had been AWOL for more than thirty days. Or so I heard. So, I suggested to Phil, "Let's take the TR down to San Diego, buy a kilo of weed, and bring it up to San Francisco and sell it. We'll make a killing." Now I guess Phil was not thinking, or he really didn't care, but he said, "When do we leave?"

"Well, payday is tomorrow…"

Next day we packed our stuff in the trunk and tied our rolled-up sleeping bags to the trunk rack. Damn, we both agreed. That looked cool as hell; reminded us of that old TV show *Route Sixty-Six*. We cashed our checks and split. We were on our way to San Diego and we couldn't have cared less about the Navy at that point. Now driving down is completely cool; we took turns at the wheel. We followed the Pacific Coast Highway south. I told Phil stories about my adventures on that very same road, showing him points of interest, like I was a tour guide.

"And around this next corner is where James Dean got killed."

"No shit," Phil said in amazement.

"That's right," I said. Making things up on the fly was my specialty. Hell, I would even start to believe my own bullshit; my delivery was so smooth. The scenery is as fabulous as I remembered it to be when Diane, the professor, and I were here just last year. We got as far as Santa Barbara, when all of a sudden, this grinding sound started coming from the rear of the car. I said, "It's probably just the bearings. We'll find a place to spend the night and fix it in the morning." That seemed like a reasonable plan, so we drove off the highway a little, pulled out our sleeping bags, and spent the night on the side of the road.

As we lay there gazing up at the stars, I told Phil about the blue-eyed blonde professor who picked me up at an entrance ramp and hitched with me up the coast on this very highway. Now, that was true, and after the story he said, "You're full of shit; I've heard enough, I'm going to sleep."

Well, I guess even the best adventurers can only tell so many tales. The next morning, we limped into Santa Barbara and found a small foreign car repair shop. A hippie mechanic and a couple other freaks ran it. After a quick once over, he said we had a blown differential. Our hearts sank; we were screwed. He then said, "I can get a used rear end from the junk yard and put it in for about a hundred and fifty bucks." Phil and I walked around the side of the station, and I could see Phil was pissed.

"Could you give us a minute?" I asked. He said, "Sure take all the time you want; we're not going anywhere." I said to Phil, "Look man, we'll give him the one fifty and instead of buying a key, we'll buy a pound. We'll still have enough money left." Phil looked at me as if he wanted to spit in my face, then said, "This whole idea was bullshit to begin with. What the hell was I thinking? Go to San Diego and buy weed to bring back to San Francisco. I must have been tripping." There was silence for a moment, and then we looked at each other and started to laugh, because that's exactly what we had been doing. When we calmed down, I walk back over to the hippie mechanic and asked how long it would take.

"Well," he said, "depending on how quick they can get a rear end over here... maybe I can bump you in front of a car or two, since you're traveling... say late this afternoon, if you're lucky."

"Great, we'll take it." I walk back over to Phil and said, "We'll be out of here by late this afternoon." He just sort of grumbled to himself and started to walk off.

"Hey, man, where you going?" I asked. He replied, sounding mildly pissed, "I guess we'll have to find something to do for the next six hours, won't we?" I caught up and walked off with him.

We wander around Santa Barbara for the next few hours, ate lunch at a fast food place, and eventually made our way over to the beach. Santa Barbara was a beautiful beach town— lush trees, a nice little downtown, and a ridge that ran around the perimeter of the town and overlooked the whole city. We sat on a beachside bench, watching chicks and daydreaming. We made our way back over to the repair shop and found the car where we left it.

"Ah, shit, he hasn't even started on it," Phil said, walking to where the car was parked. I went over to our mechanic and asked him, "What's the deal… is there a problem?"

"No, no problem; it runs fine. You owe me a hundred and fifty bucks."

I called to Phil, "Hey, man, it's ready." Phil hopped in and started it up.

"He can take it for a test ride while you pay me."

"Take it for a test and I'll pay the dude," I yelled to Phil, and he pulled out and hauled ass. I thought, Damn, I sure hope he comes back.

He did and we are gone again. San Diego, here we come. We didn't waste time getting there; we arrived in the middle of the night. We find a place on the beach to spend the night. Phil slept in the car, sitting in the driver's seat, and I put my sleeping bag on the grass next to the car. The next day we got up early and went to see our friend who lived on Ocean Beach and rousted him up about eight in the morning. He greeted us at the door, obviously awakened from a sound sleep. Opening the door, he took one look at us and walked back over to his couch and plopped down.

"What the hell are you guys doin' here this time of the morning? Are you nuts?" Now, Tommy was a full-on California dope smoking surfer. Gettin' stoned and catchin' waves; that covered Tommy. Oh yeah, drinking and surfer girls were a part of his world too; but that was it. He sold weed to make money, which is how we had met Tommy back when Phil and I were stationed in San Diego.

"Tommy," I began, "We need a pound of weed. Can you help us?" He lay there with his eyes closed and said, "I guess so, when do you need it by?"

"Today, if it's possible?"

"Today? Shit, that's not much notice."

"Well, we're kind of pressed for time. Can you get us one?"

"Maybe. Let me make a couple calls. Check back with me about noon." Phil and I look at each other and shrugged. Stood up and walk out. I said, "We'll be back at noon," and shut his door. I then ask Phil, "What do you think?"

"I think we're fucked if he doesn't come up with one today," Phil said.

"Ah, he'll find one. That's how he makes his money."

We drove out to the beach parking lot to kill some time. We sat there near our car, waiting for noon. Then up walks a very long-haired freak, just boppin' along, and he said to me,

"Need a lid?" I looked up and said, "Not really." Then I half-heartedly followed that with, "we need a pound."

"I got one," he said. "One-thirty, some killer Mexican." Phil and I both sat up.

"No shit, can you really get us a pound for a hundred and thirty bucks?"

"Hell, yeah," he said.

"You're not the mod squad or nothin' like that are you?"

"Hell, no," I said. "We're AWOL and trying to get a pound to take back to San Francisco.

He said, "Cool, if this works out they'll be plenty more." Phil and I looked at each other nodding our approval. He then said, "You got the one-thirty on you?"

"Yeah, we do." "Good. Let's go. My bikes over here… Just follow me in your car… It's not far at all."

He got on this rusty old beach cruiser bicycle and started peddling. We followed along slowly. As we did, Phil, always the wary one, said, "You were giving him a little too much information."

I countered, "I was trying to make him feel like he was dealing with some legitimate dopers."

We eventually pull up to a beat-up looking group of beach bungalows. He parked his bike in front of one of the bungalows and walked over to our car. Phil was driving, and he walked up to Phil and said, "I can't bring you inside 'cause the dude who sells it to me is paranoid about people he doesn't know. So just give me the cash and I'll come back out in two minutes."

"Fuck that," Phil said,

"Go get the pound and we'll be right here with the money when you come out. You give us the weed and then we'll give you the money." Our new friend said, "I can't do that man. The guy won't let me. Look the door is right there… it's ten feet away. Where am I gonna go?" Phil shook his head no.

"Where is he gonna go Phil? Just give him the money. His bike is right there," I said. Phil glanced at me with a look that said, *you're an idiot.*

"The dude then reached in his pocket and handed Phil what looked like a bag of pills. He said, "Here you can hold these hundred cross tops for collateral; I'll be right back." Phil reluctantly handed him the hundred and thirty. The dude said, "Just sit tight, I'll be back in two minutes." He went to the door, knocked, and walked in, shutting the door behind him.

Not thirty seconds went by when Phil sat up and said, "Wait a minute man, he just walked up to that door, knocked, and walked in, and these cross tops are worth maybe thirty or forty bucks at the most." He jumped out of the car and walked over to the door and knocked. He knocked again, only this time with a heavy fist, and the door popped open. It wasn't even locked. He looked in and ran back to the car and shouted, "that motherfucker fucked us!"

"No shit?" I said. For some stupid reason I trusted the guy. I was not expecting this at all.

"No shit, nobody even lives in that fuckin' place. It's abandoned." I got out of the car and ran to the open door. Sure enough, the place was just a shithole and the wall of the back of the room was not even there. You could practically see the waves crashing on the beach standing at the door of the room. There were empty cans of beer and trash, no furniture, and nothing but old garbage; we'd been had. As we walked around for a moment, we realized it was nothing more than a run-down abandoned motel.

"Motherfucker! Phil said, over and over again. "Motherfucker, motherfucker… Now what are we gonna do?"

"Be cool man… we'll think of something."

"Be cool?" Phil said. "Be cool? Are you out of your fuckin' mind? There's nothing to be cool about you fuckin' idiot! We're fucked!"

"I got an idea, but first, let's get out of here." Phil reluctantly got in the car and we drove off. After some quiet time, I began, "You know, I bet if we went to the base at San Diego, we could ask Stroud and maybe even Manny if they would front us sixty or seventy bucks apiece. They'd probably do it if they had it." Stroud and Manny were still at the San Diego base. Their ship hadn't come in. We were already in San Diego.

Phil said, "Why would they lend us money?"

"'Cause we're gonna pay them back an extra twenty apiece."

"You are unbelievable… do you really think they're gonna buy that crap?"

"Why not? They like us."

"Not that much."

"Let's go, what have we got to lose?"

We had to wait until four o'clock for Stroud and Manny to get off duty. Got on base with our Navy IDs, no problem. Found Stroud and Manny, and they bought my story hook line and sinker. Luckily payday had just passed, so they had the money. Phil couldn't believe it. It went down just like I said.

We went back out to Tommy's place in Ocean Beach. It was about five by now and we were hoping Tommy didn't blow us off. When we got there, he was waxing his surfboard in front of his shack… totally California.

"Where the fuck have you guys been? I said check back by twelve."

I spoke up, "We ran into a little problem, but we're here now. Did you get the weed?"

"I got it… you got the 'samolians'?"

"Yeah, we do."

"Let's go inside." He threw his rag down on his board and led us into his shack. He said,

"Sit down. I'll get it." He walked into his bedroom and came right back out with a huge clear plastic bag. Phil and I sat up.

Tommy said, "You wanna try it?"

"Yeah, why not." After smoking a joint as fat as a pinky, we are stoned and gone, in more ways than one. We are headed back to San Francisco with a pound of weed in the trunk of our car. As we pull away from Tommy's, I wasn't paying attention, I was just tooling along feeling good about our score and the next thing we know a cop car is heading right toward us. He had his window down and as he pulled up he motioned for us to stop. My heart is in my throat. He pulled up and stopped right next to us, looked out his window, and said, "You're on a one way street; turn it around." He made a circular motion with his index finger. I responded with a very, clear, "Yes sirrr." I made a U-turn and had to follow him out of the neighborhood, while our hearts were pounding right out of our chests. It felt as if someone were methodically punching me in the sternum from the inside out. When we get out from behind the cop and head down the highway, we spent the next five or ten minutes talking about how close we had just come to going to jail. If we'd been caught holding a pound, it would have been considered intent to sell. Even in the very liberal state of California, that would have meant serious jail time.

The TR was running well, and I am feeling good. We figure we have just enough money to make it back to San Fran'. We were about a half-hour or so out of San Diego, the sun was going down, and traffic was light. Then all at once, the cars in front of us started slowing down and we notice some spotlights set up on either side of the highway. I sat up in my seat a little so I could get a better look.

"Holy shit!" I said.

"Holy shit what?"

"It's a bunch of cops and they're checking for something."

"DWI check point maybe?

"I don't know but I hope they don't look in our trunk 'because we are sca-roooed…"

"Just be cool," Phil said, "We've got our IDs." As the line of cars passed through the checkpoint, we could see what looked like a cop, shine a flashlight in the windows and wave them on, although there were a few cars pulled over with people standing around and cops talking to them. Still, most of the cars were just being waved on through. When we got to the lights, the cop had to bend over to shine his light in the car. TR 4s are low to the ground. He shined his light in our faces and said, "You military?"

"Navy" Phil said.

"Drive carefully." He waved us on. Once again, we had to get our hearts out of our throats.

"You know what that was?" I said.

"Yeah… a fuckin' heart attack!" Phil said.

"Well, besides that. They were checking for illegals. They were immigration officers."

"No shit!" Phil said.

"Yeah, I read his badge. Didn't Jimmie Shedager used to call you a wetback?"

"Yeah, you're a real funny fucker." Once again, we'd got away with one. How lucky can two guys be?

We got up to the Irvine College area and pulled off to get something to eat at a burger joint. We ran into two girls on their way to a concert. We asked them who was playing, and neither of us recognized the group. I got the idea to go by the concert and try to sell some of those cross tops we had got from our rip-off friend. We ask the two girls where the concert is, and head over there. Phil didn't think it is such a good idea, so he hung back at the car. I walk on up to where everyone was going in and found what seemed to be a good perch to hawk my wares. As people passed me by, I quietly but clearly said, "Speed? Cross tops? Speed? Nobody was biting, and I began to notice they were giving me funny looks like, *what planet are you from*? They also were not very hippie looking at all— more like Beaver Cleavers. Finally, after about fifteen minutes of sneers and frowns, I went up to a couple of young dudes and said, "Hey you guys, who is the band playing tonight?" They looked at each other, and then back at me, and one of them said, "It's not really a band. It's more like a show."

"A show?" I said. "What kind of show?"

"A Christian Music Show."

My eyes must have got as big as almonds, because the two young dudes were backing up. A Christian music show?… No wonder everybody is looking at me like I'm crazy. They looked at each other again and scooted away.

When I get back to the car, I walk up to Phil and said, "Let's get the hell out of here."

"Why, what's wrong?"

"This is a Christian rock show."

"You're shittin' me?" By now Phil had a big smile on his face and he followed that with,

"You idiot..."

"Well, you didn't know any better your damn self."

We make it all the way back to San Francisco without incident. We went to this dude's place in Oakland. We had met him with Danny. We knew we could unload the weed for at least two hundred and fifty. He was home and we did the deal… no problem.

Then Phil said, "Shit, man… this ain't so great. I think I'm just gonna turn myself in and do a little brig time."

"No," I said, "You can't do that for at least thirty days. If you turn yourself in now it'll just be a little brig time, and then right back to chipping paint. You need to be AWOL for at least thirty days. Then turn yourself in and they'll kick you out."

"So what the hell are we gonna do for the next twenty days?" Phil asked.

"Do another run to San Diego," I said.

"That doesn't sound so great. What if the car breaks down again, or we get ripped off again?"

"Phil, you worry too much. Let's go." He reluctantly agreed. Off we drove, right back down to San Diego.

The drive was faster this time. We took the 101 and avoided the coast highway. It wasn't nearly as scenic a ride, but it is a lot quicker. When we get to San Diego, Tommy wasn't home, so we went out to the beach to kill some time. We pull up in to the parking lot at the beach and park. No sooner did Phil turn off the motor, when we noticed one lane forward and two cars over, a two cops, sitting in his car. We both agreed it was no big deal; we were clean and had our Navy IDs. Even though we were AWOL, they had no way of knowing. So we sat there smoking cigarettes and watching for girls. Then without any warning, the face of some hippie was in Phil's side window. Phil jerked back and I looked up.

"Hey dudes, wanna buy a lid?" Phil looked at me, and then it hit me… It is the exact same dude that ripped us off just last week— the phony motel room dude. Phil reached down for the metal pipe we kept between the seats. I put my hand on his to keep the pipe down and nodded toward the cop. Now our rip-off artist was leaning with his elbows against the door and waiting for an answer. He didn't have a clue that we are the dudes he had ripped off not eight days earlier.

"Well, do ya?" He asked again, Phil was fuming. I could feel his blood boiling right next to me. I was thinking, please don't do anything stupid...

At that, I said, "No, we don't need one." He stood up, turned and walked away. Phil is hot and has blood in his eyes. Phil said, almost yelling "DIDN'T YOU SEE WHO THAT IS!?!"

"Yeah, I know who it is; but what the hell are we gonna do with those cops right there?"

"Motherfucker... Goddamn! So he gets to just walk away!?! Phil turned to stare a hole in me.

"Like I said, there are the cops." In an instant, the thief was gone... just disappeared down the beach. I didn't think Phil would ever cool off.

We drive back over to Tommy's and he was home, so we scored. We drive back to San Fran and made some decent money—Now after that trip back and forth, we decided to just hang out down in Santa Cruz, about an hour south of San Francisco, for the remainder of the thirty days. Never did pay back our buddies in San Diego. That always did bother me. We took the money we made selling this last batch of weed and get a cheap motel for the weekly rate, then just wandered around town. It is a great little college town with cool little bars and little cafés, I panhandled a little money from time to time. Thought about Diane, the U.C.L.A. professor I had hung out with just last year. For the life of me I couldn't remember where she lived. I said to Phil, "Remember the story I told you about that professor chick I met when I came out to California the last time?" Phil seemed to ignore me. "Well that girl used to live in this town. I've been to Diane's mother's house, but I'll be damned if I can remember where it is." Phil could not have cared less.

After knocking around Santa Cruz until the thirty days were up, we had just enough money for gas to get us back to our base in San Francisco, where we turned ourselves in. We both were immediately thrown in the brig.

Both My Moms

The brig is run by Marines, jar-heads to us, whom are completely unsympathetic to our plight. They treat us like criminals. I guess we were of a sort. They yell and make us shine doorknobs and brass fittings for hours on end. They shake us down in our cells. We are in the Brig, the Navy's version of jail. The cells are small; about five feet wide, eight feet tall, and nine feet deep, with three bunks in each. Phil and I were in the same cell, so we talk the nights and days away.

One of the guys in the brig is Joe Barazono. Joe is from Jersey. He is medium height, relatively stout. Joe is pissed off about everything. He causes so much trouble the jarheads had it with him. He fights with them more than a few times, and they were more than a little unhappy with his bullshit. They stripped him to his boxers and pulled the bunks out of his cell. His light was on 24/7 and he had to sleep on the floor. Joe would talk to Phil and I. We are in the cell next to his. In his thick Brooklyn accent, he said, "Dese fuckin' jaw heads think I'm crazy and dat's da way I want it. In a couple of days, dare gonna cawt marshal me and I'm out of heah. Fuck dis man's Navy." "Yeah, we feel the same way," I told him. "We went AWOL for thirty days, so the rule is, we'll be kicked out; at least that's how we planned it."

"Shit, dat's what I shoulda done," Joe said.

"What did you do to get in here?"

"I climbed to da highest point on da ship and wit about five or six guys trying to tawk me down, I jumped, hit da wawta 'n broke two ribs, so day troo me in heah."

"Damn," I said, "No wonder they think you're crazy... you are," he laughs.

At any moment during the day or night Joe would break in to a Beatles song complete with his Brooklyn thick accent and all..."Pitchur ya self in a boat on riva, wit' tanjarine trees an mommalaid skys..."

I can see why the jarheads hate Joe, because it did get old. Phil and I, of course, would egg him on. After a few nights of hanging out with Joe and polishing brass doorknobs, the executive officer summoned me to his office. I thought, well this is it... what I've been hoping for. I was escorted by one Marine no handcuffs. Guess I wasn't much of a threat. When we got to the X. O.'s office, the Marine knocked and stood back. We then heard, "Enter," and my Marine escort motioned for me to go in. Opening the door, I stepped inside and stood at attention. The X.O. was sitting behind his desk, leaning back in his chair with his hands clasped behind his head. He began, "Martin, what the hell's wrong with you, boy? Don't you like being in the Navy?"

"No, I don't...sir," I said, nervously.

"Why the hell not... you joined didn't you?" he said, in an accusatory tone. He pulls out a lighter and flicked it, then slowly passed the flame under a leaf on what looks to be a plastic plant sitting on the edge of his desk. A tiny puff of smoke rose into the air and, by God, it smells exactly like weed. Now I am more nervous. He snapped the lighter shut and leaned forward in his chair, not making any reference to what he had just done, and looking at me square in the face, said again, "Well, I'm waiting..." I ignored the smell and pull my thoughts together.

"Yes, I joined, but I was told I would learn a trade, and I'm not learning anything but how to chip paint, sir." I felt righteous with my response.

"A trade? We're gonna make you a man. Don't you want to be a man...? Martin?"

"Yes, sir. But life will make me a man; I joined the Navy to learn a trade."

"Look, Martin, I'm gonna give you a choice: you can do six months at the Red Line Brig on Treasure Island, then if you fly right and finish out your hitch, you'll get an honorable discharge. Or you can sign right here and now, and we'll get you out tomorrow with an undesirable discharge and no benefits; the choice is yours." He shoved some formal looking paper across his desk at me. I thought, Hmmm, door number one or door number two? I went for number two and signed my name. An undesirable discharge didn't mean shit to me; I just wanted out. I had been misled and was not happy about it. Tomorrow, he says, I can pick up a voucher for a plane ticket home.

I am more than glad to hear that; I am getting out. I decide it was they, who were the "undesirable" ones. I felt somewhat embarrassed about giving up on the Navy when it came to my mom and dad. I knew they would not be proud, although I had been telling them since after boot camp I was not learning a trade. I could imagine their disappointment. It is just something they would have to accept… or not.

I hardly slept that night. I am going home tomorrow, back to Miami, and it feels good to be going. No— I am elated—bursting at the seams! I have spent the last ten months disgusted, disappointed, pissed off, and sorry I ever joined. The next day I awoke, someone had stolen my duffle bag; it was all packed up and ready to go, right at the foot of my bunk and now it's gone. I thought, isn't this some shit? What a great group of guys I'm leaving behind. Well, screw it. I picked up my voucher for a ticket home and left the ship with the clothes on my back, never getting to speak with Phil before I left. Figure he would not be far behind. Take a bus to San Francisco International Airport and make my way to my departure gate.

On the plane ride home, I find a Reader's Digest in the pocket of my seat. Leafing through the magazine, I came upon a story entitled The Littlest Hero. As I read, the story draws me in. It is about an eight-year-old boy home alone with his mother. She was taking a shower when she fell and hit her head. Finding her bleeding on the bathroom floor, he picked up the phone and called the operator. The operator got him to emergency services, where the emergency dispatcher was able to calm him down and get his address. The ambulance arrived in time to save his mom, who was seconds from death. The story went on to say what a brave and smart boy he was and how proud his mom was of him for having saved her life.

I looked out the small window of the jet and felt a wave of pain and guilt rise up within me. My eyes wanted to tear up and since there was no one in the two seats next to me I did not hold back. As the tears came, I slumped in my seat, leaned my head against the window of the jet and let my tears flow. I was a spewing garden spigot. The more I let them flow, the more they came. When I had the chance, I was not a little hero; I was not able to save my mom. I was watching TV while less then fifteen feet from me, my mom drowned in her own vomit and died. The thought of that scene in my mind's eye had been tormenting me for quite some time.

Why didn't I pick up the phone— oh yeah, it was disconnected. No, that's just an excuse for not having done anything. Truth is, I could have walked next-door to a neighbor and asked for help; but I did nothing. I was so accustomed to my Mom drinking herself into a stupor and then passing out, I thought, she'll wake up, she always wakes up…

I really missed my mom after she died. At the time, I put it out of my mind, to avoid facing her death. Now, ten years later, on a jet ride home, thirty thousand feet in the air, I felt the sting of her death like it had just happened. Like the blade of a razor had just been dragged across my heart. Up until this moment, I had never cried for my mom. I ran, and have been running ever since, searching for ways to avoid reality and the truth. I used dreams of adventure, eighteen-wheelers, drugs, alcohol and girls—anything to mask the pain. Acting like everything was okay, denying the pain and the shame that was eating at me like a cancer. Suddenly I was no longer looking for a place to hide, a way to forget; I was facing the truth. The truth that I was damaged and in pain and had been for years. The truth that I was mad at my birth mother for not caring enough about my sister and me to take care of herself and to be there for us. I finally allowed all my feelings to rise up and burst out. The tears shame and hurt filling me up and spilling out. I can see my early childhood clearly in my memory; the face of my birth mother, Marie, sitting on our stoop with my friends serving Kool-Aid; the single black and white photograph of my real dad; my Grandmother's home in Brooklyn; Our house in Bayport. I had finally allowed my feelings to come to the surface and I was feeling a release. My soul felt liberated from the torment of my guilt-laden thoughts; thoughts that had been getting the best of me for years.

Eventually I have no more tears to cry. Wiping my eyes, I decide to accept what happened to my mom, remembering all the pleading I did, begging my mom to stop drinking, and my refusing to go to the store for beer. Her getting mad and yelling at me and shaking me by my shoulders and slapping me. Thinking she doesn't know what she's doing, she doesn't mean it. Thought about telling someone but who could I tell. And why would I want to tell on my mom? Could I get her help or would I get her in trouble? I was confused and hurt all the time. Maybe I could have done something, but I did not. My mother's demise was a slow chugging train that moved through the blackness of her depression, never hitting the breaks and finally simply running out fuel and stopping dead on the tracks. It was time now to accept the truth for what it is and not what it could have been.

I notice the stewardess working her way down the aisle with the beverage cart. I did my best to compose myself. I tell myself, your mom loved you and you loved her and that's all that matters; don't ever forget that. I knew the remorse of my mother's death would probably always be with me; but I suddenly felt better about it. I will need to remind myself to accept what happened as a part of my life, a pivotal moment, a painful memory, just as I have many joyful memories. They are all a part of my past, and collectively they define me. No one owes me anything because of my past, and I have no right to act out because I have experienced tragedy at an early age. Life can be difficult — in fact it can be heartbreaking, disappointing and downright awful— but that's life, and not an excuse for being an angry, obstinate, self-centered jerk.

It is not long before the plane touches down in Miami. My brother Johnny met me at the airport. It was good to see him. He gave me a ride to our house. My mom was happy to see me, my dad, not so much. I'm sure he thought I was a quitter. I am not home five minutes and he is off to play golf. So much for a warm welcome home; but then again, what do I expect?

So here I am, back with my folks, sitting at my usual place at the dining room table— the very same dining room table where I sat when my dad had asked me to show him how it's done, almost two years ago. Well, I did show my folk's one thing— I knew how to stay away, although now that I am back, it is not as a conquering warrior— not even close. More like a runaway puppy who found his way back home.

My mom asked, "So, now that you're back, what are your plans?" I thought, first and foremost, I would get a job and a place to live. I was not about to give my dad a chance to ask me what I was doing back home.

"Tomorrow I'll find a place to rent, then I'll get a job."

"Well, you can stay home until you get on your feet. You don't have to rush off."

"Thanks, Mom; but yeah, I do need to rush off. I'm a man and I need to make my own way, the sooner the better. I love you and dad for everything you've done for me, but I need to be on my own now." She was beginning to tear up, so I got up from the table and walked into the kitchen and hugged her. I really did love her. I no longer had an attitude toward my mom.

The minister I met in Pascagoula had given me good advice, and I did learn to appreciate my folks after living in New Orleans. I felt guilty about how I had treated my mom and my dad for the last few years. Well, that was going to change; I had a new-found respect for them, for myself.

My adventure began with five dollars, twenty-two months ago. I was so confident and self-assured when I took off. Only to discover just how little I really *did* know. As Socrates once said, "I know nothing except the fact of my ignorance." I learned that there are all kinds of people in the world, of whom I knew nothing about. I found myself becoming not quite so judgmental and critical of others. Gay is not perverted and a hippie hobo is really not something to aspire to be. Also, I realized that listening to someone else's opinion might just help me and not to take their advice as an invitation for a debate. I am still a free spirit, and an optimist, but I am also humble. At the same time, I seem to have lost my desire to escape from reality. The thought of tripping seems almost like I would be ripping myself off form how cool reality really is. It dawned on me to consider the feelings of others, especially those of my Aunt Frances, who became my mother at a time in my life when I needed all the help I could get. I really did want to pay her back for the unconditional love she gave my sister Judy and me. I want her to see me as a successful man, a respectable man. As well I thought my birth mom might be looking down and I also want her to be proud of me. I want to make both my moms proud. I wanted to be proud of myself.

So instead of being mad and bitter about my birth mom dying while I was so young. I decided to feel grateful to have known her as long as I did and the beautiful memories that were mine. And to be just as grateful to have my aunt come along and take up where she left off. Yes, I was quite a fortunate kid, and it was time I appreciated that fact and felt good about it. Whomever it was spoke the truth when they said…life is beautiful!… I agree.

CPSIA information can be obtained
at www.ICGtesting.com
Printed in the USA
FSHW010846030521
80976FS